P9-CAJ-440

85A

KYLE THOMAS SMITH

BASCOM HILL PUBLISHING GROUP

Minneapolis

Smith

Copyright © 2010 by Kyle Thomas Smith

Bascom Hill Publishing Group
212 3rd Avenue North, Suite 290
Minneapolis, MN 55401
612.455.2293
www.bascomhillpublishing.com

All rights reserved. No part of this publication may be reproduced,
stored in a retrieval system, or transmitted, in any form or by any means,
electronic, mechanical, photocopying, recording, or otherwise, without
the prior written permission of the author.

This book is a work of fiction. People, places, events and situations
are the product of the author's imagination. Any resemblance to actual
persons, living or dead, or historical events is purely coincidental.

12/10

ISBN - 978-1-935098-26-3
ISBN - 1-935098-26-8
LCCN - 2010901984

Cover Design by Jenni Wheeler
Typeset by Kristeen Wegner

Printed in the United States of America

BASCOM HILL
PUBLISHING GROUP

3 5991 00077 4744

To Julius Leiman-Carbia,
With Love

ACKNOWLEDGMENTS

I'd like to thank my partner, Julius Leiman-Carbia, for his endless inspiration and support throughout the writing of this book; the Tea Lounge in Brooklyn for being infinitely patient with me as I sit writing for hours on its couches, almost every day, after ordering only one or two cups of coffee; Mike Levine for his friendship and unqualified backing in tough times; Mark Levine for helping me get published; Rachael Dean Scholes for her friendship, feedback and expertise on all things English; Joe Flood for his artistic excellence; New York Insight and Vajradhara Dharma Center for priceless instruction in meditation and the dharma; Shell Fischer, Gail Martin, Randy Peyser, Sarah Getty and Rachel Fichter for pivotal editorial support; my illustrious cats, Marquez and Giuseppe, who love me more than tuna; and my mother, Maureen Ann Smith, for encouraging me to be a writer when it wasn't even a thought in my mind.

CHICAGO
Monday, January 23, 1989

PART ONE:

NORTHWEST SIDE

"You must've heard of them, a kind of screwed-up blend
Split personality
Two sides to fight and argue all night
Over coffee or tea...
I've got four hang-ups I'm trying to beat
Four directions and just two feet
Got a very very secret identity
And I don't know which one is me"

The Who, "Four Faces"

CHAPTER I
Bus Stop
(January 23, 1989)

Every detention, every chip of glass piercing my forearm from the inside, every minute the 85A is late drives me that much closer to London. I repeat: London, London…

Andy Payne broke my window last Thursday with a Jack Daniel's bottle. Must've got it from Matt McCaskey's Dad's liquor cabinet. He's over there all the fuckin' time, right across the street. Only hangs out at Matt's to get better aim at me. When I got home from school that afternoon, I opened my bedroom door to find the bottle in a pile of glass on the shag carpet. The bottle was empty and, unlike the window, still in one piece.

But, man, Payne didn't drink that whiskey. I know he didn't. He's too much of a pussy. Probably just poured it down the drain in McCaskey's workroom sink before heading to our house. The inside smelled like water, not alcohol, so I'd lay any bet he didn't drink it before he threw it. Back in seventh grade, Payne was too scared to even take a drag off a Newport that Mike Koncz picked out of a St. Aloysius church lobby ashtray. He made excuses. Said the filter had lipstick on it and he didn't want anybody spreading rumors that he was wearing lipstick when he smoked it. But he'd see me standing around smoking Marlboros, so he'd stand behind some Aquinas North wrestling jocks and shout, "Hey, Seamus! Smokin' fags, fag?"

But look what a man Payne is now, hurling Jack Daniel's bottles at my window. Still, he's too much of a pussy to *drink* Jack. But he did plug a note in the bottle. I fished it out with my Bic pen. It said, "DIE FAG." He wrote it in big scrawl with black Magic Marker.

I wish I wasn't the kind to cry, but I do, every time—and way too many times back in grade school, I let pussy Payne see me cryin', even after I was done whipping his candy ass. It made me cry that Payne and everyone else called me fag. Couldn't help it. Tears just welled up and dropped. And seeing me cry made them all do it more. So, I just stopped fighting. If I didn't, fuckin' fighting's all I'd fuckin' do. I'd get no peace in this neighborhood. So now I'm fuckin' Ghandi. And now Payne's vandalizing our house. We don't even go to the same high school. If he hates me much, why doesn't he just avoid me? That's how it goes in every other neighborhood. Still, I can't bring myself to beat him unconscious. He'd just come back for more, like he always used to, and his words could crush me worse than any bottle of Jack to the head.

Last month, it was our living room window. Payne must've spent all afternoon packing snowballs hard with gravel and ice. That's another thing that happens in a neighborhood where nothing happens. Here in Jarvis Park, kids got all afternoon to do shit like pack up ice balls and blow out windows. Not that they ever own up to it. They just take off running like pussy Payne. His ice ball shot straight through the second pane. Mom says, after she heard glass break in the living room, she tore in and saw Payne's wussy ass through the window, tearing over to the Moores' backyard. Once he jumped the fence, he turned around, flipped Mom the fuck finger and scampered away, laughing like a hyena. Mom called the cops. Fourth time she had to, too. Never wanted to, but there was no way around it.

First time she called was that time I was in the den watching *Night Court*. One minute Roz is jawing with Bull in front of Judge Stone's bench and the next a rock from Mrs. Madden's front garden crashes through the south window. Slams right into my left arm with a shower of glass. I shot straight out of my seat, slipped on some shards that'd hit the floor, and landed on my left arm, right onto more jagged glass that was hanging off the side of the window. Had to go to the emergency room. Nothing got broken, but I had to sit there nine hours. Got bruised up pretty bad, six stitches. To this day, I'm digging glass out of my arm. Every time I think I got all the glass out, I see more glimmering coming up from under my skin. Before I can start picking out the buried pieces, I have to wait for them to rise up on their own and pierce my forearm from the inside. Some's rising up right now, right as I stand here waiting for the 85A.

We're not stupid. We know Mrs. Madden didn't take a rock out of her own garden and smash our den window. Please, she's president of the Altar & Rosary Society. She's Mom's bridge partner. For fuck's sake, she wears saddle shoes! The cops knew it wasn't Mrs. Madden too. They tracked Payne down at his house on Hiawatha Street. When he told them he didn't do it, they told him he was a lying little punk. But his mom threatened to sue the Chicago PD for harassment and, y'know, battery or some shit like that, so they got back in their squad car and hightailed out.

When I was eleven, Mrs. Payne called all the moms in the parish and told them I had AIDS and that they shouldn't let their sons hang around me. Said I masturbated in front of Andy in the locker room at the Y. All I did was change out of my Speedo in front of him after a swim meet—one where I took home the blue ribbon while he only walked off with the yellow, a ribbon to match his belly. Mrs. Payne called our house telling Mom I jerked off. I denied it, but Mom still slapped the right side of my face and backhanded me against the left.

Soon Mom found out Mrs. Payne was sending out APBs and AIDS alerts to everyone in the school phone book. Suddenly, it's not about me anymore. Mom thinks AIDS patients should be shipped off to leper colonies; fucked if she's gonna let the

O'Grady name be linked to a homo disease. Mom threatened to take Mrs. Payne to court, but she never went through with it. God forbid the papers catch wind of it on a slow news day. She let it rest and now Payne's free to run his mouth, and all the assholes calling me faggot also started screaming I jerk off in public and spooge AIDS. I was eleven! I couldn't spooge anything yet.

No use correcting them. They'll all go right on thinking whatever the fuck they wanna think—or whatever the fuck people tell them to think. They're just gonna keep screamin' it. And if there's one thing his nauseating cunt-drip of a mom's good at, it's screaming. After she got divorced, you could hear her screaming for three blocks while her vibrator broke the sound barrier in her pussy. Screamed so loud about me to all the parents, I had to quit the swim team. Ain't seen a pool since.

Now she's screaming such bloody fucking murder at the cops they won't ever book Andy, no matter what he does. Didn't dust for prints on the rock he threw. Still claim they did everything they could to dig up evidence. That's what the pigs say every time: not enough evidence. Every time Payne trespasses on our property. Every time he stares into our windows, flicking a Bic over a gas can. Every time he runs and jumps the fence into the Adamczaks' backyard, trailing gasoline. Every time he calls the house and calls me faggot or tells Mom he's gonna rape her.

Mom hangs up every time, and, every time, he calls back and lets the phone ring for another hour and a half. Mom won't just take the phone off the hook. Keeps thinking it might be Calvary Hospital calling to say they just heard Grampa's death rattle. We used to think we could get enough evidence for the pigs if the operator could just trace the call. But whenever we call the operator, she tells us she can't trace it: "All I can do is connect you with the police if you want to report a crime." The police? The same ones who set Payne loose every time? If Andy Payne was a black kid, the Chicago cops would have him packed off to Joliet by sunrise—all for so much as breathing within a hundred yards of Ponchitrain Street. But, no, they can't do that to a white kid. Not one from around here anyway, no matter what he does. He'd get a record. How would that look on his college apps?

That's why Mom backed off too, at first. She couldn't watch a white kid suffer. But after a while, she started waking up every night, waiting for the next window to break or for a match to strike next to whatever spot of gasoline the little prick might've splashed onto the side of our house. Still, Mom and Dad refuse to move. They're all into that "preserve the neighborhood" shit. We already know they can elect a black mayor here in Chicago. There's no telling what could happen to a "safe" neighborhood like Jarvis Park, especially if good and noble homeowners like Mom and Dad—and don't forget Mrs. Payne—don't keep their houses and stand their ground.

A long time ago, the community voted Jarvis Park dry. You have to drive a mile and a half down Devon to pick up beer. The vote was unanimous. They say going dry "helps keep the riff-raff out." They mean it keeps the malt-liquor-buying kind out of Peterson's Groceries. That's all they're saying. They don't want to start seeing Colt 45 billboards with Billy Dee Williams' face going up on Caldwell Avenue. If anyone here catches that malt-liquor riff-raff darkening an open house, they call McKee & Pogue and tell the agent that, if she even dreams of taking a bid from those people, they'll have her license revoked. If she stands her ground and squares the deal anyway, they'll slash her tires. If they close on the house, they turn a blind eye when their kids go beat the fuck out of her kids. They send the cops to the new neighbor's door every night, or the cops just show up on their own; we got Chicago police captains living on most streets in Jarvis Park.

Two days after the new neighbors move in, they'll walk out front to see For Sale signs on half the lawns. The malt-liquor riff-raff knows it's not wanted here. They wouldn't buy houses in Jarvis

Park even if they could afford them. The result: a neighborhood full of honkies who can't handle anything but their own kind. And the same assholes drawing these red lines are the same ones at Mass every Sunday. The ones singing "On Eagles Wings" in the choir. I know. My dad's fuckin' one of them, even though he though knows I got Tressa in my life, my African queen, my one true friend, my savior, the one he refuses to set eyes on when she's at the house.

After I busted up a cardboard box and taped half of it over my bedroom window last Thursday—Jack Daniel's Vandalism Day—I vacuumed the glass off the carpet and took the bottle to the curb in a Happy Foods bag. That's when I overheard Mom talking to Dad in their room while he was changing out of his gray flannel suit after work:

MOM: Phil, take a look at this note. It's a death threat. We have a *note*, Phil! Surely, the police can intervene this time.

DAD: Well, what the hell's wrong with Seamus that he's getting death threats and you're getting these calls? Seamus walks around with that goofy hair, that long black coat. You hear that delinquent...*weirdo*...music blaring out of his headphones from all the way down the street. He's a disgrace.

MOM: Don't say that!

DAD: Oh, please, Mary. Please. You know it and I know it. Everybody knows it. He's flunking out of school. He can't make friends there. On Sundays, we catch him hiding out in the Forest

6

Preserves with his Walkman, smoking cigarettes when he should be at Mass. He says he doesn't believe in God. He's got that mouth on him. We never talked like that. Where the hell did he learn to talk like that? People are going to think we talk like that, Mary. And it never stops, no matter how many times I take off my belt.

MOM: He might have Tourette's, Phil. Barbara Walters had this special—

DAD: Oh, horseshit, Mary! He's just willful. He puts all that concrete in his hair. I'd put his keister in St. John's Military Academy right this second. Have them make a man out of him. But that's beyond anyone. They don't take his kind in the military. I'm sure they won't take him in military school.

MOM: What are you saying, Phil?

DAD: Please, Mary. Please. Open your eyes! Everybody sees it. Everyone's saying it.

MOM: It's not true!

DAD: I can't tell you how many times I've wanted to trade him in, but they don't have places you can go do that. We're stuck with him till he's out of high school. That is, if he finishes. He sure as hell isn't college material. And if he doesn't finish high school, he sure as hell isn't living here! Got that, Mary? If he isn't still at

St. Xavier's the day he turns sixteen, he can go
down to the missions. If he gets there early
enough, they'll give him a bowl of soup and a
cot. They'll take him. They take anyone.

MOM: Pray for his soul at least, Phil.

DAD: Oh, I do, Mary. I do. Every day. But I can't take
           any more of these 9-1-1 calls. He's got to shape
           up. Maybe if he'd pray for his own soul once in
           a while, he would.

It's 6:51. Where's the fucking 85A? It was supposed to
be here thirty-five minutes ago. I've been at the bus stop *forty*
minutes already. It's five below zero. Forgot to wear long johns
again. I'm warming my balls between my thighs and they're still
going numb. Hear that 85A? I'm Warming My Balls Between My
Thighs! Where the fuck are you?

I'm gonna get detention, you know. Oh, I'm sorry, JUG.
That's what St. Xavier calls it. JUG. Justice Under God. You know
what, if I do, fuck it. I'll just skip it. But, if I skip, they'll give me
double JUG. You know what, fine, I'll take two JUGs instead of
one. They're not going to let me out for a doctor's appointment. I
can't miss Dr. Strykeroth. Not today. I need my fix.

The sun's not even out yet. The sky still looks as dark
as that pile of lead cylinders across the tracks. Does anyone even
work in the warehouses over there? I think I saw a forklift driving
around the grounds once, but it disappeared behind one of the
warehouses never to return. It's about as much life as I've seen
going on in Jarvis Park. Maybe I'll walk over there some time and
look for it. Jesus, am I that bored? Besides, you couldn't pay me to
walk around Jarvis Park. No matter how much I hate St. Xavier, at

least it's on the south side. At least I don't have to be in a white-kid carpool out to the suburbs like Payne and the rest of the lame-oids around here.

I do have to wait for the 85A, though. If this were any other neighborhood, the bus would be here now. Fuck you, 85A. Think you can take your own sweet fuckin' time around here? Why? 'Cuz Jarvis Park's a nothing neighborhood? Well, you got that right enough. The only stores we have are Peterson's Groceries, Happy Foods, Pabis' Pharmacy, Cumquats Stationary, and Drymiller's Diner. The only chain store is the Shell station at Devon and Central.

Chain stores might be the brood of the corporate monster, but at least they attract crowds. We've got those fuckin' Smolenski brothers, though. They own that whole strip on Devon and won't let any new merchants in. The Smolenskis are in league with the rest of Jarvis Park to ward off all outsiders and keep us separate from the rest of Chicago. Last year, they went to court and blocked a proposal for a Venture store—a fuckin' Venture store—saying they don't want no dot heads flocking around here in saris and turbans.

Shit, other neighborhoods got hustle. They got three or four bus lines per street, one coming right after the other. You miss one, you can always catch the one behind it. And the bus stops are packed.

Other neighborhoods got apartment buildings, not just these single-family dollhouses. Just being around apartment buildings is enough to expand people's minds. People who live in apartments, they look out their windows and see hordes of people they don't know—people they'll never know—going about their lives. Wherever there are apartment buildings, there are blocks and blocks full of businesses, shops, restaurants, traffic jams, nightlife, and, of course, bus lines. Once you start seeing enough of that shit, you start thinking, shit, maybe I can just go about my own life too. Maybe I don't have to know everyone's name. Maybe I don't have to check in with my cunt neighbors about who I could or should fuckin' be. Maybe I can mind my own fuckin' business. And maybe other people will mind theirs. Maybe I can be my own self for once. Maybe no one will bum-rush me off the block for it. Then you go off and you just do it: you go off and you just be your own fuckin' self.

People in other neighborhoods don't have time to go around harassing everybody else in the neighborhood. That's all they have time for in Jarvis Park. Especially if you look like me: lanky, dressed in black, rust-red hair—tossled, spiked, shaved on the sides and back. Can't tell you how many mornings I've stood right here at this curb and had some car skid right up to my shin. Then some fuckin' redneck or some fuckin' jock or some fuckin' prep boy sticks his fuckin' head out the fuckin' window and yells, "Fuckin' faggot!" That's another reason I wish the 85A would get here on time. Besides the fact that it's five below zero.

Where the fuck are you, 85A?

CHAPTER II
85A Cometh

Finally! The 85A's rounding Touhy Avenue. Just when my thighs are freezer burnt and my balls have turned to dry ice.

Last time I asked the driver, "What took you so fuckin' long?" he ordered me off the bus. Refused to move till I got off. Everyone's screaming at me. He threatened to call the cops, so I got off. Had to wait for the next bus. Ended up thirty-five minutes late for school. Got JUG. Had to write out the St. Xavier Norms of Conduct twice and the tardiness policy three times. It's the same asshole bus driver every morning. So now, no matter how late he is, I have to just suck it up, flash my Student ID, deposit my token and fifteen cents and take my seat like a good little cunt.

I'm getting two JUGs for sure today. One for tardiness and another for skipping the first JUG to go see Dr. Strykeroth. Can't afford any more after this. St. Xavier's already spoiling to kick me out for grades.

Last Wednesday, Mrs. McKenna asked if I want to keep going to Xavier. I shrugged, said, I dunno. I hate that school. I don't know why I can't keep up in class, I just…can't. It's just impossible for me to pay attention. The second the bell rings to start class, my mind checks out—just packs its bags and flies off to some fuckin' Never-Neverland. I never can seem to bring it back to what's going on in class, no matter how much I try to force it. I just get more and more lost by the day.

"Your GPA is a 1.4!" Mrs. McKenna squawked in the guidance counseling office, "You'll never get into college with grades like this, Seamus. And, if this keeps up, you won't be able to come back third quarter—let alone next year."

I don't give a fuck if I don't get into college. I don't even want to be in high school. The only reason I got into St. Xavier in the first place is I was a legacy—Dad went there, Brody went there, Uncle Bob and three of my cousins. Plus, Dad's the Chair of the Alumni Association. They had to let me in—much to Dean Russell's dismay. But I flunked the entrance exam. You had to get a 98 percent and I got, what, a 63? Dad's right. I'm not college material. But Mrs. McKenna and a blue million others are all out there saying if I don't go to college, I'll have no future. Well, what kind of future will I have if I do get into college? Will I get to be a yuppie then? Some stress-infested yuppie like Brody? Is that what they call a fuckin' future?

Of course, Dr. Strykeroth had to go to college to get where he is. Okay, that's true, but Mark Twain never went to college—one of the few things I ever learned in Mr. Banaszak's class. Princeton gave him an honorary degree. Maybe I can get one of those too—after I write a lot of books and show Xavier who they fucked with: boot their name into the fuckin' papers, blow the lid off how they treat struggling students. Fuckin' shut 'em down till that kingdom they keep saying's coming fucking comes.

Thing is, I know I'm not stupid. But the teachers at Xavier figure, if you're no good at grades, you got no business being in a top-ranked school. So they keep letting me fall behind and fail, fall behind and fail—that sink-or-swim shit they're all into. And I wish I could swim like the sharks at Xavier but I can't. I can't.

I could leave—go to Taft. But kids get killed every day in Chicago public schools, especially white kids, if they don't drop out first. We have the worst violent crime rate of any public school system in the country.

Plus, Dad's already made it clear: I gotta be at St. Xavier, nowhere else, if I still want a home when I turn sixteen. And my folks won't pay for me to go to the Academy of the Arts, even though it's half the price of fucking Xavier. I know I'd do better there. I mean, I know I got brains and shit when it comes to the arts. Besides, there are freaks like me at the Academy. I mean, real fucking freaks—artists, poets, actors, punks, death-rockers, guys who show up to school in skirts and makeup. I could make friends there!

Dad just brushed me off when I asked to go to the Academy. Never even looked at the brochure. "You got to get an education, mister!" An education? Am I getting one now? At Xavier, where I can't keep up and all they're doing about it is flunking me out? I mean, I squeaked by with Ds last year but this year's a different story. I'm a fuckin' sophomore now and they're not cutting me any slack.

Last week, Mrs. McKenna put a call in to Dr. Strykeroth about me, saying I was an emergency case. She referred me to him last year, after Mom called the dean's office, saying there was something wrong with me but she didn't know what. St. Xavier sent me to Dr. Strykeroth, told Mom they highly recommend him. Little did they know how much Dr. Strykeroth would be on my side in all this shit.

A few weeks ago, I went to see Dr. Strykeroth and he laughed at Mrs. McKenna. Told me she's full of shit. Put his hand on my knee. Held it nice and firm there. Told me, "Just play the game two and a half more years, Seamus. Two and a half more years. Then go away. Go away. Wave good-bye to them, to your family, and to all the other lowlives. Make a life for yourself. Make a *name* for yourself. And never come back."

Hello, Mr. Bus Driver. Why the evil eye? Here's my bus token and here's my fifteen cents. You know I'm good for it. Here's my Student ID.

Same one I show every morning, no need to look me up and down. What, you don't believe I'm in high school? Do I look like an adult? I sure don't act like one. Yes, that is me in the picture. I'm even smiling in it. Never saw me do that shit before, huh? Yes, I will need a transfer. Just like I do every morning. Thank you, thank you so fucking much. Now I'll just go sit down like a good little cunt. I won't move a muscle. I won't say a fucking word about how you were over a half hour late, you bastard. I won't say a word about how this'll set me back two JUGs and how I'll be signing my expulsion papers by May. Not that I can say any of this shit aloud. You'll throw my ass off the bus and make me later than I already am.

CHAPTER III

Forest Preserve

Yes! A window seat! I grab one whenever I can. I lean my head against the window and listen to my Walkman. The Forest Preserves slide by in a rocky, bumpy kind of blur. I love when trees blur. Reminds me of the Monet book that Tressa bought me at the Art Institute. Whenever I let my eyes go out of focus, the trees turn into something way beyond this world. Even in winter, they look like something you can walk into bucknaked, like you can come in off the street and lie down in the snow without getting cold or frostbite. You can roll around in the grass and on the roots of trees and all the mist and miasma will swallow you up and spirit you away.

The Forest Preserves are the one thing I like about Jarvis Park. England's got better forests, though. Sherwood in Nottinghamshire for instance. At least they seemed much better, more magical than the Forest Preserves when Mom would read me *Robin Hood*, way back before I started reading shit like *Lady Chatterly's Lover*. Maybe I'll take a trip to Nottinghamshire some weekend after I move to London.

I'm listening to Mozart. That'll warm me up on the death trek to the L. Tressa made this tape special for me. Must've spent weeks on the cover. It's just red construction paper, but she did all sorts of stenciling and engraving and shit. Makes the cover look like silhouettes shimmying behind whorehouse curtains. Her bedroom kind of looks like that too when you see it from the sidewalk on Logan Boulevard. She has scarlet curtains. *Miss*

Scarlet! Miss Scarlet! Says 40-year-old men ring her doorbell and offer to pay to come up, even if her mom Agatha answers the door. Agatha turns them away but she never makes Tressa change the curtains. Shit, she helped pick 'em out and put 'em up.

Her folks fuckin' rule! They exposed her to Mozart and all this other music and art and shit. I always look at the paper Tressa folded into the cassette case. She wrote the song titles in calligraphy: "Rondo Alla Turca," "Theme for Elvira," "Minuet from *Don Giovanni.*" That's the first side anyway. Her folks taught her calligraphy. Fuckin' calligraphy! Jesus. They enrolled her in drawing and drama classes. Signed her up for Russian ballet when she was practically a fetus. Now she draws like…um…Leonardo Da Vinci and pirouettes like…like an angel on a pin…even got to go to Moscow with The Chicago Russian Ballet in eighth grade. Even with all the homework and shit she's gotta do, she's making big bucks as an actress, getting parts all around town, and she's only seventeen! A fuckin' child prodigy, just like Mozart! But still she shaves her head and listens to Black Flag and Social Distortion. She's fuckin' punk rock!

She's half black too—suck on that, Mom and Dad. Agatha is from somewhere in the Caribbean, so that makes Tressa half black, and she looks full-on black too. And she's way up at the top of her, waddyacallit, IB—International Baccalaureate—class at Lincoln Park. Yeah, suck on that too, Mom and Dad. Blacks aren't as dumb as you think; might try talking to one someday. Agatha can speak the King's English even though she slips into Carribean patois just as often, and, yeah, Tressa slips into black street talk a lot but that's just so she can get by in public school, and she knows how to slip right back out of it.

Tressa's going to school in Switzerland after she graduates this year. Her folks groomed her to succeed. Mine didn't. Just told me I *better* succeed. Never told me why or how, just went right back to watching TV, shaking their heads at how I'll never be a lawyer like my brother, Brody. I'll never have a fucking future like fucking Brody.

But I'm listening to Mozart. That's gotta count for something. *Amadeus* was on Channel 9 last week, all uncut. You even heard Mozart say "shit," right there on network TV. Censors let it slide. What else could they do? It's a movie about classical music. They can't encourage that shit and call it dirty at the same time.

I love the way people dressed in Mozart's day. Doily cuffs and collars, powdered wigs and patterned coats with tails. Mozart wore a pink wig before the imperial court of Austria. Two hundred fuckin' years before punk! People in America today, people like Brody, would call them all faggots. People in America, people like Brody, are a bunch of fucking rednecks and yuppies.

They wouldn't call them faggots in England. They're more colorful there. They're more *open-minded* there. There are enough people walking around in loud outfits like that in London. Their punks do it to the fuckin' hilt. I hear it's so bosses won't hire them and they can go on living off government relief. Even when it comes to non-punks, though, I love the way people look in London. Never been there, but I love how they look on BBC shows on Channel 11. I love the way they talk too. I could listen to it all day. I wish I had their accent. I can do a good one. When I move there, I'll talk like them. They watch so much American TV in England, though, they say that by the year 2000, the English will lose their accents and start using ours. I better get there before that shit happens. Stop them all from making a huge mistake.

Mozart will last longer than English accents, though. Hate to say it, but...yeah, he'll probably even outlast Johnny Rotten. I hope to be Mozart one day. I mean, I don't want to compose symphonies or anything. I'm no good at music. When Uncle Bob died a couple summers ago, Aunt Delores said I could have his old acoustic guitar. I tried teaching myself. Practiced all year. By last spring, all my calluses and cuts hardened into bumps bigger than Buddy Guy's. But, no matter how much I worked on it, I could never get past the three-chord progression in the Mel Bay book that Uncle Bob stowed in his guitar case. After a while, after you try and try like that and nothing happens, it's best to just lock that acoustic axe back up in its case and say adios. Still, I want to do something like what Mozart did. Sit at a desk, write hour after hour after hour for a living without stopping, not even to take a piss.

Mozart couldn't stop. Thousands of webs of fantasy spun in and around his head at all times. He dreamed up enchanted forests, wicked queens, Turkish harems. He had inspiration. It poured out of him like rain out of the fucking sky. I'd like to live in dreams. And I want to have everything I set down on paper be perfect. I want the muse pumping inspiration straight from her brain to mine. That's one way to have a future.

I left Public Image Ltd's *Happy?* in my tape drawer this morning. I was going to bring it with me, just in case I got bored listening to Tressa's Mozart tape. But, no, it's time for Mozart now. Time to put away my old tapes for a while. Time to get some culture. Raise my IQ.

All the same, it's tough leaving Johnny Rotten at home. Rotten's a fuckin' rottweiler! He's a fucking god! Nobody could ever keep him down, not even the National Front…not for long anyway. And he's Irish too. Or his parents were from Ireland, just like my grandmas and grandpas on both sides. I hate being Irish. Once the Irish stopped being pagan, they just signed up to be the Pope's slaves. But the English didn't. And Johnny Rotten didn't. He got luckier than I did, though. He got to grow up in England. I wish I could get away with being like him. Fuck knows I tried! We even have the same red hair. I just can't fuck mine up as good as he used to, no matter how much I work the Dippity-Do.

I'll never forget the first time I rented *Sid & Nancy* from Jarvis Park Video. They only card if you rent something, like, triple X. I slipped it past Mom and turned it on in the basement. There was that scene where Rotten gets Sid Vicious to stomp in that Rolls Royce's windshield. Didn't even know whose Rolls Royce it was, just fuckin' stomped the windshield. I never saw anything like it. Behind them, you see all those Kings Road flats that Tressa showed me in the coffee-table book that Agatha has from when she lived in London. Vicious and Rotten tear off all the impacted fiberglass and find that terrier whimpering behind the steering wheel on the right side of the car. Johnny hands Vicious the spray-paint can, says, "Go on, Sidney. Spray the beast." When Sid goes to pet the doggy instead, Rotten stomps away hissing, "Boring, Sidney. Fucking boring." Sid tosses the can on the dash, stomps back down off the Rolls hood, and kicks the RR decal right off. Johnny and Sid got away with stomping in car windows! It's a fuck lot cooler than what Payne's doing with iceballs and Jack Daniel's bottles. Rotten would eat Payne for breakfast. I saw that scene and I thought, that's it! "I am an Anti-Christ/I am an Anarchist," I'm fucking sold on England!

Mom and Dad wanna know where I get my fucking mouth. I say fuck all the fucking time. Mom says it's Tourette's. It's not fucking Tourette's! It's Rotten! Johnny fucking Rotten! That's where I fucking get it! That's why I fucking say it!

Fuck this and fuck that
Fuck it all and fuck the fucking brat!

I never used to fucking talk this way before Rotten. Tipper Gore's fucking right! If anyone tells you TV, music, and movies won't fuck up your kids, they're fucking lying! By now, I must've rented *Sid & Nancy* fifty times. Fuckin' look at me now. After the first time, I went out and bought motherfucking *Never Mind the Bollocks* and played it and nothing else for a whole fucking year! I'm the only one in my whole fuckin' neighborhood who owns it.

Brody confiscated my first copy when he came over to visit Mom and Dad one day. He said only fags listen to Sex Pistols and that, back in the seventies, if you listened to them, they called you fag. He said Pistols' fans were these creepy anti-social sickos, wearing chains, leather and their Levis backward. I told him, "I don't care. People call me fag anyway—and, anyway, I don't see what's so fucking wrong with being a fag." He clocked me across the face, told me I was a fucking fag myself. "You walk like a floozy," he said, "a streetwalking little floozy. What is this? *Midnight Cowboy*? Oh, I'm sorry, Cowgirl? You always did swoosh around like a pansy. Face it, you're nothing but a fag, Seamus. I don't care how tough you talk." He smacked me again.

Brody got me on the ground and got his fist ready to pound my fuckin' lights out, just like he did that time I was nine and showed up for supper looking like Adam Ant's Prince Charming, wearing Mom's eyeliner and lipstick with lipstick streaks war-painted across my cheeks. Not two seconds later, Brody dragged my nine-year-old ass over to the sink, scrubbed all the makeup off my face with a bar of Dial soap, and force-fed the Dial bar to me through my clenched teeth before body-slamming me into the tub and turning on the shower. That's where he punched me in the gut and slapped the shit out of my face. Mom wouldn't let me watch music videos on Channel 60 for a whole summer after I pulled that stunt.

Four years later, when Brody got me on the ground after the Sex Pistols rap, I didn't let him get at my mouth. I crossed my arms right in front of my face as he got his knuckles up and ready. But he stopped. Just stopped. Got up, looked at me, huffed, walked off with my tape in his mitts, got in his bronze Jaguar, and drove back to his condo. Bet he took a hammer to *Never Mind the Bollocks* on his kitchen island. But I went to Coconuts the next weekend and put the last of my Confirmation money down on another copy and he never did shit about it. Guess he figured, no matter how bad he could bruise me, I'd still go off and do my own thing, even if it included getting my ass fucked. Now when he visits, he just minces around in front of me with a limp wrist, and I don't say Word One to his *Thirty Something* ass.

After Brody took my tape, Johnny Rotten became more my idol than fuckin' ever. Soon as I got the money, I went to Rocket 69 and picked up a poster of Johnny shoving his face into the camera, fucking diabolical eyeballs popping out; safety pins all up and down his ripped-up, raggedy coat; T-shirt split down the middle, holes every which fuckin' way on it. He's everything the old guard was ever scared of. He'll throw his scrawny, scavenger dog's body at any nightstick. I hung him on my wall and bow down to him every night. I'd do it every morning too if I wasn't always so fucking tired, waking up before dawn to get all the way down to fucking Xavier on time—when the 85A's on time, that is. Rotten'd probably spit on me for worshipping him. Go ahead, Johnny. Baptize me in your spit, Johnny. I'll be your disciple, Johnny. They'll never get Rotten on a cross.

But the band Johnny formed after the Pistols, Public Image Ltd., is different. Way different. Rotten can actually *sing* in PiL. He's grown up. He's not even Johnny Rotten now. He's back to being John Lydon. Just as cool, though. Cooler even. You get to see Johnny's smart side in PiL. They're my favorite band, I think. They're not fast and loud like the Pistols, though. They're not even punk. Kind of New Wave actually, but deep New Wave. The lyrics are deep—deep concept, kinda-sorta New Order but rougher, much rougher. Rotten's way past his punk days with PiL.

But still, it's not Mozart. That's the groove I'm gettin' with now. Trying to get smart. Trying to expand my tastes, learn from the true greats. Tressa said she'd teach me. She knows everything about everything. I want to show her I'm not fucking off. Yes, Tressa, I *have* been listening to your Mozart tape. Yes, Tressa, I'm gonna get my hands on that pipeline, that pipeline that'll run inspiration straight from the muse to my brain, and I'll run all that inspiration right on to the page in fulfillment of my dreams. Or maybe it'll run through my body as I'm acting on stage. The stage or the page, whichever!

Brody says, the way I'm doing in school, the only thing he sees me pumping is the gas I'll be pumping for a living—and maybe some faggot's ass too. Now that he's a big-bucks lawyer, he can look down on future grease monkeys and ass bandits like me. Who knows? Maybe he does know what he's talking about. Maybe he's been gaming the system this whole time with his white collars, cufflinks, wingtips and easy-ass smile. Maybe his fat-cat credentials can save his soul.

Brody always did know which side his white bread's buttered on. He went to Xavier fifteen years ago, did his homework, aced his tests, learned fuckin' nothing—didn't get culture like I'm getting now with Tressa and Mozart and Monet and shit. But Brody got As; that's what gains the world on the world's scorecard. National Merit Scholar. Scholarship to Notre Dame. Stayed for law school. Graduated at the top of his class. Now he's up for partner at Dryden, Weber & Simon and he lives with his yuppie lawyer wife, Sylvia, on One Mag Mile and he's Mommy and Daddy's one and only, forever and ever the fucking fair-haired boy, amen.

When Tressa hears me talk about Brody, she says he's full of shit. Tells me hang in there. He'll be eating my dust by the time I'm his age. She says there's something to me. She sees a poet, a playwright, *and* a novelist in me, she says. Says she bets her tits, ass, and twat she'll be hearing about me. Better get to it then. Don't want Tressa losing her tits, ass, and twat. She says I'm sensitive and gives me all these books to read so I'll be a writer—Balzac, Kafka, Hesse, Henry Miller (fuckin' love Miller),

D.H. Lawrence, and Nelson Algren (he's dead now, like the rest of them, but he lived about a mile down from Tressa and wrote about junkies). I don't finish reading them all (except Miller; fuckin' love Miller), but I do get a good way through them and I look up all the words I don't know and write their definitions down on flashcards and study them instead of studying my fucking biology book or doing homework. I'm a helluva lot more scared of flunking one of Tressa or Agatha's pop quizzes than I am of flunking any midterms or finals at a school that's flunking me out anyways.

Dr. Strykeroth says he'd throw his balls in Tressa's tits-ass-and-twat bet too. He tells me he learns something new every time I come by his office. Says not to worry about school. He says, "You'll make an *outpouring* some day." He said an outpouring. Even called it "supreme." "A supreme outpouring" is how he put it. That's what he told me when I told him I found a long, sharp razor near UIC-Halsted. I keep it in the top drawer of the desk in my bedroom and I take it out all the time and stare at it, thinking I can cut deep and do a fuck lot better job than the last time I tried offing myself. He told me, "I don't want you to die, Seamus. I don't want you to die." He brushed the side of my face with the backs of his fingers. My tears rolled on to them. He had such beautiful fingers. They're dark—dark German, not pasty Irish—and they glide so gently.

CHAPTER IV
Minimum GPA

Lately, all I've been doing on the 85A is looking back to last year, freshman year...

The old man was wearing an ascot. He had this deep, cultured, kinda-sorta-but-not-all-the-way English voice. He said, "Young man, are you seeking a career in *acting*?"

I smiled and nodded. That nod was the truth. On Sunday nights when I was little, I used to sneak downstairs when Mom and Dad were in bed to turn on *Dr. Who*. It used to come on at 10:30 on Channel 11. I never understood any of the shit that was going down on that sci-fi show but, man alive, could those limeys act! Even as young as eight years old, I watched every BBC show that ever came on here, even the real fuckin' boring ones. The accents, why the fuck weren't we using those accents? Why the fuck weren't our vocabs that good? Why the fuck weren't our actors anywhere near as good as theirs? Why the fuck weren't we that fuckin' cultured? Lots of Americans want to go to Hollywood to be movie stars. Even back when I first started thinking about acting, I couldn't give a flying fuck what was going on in Hollywood. Or even on Broadway. None of that shit was art. It was all sales. But the BBC and the London theater scene—from everything I saw in the Sunday *Trib* and on PBS— that was all *art*, and ever since I was eleven, I planned to take off and join up with it. And now somehow Mrs. Wesley got this theater vet with an ascot and an accent to sit in on auditions and he recognizes my spark. Maybe this was my big break, maybe I just got discovered, right here at my first high school audition. Well, I said to myself, wasn't that fuckin' easy!

It was last year at the first round of auditions for *The Importance of Being Earnest*. For a second or two after my last monologue, Mrs. Wesley and the old guy, who stroked his chin a lot, stopped dead cold and silent. I breathed hard and stood in place. Mrs. Wesley took a deep breath before saying, "Well, you scared the bejeezus out of me...but you blew everyone else out of the water." The old man nodded in agreement.

"Freshmen don't typically bowl me over," Mrs. Wesley continued. "Never seen it done, not in all my years of teaching here. You did, though. Have you acted before, Seamus?" I shook my head no. The old guy pinned an eyebrow up at her and she raised hers back. She turned to me, "Could you maybe stick around until after 4:30 today? I'd like you to do a scene, reading the part of Algernon." She handed me a photocopied script and pointed to where Algernon's lines begin, which is also where Wilde's play begins.

Yes, it was second quarter, last school year at Xavier and I was the only freshman with balls enough to try out for the drama club's spring production. It's common knowledge that freshmen never get cast in shows. Never, except maybe a walk-on part here and there, and there ain't a helluva lot of those in *Earnest*. Hardly any freshmen even audition. Most every sophomore shrinks back too, but juniors and seniors line up for two or three hallways.

It was a snowy afternoon. Upper-classmen milled outside the multi-purpose room running lines and adding on all sorts of phony-ass gestures and accents—all them spending all their energy psyching out the competition with glares, tisks, and other mind games—none of them getting at the meat of their monologues. I saw through all their shit when they tried it on me. To them, this was just a high school play, but, to me, it's art—or could be—and I'm an artist. I know I am. I'd be at the Academy of the Arts if Dad wasn't such an asshole. But these little Xavier browbeaters, they're nothing but future fuckin' yuppies, a herd of capitalist swine who'll never act again after high school. Wilde is just another extracurric they're gonna tack on to their college apps. So nobody, least of all Mrs. Wesley and that old theater dude, ever saw my tsunami coming.

For first rounds, we each had to recite two five-minute monologues. This senior bitch, Beth Schiller, turned out these cutsie little girly girl monologues from *Our Town* and *Little Women*. Toby Drymiller, a class-clown senior, was prating some safe-safe chuckle-chuckle bullshit from *Brighton Beach Memoirs* and *Willy Wonka & the Chocolate Factory*. Jill Sibley, a junior on the cheerleading squad, gave some flip-your-wig flourishes from *Butterflies Are Free* and *The Goodbye Girl*. Patrick McDonald, a senior wonk hell-bent on Harvard, went for grand fuckin' effects with verses from *All's Well that Ends Well* and *As You Like It*.

Me, a freshman, I was foaming at the fuckin' mouth after I did that "in-and-out" monologue from *A Clockwork Orange*, where Alex licks his chops after a gang rape, and the one from *Medea*, where Medea tells Jason that she's killed their own children, right after she sets the bitch Jason left her for on fire. "Whyyyyy!" Jason screams like thunder over his kids' bleeding corpses. Medea coldly replies, "Because I loathed you more than I loved them." Yeah, I scared the shit out of Mrs. Wesley. Plus I was the only guy with balls enough to play a chick.

I knew the *Clockwork Orange* monologue could get me kicked out of school. It's high on the list of banned books in St. Xavier's library. But, for free-speech principles alone, I figured it'd be fucking worth it. Besides, it was Xavier that taught me the sick, sick *Medea* shit in the first place. I suckled every scene down to the last dregs in Mr. Wood's class, the first month of freshman year. I could blame him for corrupting me with Euripides. Much as I hate the man, I should thank him; if it wasn't for Wood, I never would've read *Medea* and it wouldn't've motivated me to check something as lethal as *A Clockwork Orange* out from the Chicago Public Library.

After listening to about another hour or so of bone-dry bullshit from everyone else, Mrs. Wesley and the old guy thinned the second round of auditions down to a few worthy candidates. I was one. I read the part of Algernon opposite Beth Schiller, who read Gwendolyn. Mrs. Wesley and the old man belly-roared at every line I delivered. They called my accent "perfect." They thanked Beth Schiller and the others and sent them all home. They had me alone stay behind to keep reading.

After auditing me for about twenty more minutes, Mrs. Wesley said, "Are you sure you've never acted before, Seamus?"

"No, never," I said. "Always wanted to, but, no, this is my first time."

Mrs. Wesley and the theater guy exchanged knowing looks and smiley nods. "Well, we still have some formalities to go through," Mrs. Wesley told me, "you'll still have to come to callbacks Friday, but...You any good at keeping secrets?" I crossed my heart with my forefinger. She came over and gripped my arms, "You're the lead. You're Algernon!"

I didn't sleep for two nights, I was in so much fuckin' glory. And, even on no sleep, I felt alive for the first time since I walked through Xavier's prison gates. I thought, maybe I'll even learn to concentrate in class. I mean, I know I didn't know jack shit about what Mrs. Pischke was doing with the numbers or symbols in that fucking *Through the Looking-Glass* world of algebra. But for once, I started thinking, if other kids could catch on in class, maybe I could too. So what if I flunked Xavier's entrance exam? I liked to read a lot, so maybe I could find a way to finally wake up in Mr. Wood's class. Maybe there were some hidden gems in all that boring bullshit he made us read in our textbook. Maybe it could help me act and write. I could learn newer and bigger words. I mean, y'know, that shit can help your art out a lot if you study it enough, right? I started feeling like, even though I got off on the wrong foot with school, maybe I could scrape up the brains I didn't have at the entrance exam. Maybe there was still time to pick up all the slack I left behind since the first day of freshman year.

And callbacks were a fuckin' cakewalk. I mean, I could've rested on my laurels. Could've sat there thinking, well, I already got the part, so fuck it. But, no, I was real fuckin' dedicated. They had me read more *Earnest*. Once again, I *devastated* the multi-purpose room. Mrs. Wesley even brought a couple other teachers in to watch me. Still don't know their names, even though I see them around school all the time, but they all gave me a huge fucking round of applause. One of them, Mrs. Something-or-Other-or- something, she even went up to Mrs. Wesley and said, "Oh, Barbara, you're right. He's a natural." Then Mrs. Something-or-Other-or-Something walked up to me, patted my shoulder and said, "Good job, Seamus."

My name was out there. My name, Seamus O'Grady, was fuckin' *out* there! Two days later, the cast list went up. Jeff Hawking—that prick from Oak Lawn who got kicked off the football team for twelve counts of "unsportsmanlike conduct"— he was one of two sophomores who tried out, only he didn't make the cut like I did, so he got up in my face and said, "Figures they'd make an Irish fag the lead in an Irish fag play. Right, O'Grady? Oscar Wilde was a fucking fag and so are you." Hawking bumped his chest right into the bridge of my nose—one of the few assholes tall enough to do that. He always leaves his shirt half-unbuttoned too so everyone can see what a worked-out chest and bod he's got and how many hickeys he's got riding from his neck to his sternum and probably lower—at least he'd like everybody to think they go lower. Hawking calling me fag hurt like hell like it always does, but my mood was high enough and my wit quick enough for me to say, "But, gee, Jeff, isn't that the part you wanted? In this faggot play? Too bad callbacks didn't work out for you, big boy." He smacked me upside the head. Mr. Mailer saw it, though, and JUG'd him for it. I walked off laughing and went home to memorize lines.

First week of rehearsals, I was the only one with my lines down pat. I'd get home late from scene study and, instead of doing homework, I'd walk around my room, trying to bring every word from Wilde into my bloodstream. My shanty blood was becoming more lace-curtain with every line this Irish Protestant jailbird bugger wrote. Every day, Mrs. Wesley gave me directing notes and I'd go home and try matching them up with the script. I couldn't wait for the day that I could stride right out on to stage. I already knew Xavier's wasn't the place for me, but I fantasized that, if I could kick ass early and get discovered by casting agents, I might get a part in some movie or traveling show and never have to finish high school or live with fuckin' Mom and Dad again. Oprah has shows about whiz kids that shit happens for, so why couldn't it happen for me?

The second Friday of rehearsals came. Mrs. Wesley asked me to come in early. Soon as I got there, she sat me down, "Seamus, I'm afraid I have some bad news." She took a sighing breath, "I had to submit the cast list for Dean Russell's approval. He saw your name and went over your file. Now, Seamus, to be in a play at St. Xavier, you need a GPA of at least 2.5. Your first quarter grades show that your GPA is…well, much lower."

My body shot up, "What does that mean? Are they gonna let me do the play?" She put her hand on mine and looked down, not saying a word. I screeched, "Isn't there something I can do? Can I…? You know what, tell him I'll bring my grades up next quarter. I swear."

She shook her head, "I did my best to persuade him. Believe me. I was in the dean's office for an hour. I pulled every rabbit out of my hat. There's nothing I can do, Seamus. Dean Russell strictly forbids any student from participating in the drama club or on sports teams unless and *until* they reach the minimum GPA. It didn't used to be this way, but ever since Dean Russell came on board two years ago, he's been…oh, Seamus, I'm sorry. I'm so sorry. I cried when I heard. Just like you're crying right now, sweetheart. Believe me, I underst—oh, look, you got me crying now too." She handed me a Kleenex and got some for herself. She dabbed her eyes. "I'm sorry, Seamus. You have the most potential of any student I've seen in a long time. In fact, I can't remember anyone with more. Maybe this coming spring, huh? If you can get your grades up. Please try, honey. I want so much to see more of you."

She gave me a hug, but I was too fuckin' stunned and too fuckin' limp to hug back. I walked out and, for a while, just sat on the icy sidewalk on Racine Street. The wind pushed me over on to the concrete, both ways, at least three times. Even the gangbangers from the Abla Homes across the street took too much pity on my sorry ass to shake me down as I sat there crying in the cold. It wasn't until a long time later that I made my way to the L station.

And wasn't it fucking humiliating announcing to Mom and Dad that I just got kicked out of the play on account of my fuckin' grades. Of course they took this as an invitation to trounce me. What hurt most was, Dad ended his rap with, "But I'm not surprised."

But, no, what hurt way worse, wa-a-ay fuckin' worse: Mrs. Wesley went back and cast Jeff Hawking as Algernon. Fucking Jeff Hawking! Guess he wasn't so above taking a faggot part once it was his to take. But I hear he was an absolute twat on stage: couldn't do an accent, kept fumbling over his fuckin' lines. People got up and left. Who walks out of a high school play? I mean, you really gotta suck for that shit to happen. But I never went to see him butcher

Wilde. Fuck no. Never went to see *Earnest* or any other Xavier play. Never auditioned for anything else either. Get to 2.5? That's like asking me to bend down and suck my own cock.

It was a Tuesday, two days after *Earnest* closed, that my second quarter grades came in the mail. One C-, three Ds, two Fs. Landed my ass on academic probation.

Next night, Mom and Dad were heading downtown to the Palmer House for St. Xavier's Annual Gala Dinner. Mom was making up in the bathroom for more than an hour trying to put a pretty face on the O'Grady name and salvage the rep I was ruining. She put a plush green overcoat on over her cream-colored Chanel suit. Dad put his London Fog trenchcoat on over his best suit, a gray pinstripe from the Jos A. Banks catalogue. He damn near choked himself to death tightening up his burgundy silk tie for their grand Palmer House entrance. Neither would look at or speak to me on their way out. Mom's theatrics were pure shit: angling her head away from me, sticking her nose so high in the air that, if Dad hadn't pulled her back, her chin would've rammed straight into the front door. Dad followed Mom out and threw his voice so I could hear him say, "If we're gonna keep this little puke in school, Mary, we're gonna have to write a bigger check than ever to Father Mahoney. And, God-Almighty, the money couldn't be any tighter than it is now." The door slammed shut.

I crept over and stood off to the side of the white curtains so they wouldn't see me watching as they pulled out of the driveway in Dad's Corsica. Dad backed out to the west and pounded on the gas east toward the Kennedy Expressway. A gust of heat rushed to my head. I stood, shook, and breathed.

My little tabby, Puddles, walked over to me, meowing and rubbing against my legs. I named her Puddles after I found her by a puddle on Ionia Street two years ago. In fact, Puddles had crouched right under the wheel of a parked car, and it didn't look like she was in any mood to move, not even if the owner came out and started the engine. She was an abandoned kitten, two months old, and had the look of a dying deer who was about to turn its belly up to a pride of lions. I decided to pick her up and give her something to live for. And, fuck, did I have to fight to keep her in the house. Dad only let her stay because, right when he was about to turn her back out on the street, he decided to take a nap in the den. I sat upstairs, crying, cursing his name, plotting his death even worse than usual. But Dad slept on his back and woke up to find Puddles snoozing on his stomach, her little white chin resting on her little gray and white paws. Not even he could deny how cute it was the way she went up and down, up and down on his beer belly. Not even Dad had the heart to kick her out after that. Still refuses to call her Puddles, though. In his book, it does a cat too much dignity to give it a name. At most, he says, "Out of my way, stupid." But at least Asshole let her stay.

I turned away from the door, picked Puddles up and gave her a big kiss on the forehead and cheek. "Daddy loves you, Puddles," I told her. "Never forget that." I thanked her for how she slept on my leg every night, looking out over the edge of the bed, protecting me from any ghouls and burglars who might be coming by. I hugged her close, kissed her again, and put her down across the kitchen threshold. She pitter-pattered over to her bowl of Meow Mix. I smiled watching her but stopped smiling as my eyes hit the floor. I had so much to take care of now.

I padded a few feet over to the laundry room. After school, I'd put a couple raggedy towels, a pair of scissors and a roll of masking tape behind the trash compactor. I picked them up, stepped back into the foyer and peered through the door window one more time. Our front lawn bloomed like a misty emerald rose. In fall, it's never a flush green, but now, in the moonlight, it looked riper than summer grass. I stood, held the image a few more seconds and looked back to the floor, letting our yard fall out of sight and mind. I turned toward the kitchen. Puddles had turned away from her Meow Mix; she was standing a few feet away from her bowl, making cow eyes, cocking her little tiger-striped head. I put my supplies on the floor, ran back into the kitchen, and scooped Puddles back into the air, kissing her over and over as she closed her eyes, barely tolerating my mushiness. I told her one last time, "Daddy loves you, Puddles." I put her back down, picked my supplies back up and opened the door to the garage. I said to Puddles, "Don't follow me, now, sweetheart. I love you." She cocked her head again.

I walked into the garage, shut the door behind me, and tucked the towels under the door. Tears came but I didn't let that stop me from tucking. Part of me wanted to walk back into the foyer, put everything back where I found it, and take Puddles upstairs and fall asleep petting her. But I stayed on my knees.

I cried some more, bowing my head to Puddles, who, by now, was meowing for me on the other side of the door. I didn't leave a note for Mom and Dad. There was nothing to say. They'd find me and look back on everything they'd ever said and done. That'd say it all. I should've had some more last words for Puddles, but I didn't. I tried coming up with some, but nothing came. All except for Pink Floyd's "Brain Damage." I tried fighting the song back, but it was too strong for my sappy little mind. I know Johnny Rotten used to walk around London with a T-shirt on that said, "I H8 Pink Floyd," but I don't. I hoped Puddles didn't either:

And if the dam breaks open many years too soon
And if there is no room upon the hill
And if your head explodes with all the bones too
I'll see you on the dark side of the moon.

Pink fuckin' Floyd: not very punk rock of me. Still, it was a fuck

lot better than anything the Misfits or any other hardcore band I
could think of had for a time like this:

And if the dam breaks open many years too soon...
I'll see you on the dark side of the moon.

        I stayed on my knees a couple minutes longer, got up,
dried my eyes, and plied masking tape along the edges of the door.
Puddles was happy in her feline life, a fuck lot happier than she
was under the wheel of that car. There was no reason to take her
into the garage with me. My muscles and bones were as bloated
as a drowned sailor as I dragged my feet over to Dad's station
wagon. I unlocked the door, hopped into the front seat, and shut
the door after me, remembering Frank Seaberg.

        Frank lived a block over on Wildwood Avenue. He'd
been a boozehound since sixth grade, when he first started taking
swigs of Jameson out of his parent's liquor cabinet. Like me,
Frank wasn't much of a student. At morning free period in his
last two years at Aquinas North, he'd slam a couple six packs of
Old Style in the parking lot with his buddies and black out by
lunchtime. Ended up, after senior year, he had to repeat three
classes in summer school to graduate. Couldn't get into a four-
year school, so he had to go to Oakton Community College.
Didn't score any higher there his first year, but that didn't make
his folks love him less. Plus, he got on okay with the boss at Golf
Glen Auto Body & Repair, so his mom and dad figured he could
at least stay on and learn a trade if he didn't pass at Oakton.

        Three years ago, Mr. and Mrs. Seaberg went on a two-
week tour of Europe for their silver anniversary. Frank was
supposed to stay home and look after his little brother, Mark,
who was only a freshman or sophomore and already MVP on
the Aquinas North wrestling team. The first Saturday his folks
were gone, Frank took their panther-black, mint-condition 1970

Corvette to a party. I guess he thought he could pick up chicks with it. I'm sure he got blasted out of his mind, though, and didn't pick up any, but he didn't get in any accidents on the way home either, so, in that way, he still got lucky.

Only, on his way out that night, Frank forgot his house keys. He didn't know it, though, until he put the Vette back in the garage and checked his pockets. He rang and rang and rang the front doorbell for Mark to wake up and let him in, but Mark wasn't home. He'd left a note on the kitchen table saying he was staying at a friend's. Frank never saw the note, but, after throwing enough rocks at Mark's window in the freezing cold, he put two and two together and figured Mark was either staying out late or not coming home till morning. Frank slept in the Vette, deciding, I guess, not to push his luck by driving back to the party and risking more accidents.

Should've took his own Ford Escort. It wasn't a chick-charmer—he bought it used a few years before and it was only about five grand, new—but at least he would've parked it on the street like he always did and had more chances with the ladies next time. But, no, he had to show off the Corvette and put it back in the garage. It was about as cold that night as it is this morning, so Frank let the garage door down with the remote, turned the engine on for heat, and fell asleep in the backseat. He wasn't a sad guy or anything, he was just a dumb-ass drunk. He didn't know he'd wake up dead. From what the police said, car exhaust puts you to sleep. You doze off as you swallow it, then you suffocate. It's an easy death.

The week after the funeral, Mark dropped off the wrestling team and started hitting the bottle hard like dear ole bro. But to be MVP of alkies like Frank, he'd have to practice night and day for years. Mark's folks checked him into rehab before that shit could happen. They also got Mark a shrink so he could learn to live down not staying home the night Frank forgot the front door keys and died. The Seabergs thought nothing of selling the Corvette for parts. They loved Frank too much to wait around for the highest bidder to come along and take the vintage exhaust-trap off their hands. But getting rid of reminders isn't the same as getting rid of memories. Three years later, Mr. and Mrs. Seaberg still look like they got about as much blood left in their faces as Frank did in his coffin.

So what about me with Mom and Dad? Well, I figured, they'd probably have to put on a show of grief for people at St. Aloysius or St. Xavier, but aside from that, they'd probably be happy. They could write out smaller checks to Father Mahoney every year, loosen the purse strings a little. And as for me, I knew this way report cards, failure, bum deals, Andy Payne, Jeff Hawking—all that shit—would be in the past. Say what you will about my Ds and Fs, I'm no dumb-ass like Frank Seaberg. I knew what the fuck I was doing in our garage. I put the key in the ignition and turned it. Smoke whooshed up outside the windows. I closed my eyes and fell asleep to the sound and taste of smoke seeping into my ears and mouth.

People always wonder what's on the other side when you stop breathing. I just saw a lot of clouds and smoke. I mean, I seemed to be breathing just fine after a while. I didn't see what the big fuckin' deal was. There was no God or devil standing there, waiting for me with arms folded. Father Griffin told us in seventh grade that the Church doesn't believe anymore that people who kill themselves go to hell like people who kill other people or fuck before marriage. But he didn't say they go to heaven either. Not that I give a shit what him or the Church say. But it's true. As far as I could tell, there was no devil and no God waiting for me. Just clouds and smoke.

I got out of the car and walked through a plague of clouds, kind of walking, kind of floating. One cloud had an open door in it that was made of the same marshmallow fluff as the rest of the clouds. Everything around me looked the same: big clouds clustered together with little patches of blue and gray sky in back. The door opened. I could see Frank Seaberg standing on the other side. He looked the same as he always did: brown Members Only jacket, gray AC/DC T-shirt, Gap blue jeans, white Adidas high-tops. He just stood there, stock-still and catatonic, like he just took a bullet in the chest but wasn't falling down. What the fuck did he find on the other side of the cloud door? Whatever it was, it left him looking mighty fuckin' confused. Was he just gonna stand there with that stupid look on his face for all eternity?

When I walked up to the cloud door, it slammed shut with a crash. Next thing I knew, I was flat on my back in the dark, couldn't even flinch. Red and white lights were flashing everywhere. Air flooded my lungs. And everything went black. Pitch black. Made me wonder if death is even more of an anticlimax than life. Pitch black, only? Maybe it's true. Maybe there's nothing waiting for you after you swallow too many gulps of smoke. Meeting nothing don't sound so bad, especially if you lived your life fearing hell like Mom and Dad. But what if you have to be aware of that nothing, all that blackness all the days of your afterlife, while you're free-floating through eternity like Major Tom in "Space Oddity"?

When I was a little kid, I used to go into a deep fuckin' freeze whenever I thought about death and being stuck in a casket some undertaker drops in the ground. It scared the living shit out of me that buried dead might be the same as buried alive—and it'd be for-fuckin'-ever, just you and your lonely little corpse, stuck in one place under thick wood and mounds of immovable dirt, until the end of time, until the Second Coming—whenever that shit was supposed to happen. Later, when I was about seven, I found out you could get cremated instead, so I went and told Mom I want to be cremated, have my ashes scattered to the four winds so I can at least get some elbow room when this trip is over. She said Catholics can't. Man, Catholics can't do shit, can they? I think it's after she told me that that I first started checking apartment listings in the Sunday *Trib*, thinking I should move out. Seven years after my cremation chat with Mom, I found myself right where I didn't want to be: flat on my fuckin' back in the afterlife, in a dark place, unable to move a muscle, probably for-fuckin'-ever.

The darkness cleared after a while, though. I could feel my eyes start to open. I saw white walls. My head felt woozy. I closed my eyes so the wooziness would wear off. I couldn't fall asleep. Kept hearing a voice, "Seamus? Seamus? Can you hear me, Seamus?" I looked up and saw a fat old man's face hanging over me. He had a white coat on. I looked down at my stomach. It was under bed sheets. So were my legs. I propped myself up a bit. I saw gray guardrails at my feet. I looked all over. Holy shit! I was in a hospital bed. The fat old man in the white coat was a doctor in a doctor's coat. He had a stethoscope around his neck. "Can you see me?" he asked, "Just nod or signal with your index finger if you feel too weak."

I propped myself up on my elbows and said, "What the fuck is this? *The Wall?*"

"Good Lord, you can speak!"

"Where the fuck am I?"

"Can you count to ten?" the doctor asked me with bated breath.

I sighed, rubbed my eyes and said, "Listen, I'll count from twenty to zero if you tell me who the fuck you are and where the fuck I am."

"Good idea," he said. "Count backward from twenty." So I did. He cheered and said, "I'm Dr. Lang. Can you tell me your name?"

"Seamus."

"Last name?"

"O'Grady."

"Good. What's the year?"

"Last I checked, 1987."

"Excellent! Can you tell me who the president is?"

"Ronald Reagan," I answered, "and we still got a whole 'nother year of that fuck."

"Remarkable," said the good doctor. "Young man, do you see those monitors?"

"Yeah," I said. "What are they monitoring?"

"Your brain waves and your heart rate," Dr. Lang rubbed my arm with his cold hand. "And both are in perfect working order. *Perfect* Working Order! They weren't when they pulled you in on that stretcher last night, boy-howdy. Even four hours ago, they were both on the verge of flatlining. Young man, do you believe in miracles?"

"No."

"Well, you'd better start," he patted my arm. "The minute you're back on your feet, you drop to your knees and thank God He saved you from the shadow of death. Now I'm not here to judge you. Lord knows I've had my days. But you have to know that, after what you did, you could've wound up brain damaged *at best*."

"Too late," I replied, "have been since birth."

"I wouldn't joke about that if I were you, Seamus," Dr. Lang said. "Don't tempt fate. There's a reason God kept you alive. I suggest you find out what it is. Your parents are in the waiting room. Your father's been pacing the floor all night. Your mother's crying buckets. I'm going to go tell them God was good and they can come visit you later. Meanwhile, I want you to get some sleep. You've got a lot of explaining to do, sir. You'll need your strength to face the two of them. We're going to keep you here for a day or two to make sure everything's a-okay. From there...we'll see. But your case is more promising than any doctor would have expected. You're *very* lucky." He exhaled deeply. "You might grow a little bored between naps. Would you like the nurse to bring you something to read?"

"Got any Greek tragedies?" I cheered.

"That's not what you need right now, son. Now get some sleep."

Dr. Lang left the room. I closed my eyes. There was an IV in my arm, but I was so beat, I hardly noticed. I dropped right off to sleep and dreamed I was back in the station wagon in our garage. Only this time, the garage was open. Wind whipped in and washed out all the exhaust. I got out of the car, walked out of the garage—past Frank Seaberg, who was standing with one foot inside and one foot outside the garage—and down our driveway to the sidewalk. I walked down Ponchitrain Street to the bus stop at the corner of Lehigh. It was dark as the night before, the night I'd planned to make my last, and the streetlights were glowing. I looked far off into the distance across the railroad tracks. I saw the Chicago skyline like I always do on a clear day. I watched it for a little while. But, all of a sudden, all the lights went off on all the skyscrapers and new lights started rising up. I saw London Bridge and Big Ben. London was in sight beyond the railroad tracks, where the Sears Tower, John Hancock, and all the other downtown buildings used to be. I could feel my heart opening wider and wider. The Chicago skyline lights came back on soon after, but the London lights stayed on too. And between Chicago and London, more bridges and skyscrapers started coming up on the horizon, ones I didn't recognize at first. I recognized the Empire State Building from old movies, though, so something in me knew I was looking at New York. Looking out from the bus stop, I saw Chicago, New York, and London standing together, not as three different places, but as one continuous city. I turned my head north toward Touhy Avenue. I saw the 85A coming my way, opening its doors before it could even make a full stop. I looked at the driver. It was Oscar Wilde in his curls, a frock coat, and a lavender silk scarf. I saw there was only one passenger on the bus. It was none other than Johnny Rotten, sitting toward the front with his legs draped over the seat next to him. He was wearing a black overcoat, square shades, and a sneer. He was drinking a can of Guinness and wiping dribble off his chin. I remember thinking, I didn't get to do *Earnest*, but I didn't miss the bus either. There's still life on the horizon.

I woke up with my eyes shut, feeling like I was soaking in a warm bath of peace and excitement. It was the same feeling I got when I was still in the play, the feeling that I finally fucking found something worth living for, just like Puddles did once I took her away from the puddle and the tire on Ionia Street. At the same time, I felt a little disappointed in myself for fucking up, yet again—couldn't even get my own suicide right. But I put all that shit to the side and focused more on shit like how I couldn't wait to see Puddles again. I'd hug her close, rub my nose into her whiskers, and tell her I decided to stick around a while longer, now that my dreams were telling me that London was just a little ways across the tracks, that Oscar Wilde was driving the 85A and Johnny Rotten was riding it.

I woke up from the dream to find Mom and Dad standing by my hospital bed. I don't know how long I'd slept. I don't know how long they'd been standing there. I didn't know what time it was, but sunlight was beaming in through the windows and Mom and Dad still hadn't changed out of what they were wearing for their grand Palmer House entrance the night before. Mom stood to the right of my bed in last night's cream-colored Chanel suit, clutching her brown leather purse and, since it was a little chilly in the room, she was still wearing her green overcoat. Her face was set in a combination of fatigue and fury. Strapped under tight blankets with an IV in my arm, I couldn't just get up and walk away. I closed my eyes, hoping Mom would disappear if I couldn't see her. That shit never worked when I was five and it wasn't fuckin' working now. There comes a time when you gotta stop believing in magic. Like when you're laid up in a hospital bed because whoever's running this fuckin' show won't let you out of your fuckin' contract.

I also knew I had to abandon any hope I wasn't in deep shit, so I bit the bullet and looked at Dad. His forehead looked like someone'd raked plows across it for ten days straight. For the first time since I knew him, his tin-colored hair had lost its part and was standing up in tufts. His Jos A. Banks pinstriped coat was open wide over his beer gut, his burgundy silk tie was wrestled down into a gnarly knot that looked like a loose noose waiting for a head, and his shirt looked like a rumpled wino's with the top three buttons open over his white undershirt.

Dad spoke up first, "You never pass up the chance to humiliate us, do you?"

"I'm feeling fine, Dad," I said, stretching out my arms and legs, "thanks for your concern."

"No backtalk," Mom shot back, stamping her foot. "Who do you think you are? Who *do* you think you are? Not only making fools of us, but courting hell and damnation."

"Don't bring your goddamn religion into this," I said.

She took three or four steps right up to my bed and pointed her finger about a centimeter away from my left eye, "Don't you dare mock me, your father, or the Lord, you little heathen."

"Say anything," I spit back. "Say anything you want. Just don't bring your goddamn religion into this."

She slapped me with a roundhouse to the right side of my face. If she'd tried that shit on me while I was standing up, I would've said she had a death wish. Since she did it when I was lying down and taking food in through my arm, I just put it down to a cowardly sucker slap. After all, there were no witnesses besides Dad in the room. He wasn't gonna say anything. I didn't say anything either but I looked at her colder than she'd *ever* fuckin' looked at me. Mom prides herself on being able to glare harder than the nuns did over brick-shitting kids in the 1930s. She never dreamed I'd top her with one of my glares—not until I did—from my sickbed no less, which I now went back to wishing was my deathbed. My glare even scared the shit out of Dad, the ex-marine captain. Totally fuckin' missed his cue to halt my vibe of doom.

Mom broke eye contact with a hissy inhale. She turned around and stood a few feet away from the windows, crying with her hands over her eyes. If she was blubbering for the right reasons, I would've felt sorry for her. Might've even apologized. But I knew why she was blubbering. It wasn't about how she'd miss me if I were gone. It wasn't about her being sad about me being so sad that I went off and did what I did. Fuck no. It was about what she said: me, her own son, "courting hell and damnation." Guess she wasn't there when Father Griffin spoke to my seventh grade class. She didn't know the Church changed its mind. She still thought that, if I'd done it right and died, God and everybody else would always look on her as the mother who raised a son who took his life and went to hell. So I kept going with my glare.

"You owe Mr. Adamczak a debt of gratitude, mister," Dad said from the foot of my hospital bed. "A *lifelong* debt of gratitude. Plus an apology. He was the one who found you, you know. Now everybody knows." Dad went and told me that, the night before, Mr. Adamczak walked up to the little stretch of grass on his side of our driveway with a flashlight to see if his Ziploc bags were still tied tight enough around his perennials, which always end up dying in the fuckin' snow anyway. Normally, Mr. Adamczak has a hard time moving around, what with being, like, 70 years old with a Quasimodo hump. But when he saw smoke, he hauled ass over to our garage door, which I somehow forgot to lock as part of my grand fuckin' master plan. I was all

43

unconscious dead weight, but, with a sudden surge of strength, the kind that helps a mom pick a monster truck up off her baby, Mr. Adamczak hooked his arms under mine, dragged my body out to the driveway, and started performing the CPR he learned way back when he was a volunteer lifeguard at the Y. He called out to Mrs. Adamczak and she called the ambulance. I guess it was the ambulance lights I saw flashing above my head after the cloud-door slammed shut. The air filling my lungs must've come from Mr. Adamczak's CPR. Or maybe it was the paramedics' oxygen tank. Either way, man, Mr. Adamczak's lips were on mine. So I guess there is such thing as hell.

Mr. Adamczak could never mind his fuckin' business. Everybody knows that. People walk blocks out of their way to avoid his small talk; he'll keep it going till their bowels break and they have to book it to the nearest john. He stands on the sidewalk, leeching everyone for every last detail of their lives. I see him looking in our windows when he comes around to check his plants. That's another thing I fuckin' hate about Jarvis Park. You can't even kill yourself without someone like Adamczak sticking his nose in and stopping you.

I never went up and thanked him after I got out of the hospital. For one thing, I was too embarrassed. I'd just turn my head away if I saw him. But, by then, Mr. and Mrs. Adamczak were turning their heads away when they saw me coming too—them and all the other neighbors.

This one chick at school, Dawn Cino, made a half-ass attempt at taking her life once. I don't know what her deal was, don't know why she tried. I just know what I overheard Raza Stevens telling Stephanie Gerald when I was in line getting fries in the cafeteria one day. Dawn's dad's a cop. She knew his routine like she knew the shape of her tits in the shower. He'd head to his bedroom closet after work and hang up his pants, gun, and holster before changing into sweat pants. Once, while he was down in the kitchen making spaghetti, she went in his room and picked up his gun. I guess she was gonna blow her brains out, but the gun went off before she could even raise it to her temple. She ended up shooting the cable box. Her Dad checked her into a hospital and she got to be out of school for seven weeks. They had group therapy. Everybody told their stories. They all bonded and felt better.

I was hoping for the same luck. Thought I'd get to go to the psych ward. Thought it was the law. But Mom and Dad convinced Dr. Lang I didn't need it. They even got him to call Father Mahoney. Don't know where the fuck Father Mahoney got off saying anything about me to anybody. He knows Mom and Dad, but he's never even looked at me. Still, he vouched for how I was a stand-up young man, if a little undisciplined, but no danger to myself or others. How the fuck would he know? But somehow Dr. Lang bought it.

I spent the next two days in the hospital, sucking up an IV through my arm and reading the *Little House on the Prairie* books the nurse brought me. By the third one, I was ready to get the fuck back home. They finally sprang me that Saturday, and I spent the rest of the weekend in my bedroom.

For the next few weeks, Mom and Dad wouldn't talk to me and I wouldn't talk to them. Still made me go to fuckin' Mass, though. I'd walked into St. Aloysius and grab a Mass bulletin to show my ass was there but I'd walk the fuck out right after and hide out deep in the Forest Preserve, deeper than they ever fuckin' found me before. I'd pack a new pack of Marlboros against my wrist and suck back three or four smokes.

I'd crank up Hüsker Dü's *Zen Arcade* on my Walkman. Album's all about smashing down all the fuckin' walls that need smashing down. I fuckin' loathe how the fuckin' game is rigged. Fuckin' loathe it. Every time I try to get ahead, something stands in my way. I want to kick ass in school but my mind can't keep still. I

45

want friends but everybody thinks I'm a freak and the freaks don't think I know what the fuck I'm doing, they call me a fuckin' poseur, a Rotten-wannabe. Mrs. Wesley said I was the best fuckin' actor my age she's ever fuckin' seen, but, no, whoever's running this fuckin' show, whatever asshole up there wouldn't even let me kill myself, also arranged for Dean Russell to pull me from the play.

But none of that shit'll matter much once Oxford gives me an honorary degree for my ass-stomping work on the London stage. I'll be there soon, acting and writing and making my name. I will. I fuckin' will, if I have any shit to say about it.

CHAPTER V
Play

"Where'd you get the incense?" Dr. Strykeroth asked me a couple weeks after I got out of the hospital.

I lit a slim stick of sandalwood incense with the silver Zippo he bought me for my birthday. I took the stamp-sized holder out of the bottom of the incense box and set it on the coffee table next to his chair. "At Ortega's Pharmacy," I said, sticking the sandalwood stick in the holder hole, "right across from Café de Sade."

"You've been spending a lot of time there," he said. I blew out the flame on top of the incense stick. He went on, "You know, after you light incense, you're not supposed to blow out the flame. It's bad luck."

I stayed on my knee by the coffee table, "Great. Now you tell me." The sandalwood smoke rose between us with only an ember burning about half a foot away from the base.

"You're supposed to wave the stick until the flame goes out," he said, reaching over to run his fingers through whatever strands of my hair managed to stray loose after all the ratting, dreading, and gelling I did to it that morning. While he played with my hair, I leaned down and dug my notebook out of my backpack.

I stood up and walked over to the armchair across from him, notebook in hand. "Is something bad gonna happen to me now?" I asked, sitting across from him.

Dr. Strykeroth smiled, "No. It's just a superstition we

had in the sixties."

I lit a Marlboro, "I got something I wanna read you."

He smiled, leaned back and closed his eyes, "Oh, good! I love it when you read to me. What's this? Another poem?"

"A play," I said.

"You wrote a play?" he exclaimed. "You sure kept it under your hat."

"I'm writing one," I told him. "I just started it last week."

"What's it about?" he asked.

I said, "It's about a painter."

"A painter, you say…" he said and, with his eyes closed, passed me the ashtray next to the incense.

"In Germany," I answered, taking the ashtray and tapping the first ash off my smoke.

"Germany?" he asked. "Why not England? I thought England was your country."

"It is, but…I dunno. When I first thought up the plot, you were on my mind…and you're all German, right?"

His mouth creased into a thin smile, but a hint of worry also rippled across his face, "Nothing in this play will incriminate me, will it?"

"No," I assured him, "It's about a painter. You're my shrink. Plus, you weren't the only one on my mind when I started writing."

"Oh?" Dr. S peered in at me. "Who else were you thinking about?"

"Mozart," I grinned. "I started writing this play right after I watched *Amadeus*."

"Haven't you worn that tape out by now, Seamus?"

"Not yet."

"Keep popping in that movie, you'll break your folks' VCR."

I tapped my cigarette a few times over the ashtray. He

fanned some of the smoke away, his eyes still closed. "Well, for Mozart, it's worth it," I said, "Plus, it'll give me ideas for how to make a living daydreaming."

"Okay, so, Mozart's the German angle."

"He was Austrian."

"Let's not split hairs, Seamus," Dr. S said. "Now, where in Germany is it set?"

"Hamburg."

"Do you know anything about Hamburg?"

"Just that it's on the map."

"Good start," he said, "Did you do any research?"

"Don't need to," I said, "I got imagination."

"Yes, you sure got that. Think this story will top all that erotica you've been reading me?"

"I hope so," I said, "I'm just writing that shit for practice. Just in case, later on, I gotta go make money writing for dirty magazines—y'know, before I break into the book market or the theater. Henry Miller and Anaïs Nin, they had to do the same shit."

"So you're in good company…"

"No, but this shit right here could be a masterpiece," I told him. "We're talkin' fuckin' Princess Di herself might come to the West End and hand me an award."

"Got that Pulitzer in the bag, now, don't you?" Dr. Strykeroth said, leaning back in his chair, "So, how about giving me a rundown? Start from the top."

"Okay, so, when the play starts, a man in harem pants walks on to stage."

"Harem pants?"

"Yeah, y'know, like, Arabian—sort of *I Dream of Jeannie*—long at the crotch. The Hare Krishnas up in Rogers Park wear 'em."

"Gotcha," Dr. Strykeroth said, eyes shut tight, his face

falling into a dream state. "Now does this guy have a name?"

"No," I told him, "He's an artist."

"Starving?"

"Of course," I nodded, "Jesus hair, drags around a bean bag. Sits Indian-style on it. Meditates like The Beatles. Smokes hash. The whole trip."

"So, sweetheart, your main character is a no-name artist."

"No," I told Dr. Strykeroth, "My main character's got a name. It's Hans. Hans Heinemann. Now, as for the guy on the bean bag—"

"The one in harem pants?"

"Right. That guy doesn't have a name. He doesn't have much of a part either. All he does is announce what went on before the play began. He's like the chorus in *Medea*. Remember when I read *Medea* to you?"

"How could I forget?" Dr. S said. "The office down the hall left a note under my door asking if I should have them send security next time you're here."

"Sorry," I said. He shrugged his shoulders like it was no big deal. I went on, "So, the real action begins *after* the guy in harem pants gives the intro, uncrosses his legs, and drags his incense and bean bag off the stage."

"Ah, good," Dr. Strykeroth replied, shifting his butt in his chair a little. "So it's not just some nameless artist play."

I shook my finger, "No, it *is* a nameless artist play. I mean, most of the artists in it—and there are a lot of them—have names but they're still nameless. They're..."

"Misunderstood?"

"Yes!"

"Unknown?"

"Yes!"

"Disaffected?"

I didn't know what the word meant (I wrote it down and

looked it up), but still I cheered, "Fuck yeah!"

"Alienated."

"Er…I guess."

He kept his eyes closed but put his right leg between both of mine and brushed it up my calf before resting his foot under the lip of the cushion on my chair, "Go on."

I closed my eyes for a second, the corners of my mouth twitched up into a little smile. I opened my eyes, took a drag off my cigarette and ran my forefinger a few lines down in my notes. "The guy on the beanbag plays a sitar, like on one of the songs from the Ravi Shankar tape you made me."

His eyes open wide, "You've been listening to it?"

"Oh fuck, yeah!" I said. "I mean…at first, I said, this music is plain shit." Dr. S grimaced, but I made a nice save: "But as I played it more, I thought, y'know, there's something to this. There's no better anarchy than transcending time and space. Ravi Shankar and his gurus are all about that, right?"

"You've got the tact of a sledgehammer, Seamus," Dr. S said, once again closing his eyes in meditation.

I blew a wreath of cigarette smoke above my head and rubbed my Marlboro out in the ashtray. "The play goes on. Beanbag man tells us that Hans—the painter in Hamburg—just made his best painting in ten years."

"Ten years?" Dr. Stykeroth said, his knee knocking against mine. "He must be an old man."

"Um…middle age," I answered, "He'll be thirty in a couple years."

Dr. S's face went still as flat Coke. "If thirty's middle-age, Seamus, that'd put me in the geriatric ward."

"C'mon, forty's not so old. You still look good."

"Go on with your story."

"In the second scene, we see Hans. He just got out of jail for defacing public property. Defacing public property is the only way he can paint. He can't afford canvasses, so he's got to use the sidewalk. He can't afford paints or brushes either. He's gotta dumpster-dive for supplies outside the paint factory.

"Thing is, he wasn't always poor. He was the *shit* in Berlin. I mean, not shit, per se, but he was…y'know…"

"The *toast* of Berlin?" Dr. S clarified.

"Exactly. He won every art award you can name by the time he was seventeen."

"Seventeen?"

"Yep," I said, "He wanted to be an artist in Berlin, so he ran away from home when he was fifteen or sixteen. He got rich quick, got famous quick, more famous than Elvis. But the scene corrupted him. He started making all sorts of compromises. Played the game way too fuckin' much, did what everybody else fuckin' wanted him to do. Made the sort of art everybody else wanted him to make, but he saw he was selling out, so he staged his own suicide, gave all his money to a panhandler, and went and lived on the streets in Hamburg.

"His paintings were better than anything at the Art Institute even. Even the Monets! But he'd paint them on sidewalks for spare change. And, when I say 'on the sidewalk,' I mean, *on* the sidewalks; he paints the concrete. But the pigs always come and arrest him, and either the rain or the sanitation department comes and washes his paintings right off the sidewalk. But his best painting…his best painting stuck. No water could wash it off, it's waiting for him when he gets out of prison in Scene II."

"What was the painting?" Dr. Strykeroth asked, his eyes fluttering into REMs beneath his closed eyelids, his face tilting to the side, his voice fading out.

"An old woman," I said. I read right off my notebook page: "*Elizabeth is an old woman with wrinkly skin and emerald eyes. In fact, the eyes are real. Her eyes are real. People become hypnotized staring at them. In the painting, Elizabeth is taking a moment to rest on a boulder with a sack full of vegetables that she's carrying to her starving grandchildren on the other side of the Black Forest. Hans' career could make a comeback with his painting, Elizabeth. But he's in danger of falling back into his old sell-out ways by falling back in with his old capitalist agent, Alexander Van Jast."*

"Then what happens?"

"I'm thinking of having him commit suicide over his painting. Hari-kari-style. Death after dishonor."

Dr. Strykeroth opened his eyes, "Read me the first line?"

I said, "I didn't write it yet. I just wrote the description."

Dr. Strykeroth got up and walked over to the couch. He sat down and stared at me for a while before waving for me to come join him. I walked over to the couch. He took me in his arms and said, "It's a good plot so far, Seamus. But things we imagine often have a way of coming true. I don't know why that is, and maybe it's just another one of my don't-blow-out-the-incense sixties superstitions, but I sometimes fear that you're setting yourself up for a hard life by always writing about hard lives—in your poems, your stories, your *porn*, your plays."

"You gotta express how you feel," I raised my shoulders, "and I gotta make it somehow. It's not like fuckin' Xavier's gonna let me up on stage. I gotta write my own shit now, don't I?"

He pulled me closer.

"Could you hold me until our time's up?" I asked. Dr. S didn't answer but he held me until the session ended.

CHAPTER VI
Downtown-Bound

At least we're approaching civilization, now that the 85A's pulling into Jefferson Park. Buses from all over Chicago end up here. You can feel the onrush of commuters. Even the pavement looks more streetwise than it does on my block. Gets trampled by tens of thousands of feet all along the half-block of windows, stretching out on both sides of the Kennedy Expressway. This is where you can feel the pulse of the city start to come back after you get off the 85A. Pulse's not back yet, but it's coming back, you can feel it.

Chicago isn't London, but it'll have to do until I'm eighteen and can board the plane out. "America, love it or leave it." Well gimme a fuckin' ticket and I'll fuckin' leave. I even got nervous when the CTA started painting all the buses red, white, and blue. I thought, I can't ride a red, white, and blue bus. That's so fuckin' Reagan regime! It goes against my principles. Even though it's also the color of the Union Jack, I guess. But then I saw the buses getting all dirty and shit and then it was fine by me. Let Old Glory get good and dirty. To me, grease, gas, grime, trash, puddles, and mud marring those red, white, and blue buses is like stepping on the flag, like they did at the Art Institute last summer. Remember that? Every Republican asshole got all self-righteous and wanted the artist who put the flag on the floor arrested—the Art Institute got death threats. Fuckers never asked themselves why anyone would want to put the flag on the floor, and their ears sure as hell weren't cocked to hear why. Trust me, I got about a hundred reasons right on the tip of my tongue.

Could you believe that inaugural address, Friday? What'd Bush say again? I wrote it down. Not that I needed to, they played it back enough times on all the news shows for me to memorize. Prick said something about how it's 1989 and "the day of the dictator is over." After that, he got all poetic, said, "The totalitarian age is passing, its ideals blown away like leaves from an ancient and lifeless tree." Beautiful. That's some beautiful bullshit right there. I'm sure one of his White House mercenaries wrote it for him. What some assholes'll do for a paycheck: making it look like that fuckface wrote a motherfucking poem.

But you know how people are, right? They don't want to admit he'll get 'em in the same chokehold the Kremlin's got the Russians in right now. "Oh, no. That could never happen here. Not in the good ole U.S. of A." They buy that shit, man. They just… they just…they just…and I want to take this steel pole right here and bash their brains in with it until they're ready to wake the fuck up. But, y'know, that pole is fucking cold right now, and, besides, it's about the size of fuckin' Lawrence Avenue. But, y'know, what if I *could* lift this pole and bury it in those people's skulls? They'd still be sitting back, all saucer eyes and gooey smiles, while, with one hand, he swings a ticking pocketwatch in their faces and, with the other, steals their pockets, their pickets, their social security, their rights to free press and free speech.

But there he is, pointing his finger right at foreign leaders, tossing off buzzwords like "dictator" and "totalitarian," trying to mask the fact that he's nothing but the fascist successor to eight years of American fascism. But he's a fascist in a Brooks Brother's suit—not in jackboots or a South American general's uniform—so they vote him in for four years and they'll probably do it for four more after that. Yep, and last November, good ole Mom and Dad were first at the polls to do it. All summer, they kept that sign pitched on our front yard: "Election 1988: George BUSH for President." Fuck, I hope Bush doesn't have any kids who'll pick up where he left off! Shit, that actually *could* finish off the wold. There's *no way* I can do another three years in this country! Gimme a ticket and I'll go now.

Course, they've got Thatcher in London. Punks start riots over her kill-the-poor ass in their dole queues. Saw it on *60 Minutes*. It's kinda cool. All those Mohawks and Liberty Spikes, kicking over police barricades, crashing up against crowd-control shields, crushing spiked rings in coppers' faces before they bust out tear gas and slam rubber hoses down on rioters. If the bobbies ain't gonna fuckin' show no mercy, the punks ain't gonna fuckin' show no mercy. But that Thatcher bitch is such a cunt, her own party's asking her to step down. But, y'know, she's a fuck lot better than what we got goin' here.

Still, there are things I can do between now and the time I'm ready to defect. Right here at Jefferson Park, for instance, on my way to school, I can play Mozart and fantasize about living in a magic land. Especially when Tressa tapes *The Magic Flute* for me, which she's probably doing even as I flash my Student ID at this terminally bored terminal agent. She promised she would. Listen to that string section on "Ronda A La Turca." It lends such pomp and such circumstance and such fucking atmosphere to this sleepwalk through the turnstiles. It's foreshadowing the moment I'll be accepting all those honorary degrees from all those colleges that'll be teaching my books or taking their students on field trips to see me act or begging me to speak at their graduations.

Through the southernmost windows, you can see the Sears Tower, the John Hancock Building, and the Standard Oil Building. When I was a little kid, taking the Kennedy past those buildings in Dad's old Buick station wagon to go to the Auto Show at McCormick Place every year was like boarding the TARDIS to Andromeda. I felt like Dr. Who. But, actually, Chicago's city lights were so much more fucking awesome than the chintzy-ass special effects on that show. Back then, I used to look forward to high school. I used to think my spirits would soar every time I took the L downtown and miles past to Xavier. I Could Not Wait. Now that I see the same skyscrapers every morning, though, they just look fucking mundane. I have to set them to Mozart to give them life. But they are American buildings. That's why they're so fucking boring, no matter how hard they try not to be.

But there are some things I still look forward to on the commute these days, especially in winter. Unlike anybody else, I look forward to standing on the L platform in the freezing cold. Everybody else shrinks back into heating domes. They huddle up to keep the Windy City wind from racking their rinds. Not me. I stand right at the fucking edge of the platform till the train comes. I play Tressa's Mozart tape and keep my eyes on the other side of the Kennedy, looking past the gridlock and out on to the slopes with the glistening, diamond snow.

It makes me think of *Doctor Zhivago* and that time me and Tressa watched it at her house. If I stand out here long enough, I don't even see cars. I see Russia in the snow on those slopes. I see the ninteenth century. I imagine I'm the main character in some movie like *Doctor Zhivago* or some novel like that, even though I never read it. (Tressa's read it.) Then, if I look out long enough, I remember Tressa's copper breasts and ash-gray nipples.

Right before we watched *Doctor Zhivago*, she let me in a second time. I thought I could do it better that time. I didn't. She had to help me—again. It was on her bed, that time, the second time. Her bed has scarlet silk sheets to match her scarlet silk curtains. *Miss Scarlet! Miss Scarlet!* And, when we were in it, I crawled up and tried crawling in—both eyes shut—but, even when that didn't work, even when I did all I could to charge forward, my cock just kept shrinking back, just like the people shrinking into the heating domes over there. She didn't even make me wear a rubber that time. Must've known it didn't matter, even though we used it the first time and I just barely made it in.

She must've known I was thinking about Colby again too. I never talked about him with her. She doesn't know Colby. Hell, I don't even know Colby. But she knows about him. She must. She knows everything. Tressa reads minds. She does. Dr. Strykeroth doesn't know about Colby. He doesn't know how to read minds like Tressa. I don't want to talk to him about Colby. He doesn't have to know.

And Tressa must've known about Colby the first time I did it with her too. She must've. The first time, like the next time, all she could do while I was going at it was sigh and say, "It's alright, Seamus. Don't worry. I...I get it. Let's...I dunno...go do something else now." Guess there's not gonna be a third time, huh, Tressa? I didn't even look at her tits and nipples that second time. But I got a good look at them the first time.

The first time, she dropped perfume capsules in the hot tub water. We didn't plan this. At least, I didn't. One minute, I was looking at the library in her bedroom, picking out a book for her to test me on later. A stick of her jasmine incense burned in a cupful of dry rice on the top shelf. I admit, I didn't know the names of the writers. I just went by titles and picked out the ones I liked best. Right when I started taking *Nausea*—fuckin' awesome title—out from between two other novels whose names I forget, I felt Tressa come up behind me. She wrapped me in her arms and pressed in on me. Her big lips started gushing into my neck. I didn't move. She hooked her leg around mine. I looked down. She wasn't wearing jeans anymore. There was just a black dancer's leg, long, muscular, clamping me in. I looked over, my eyes still down. I saw her bare ass off to the side. She propped my head back up with both hands. She mussed up my hair with her fingers. I could feel her breasts squishing into my back. They felt as naked against my Alien Sex Fiend T-shirt as her ass looked off to the side. "You gotta stop wearing all that product, Seamus," she said, giving my hair a good rub. "Trust me. Let it be baby soft. I wanna run my

fingers through the red hair of my lil Irish Howdy-Doody baby." I
was in too much shock to say, "But what about my whole Johnny
Rotten look?" Thank fuck I didn't say something fucking stupid
like that. I just stood like a statue. She let me go and stepped away.

I stood at the bookshelf a minute longer. I could hear
bathtub water running from down the hall. I put *Nausea* down on
her nightstand (still haven't read it, but I saw she'd underlined the
shit out of it, so I guess it's good and I guess I should). I heard
a rush and whirl of water. I walked down the hall and into the
bathroom. Tressa stood in the tub dropping fragrance capsules
into the steaming water from a jar that was next to a line of Prell
and Pantene bottles. They were jasmine capsules. Must've been
jasmine. It smelled just like the incense she always burns. Made
the room smell like a mix of jasmine and Tressa's patchouli, which
I'm convinced she only wears to clear out L cars when she wants
a seat.

Her folks have a Jacuzzi dial in their bathtub. She turned
it all the way to the right and made a whirlpool for us. She was
naked. Her ribs showed. Her abs and arms were toned like a
gymnast's. Her color was an even copper, all the way up and down.
Her breasts were oblong. Nipples big and round as half dollars
but darker, much more tarnish than silver. She had one leg hiked
up. Her thighs were creamy and perfect like a mannequin's. But
her pubic hair, man, it looked like…tar…with all sorts of coils,
sprigs and fuckin' thistles sticking out every which way. Before
that moment, I never saw a coochie up close. My blood went faint.
My heart was giving the fuck out. She said, "Don't worry." Said
it over and over again. Don't worry. Don't worry. Don't worry
don't worry don't worry. She stretched out her hands to me. Sang
it like a song: don't worry don't worry don't worry don't worry
baby don't worry. Her palms were beige, looked almost as white
as mine, but fuckin' no one's palms, except maybe Casper the
Friendly fuckin' Ghost's, could ever be fuckin' whiter than mine.

I walked toward her. Ambled, more like. I was fuckin' Frankenstein. She just kept stretching out, telling me don't worry. I kept focusing on the light that shined on her scalp and the stubble she'd be shaving off of it the next week. That's what I kept my eyes on as I stepped into the roaring bathwater.

There was the threat of hell, of course. That's what good ole Mom always says. From the moment she found I even knew that…that…that…*word*, S-E-X (and I've fuckin' known it ever since I could fuckin' remember, it was always on the TV she's been blaring twenty-four hours a day since before I was born) she followed up with the words "mortal sin." Freaked me the fuck out when she told me what a mortal sin was. Couldn't even breathe after that. Kept expecting a molten pitchfork to stab my ass every time I was even around a kid who told a dirty joke. For the longest time, if I even accidentally popped a boner, I went about as fuckin' psycho as Norman Bates. And that's what I was about to do. Commit a mortal fucking sin. With a black girl, no less, the color Mom always told me I could never date or marry.

But I didn't fuckin' care. Or I did, I did fuckin' care. I just kept wishing I didn't. And my heart, it dropped to my stomach. But I kept stepping forward. Kept telling myself I didn't fucking care. Kept hearing Johnny Rotten in my head, kept telling myself what he'd tell himself, "I don't fucking care." And I kept focusing on her scalp. I couldn't, I couldn't look down. Couldn't look at those tits. I…I didn't like her tits. Couldn't look at her pubes. They were full of…fuckin' coils and thistles and sprigs. And I guess it was while I was fixing on her scalp that she ripped open the Trojenz wrapper. But I didn't see her rip it open. I couldn't look down.

She couldn't've been more relaxed the whole time. She was looking out the bathroom window through most of it. Her eyes seemed to graze from one tar rooftop to the next as the sun went down and I tried pleasuring her, planting my lips on her throat and neck and plunging in, that is, after she helped me find it, after she helped me in. I still don't know if condoms work under water. But she didn't look worried. She said she's on the pill. Agatha gets it for her. Still don't know why she made me wear a rubber then. Hope she wasn't scared I might have AIDS. She wouldn't know Payne or any of the other losers in Jarvis Park, but, still, you never know how far and wide a little rumor like that can spread.

But, after a while, she let me do all the work. Stopped pulling me in and moaning. Just leaned back, stopped trying to make it fun for herself. Just looked out the window. And before she said, "I get it," that she *understood* why I was having such a hard time, and before she said let's go do something else, she said, "Wow, I never noticed it before, but we do get a good view from that window. See? You can almost see as far as Lake Shore Drive. That's far!" I didn't check to see. I still had a job to do. I wanted to finish what she'd started before we'd go do something else.

And I did come. At least I can say that fucking much for myself. I was man enough to come. She never came (I hear girls can come too), but I did. I'll admit I had to think about Colby, though, in order to lose my virginity. And, yes, I crawled away once I shot my last round of cum into the condom.

And, no, I didn't feel great about sex with Tressa. I couldn't talk for a whole hour after it. It did something to me too. I don't know what exactly, but I haven't been the same since and I can't say how or why. But, I'll admit, part of me did think it'd be kind of cool if Tressa's pill didn't work and the condom broke under water and she and me'd be having a little black baby coming in nine months. That'd fucking *kill* Mom and Dad. But, man, she's not even my girlfriend.

CHAPTER VII
Black Chick Into GBH

Here's the L. Shit! It's full. I gotta stand.

This shit happens all the time. Maybe I'll douse myself with one of Tressa's vile vials of patchouli next time. That'll get people scudding to the emergency release. They'll throw themselves on the tracks like lemmings. I'll put my bag down next to me, spread my patchouli-scented body out in a row all to myself, and tell the six o'clock news I don't know what on earth caused the upset.

I was hoping to sit down and do geometry. Only got two problems done last night and I've got, like, fifteen more to go. Who am I kidding? Gimme a choice between listening to Mozart and opening the *Elements of Geometry* book, you won't see my hand flopping anywhere near a fuckin' protractor or compass. It's a fucking useless subject anyway. I don't understand the first fuckin' thing about it, and all anybody who's ever graduated high school says is you'll never use it again. They just teach it to torture kids.

At least diamonds are still glistening on the hills across the expressway. Still thinking about *Doctor Zhivago*. Russia. The second time Tressa and I had sex. Maybe I should've brought the Tchaikovsky tape Tressa made me. Right now, the ride's more like Vienna than Russia, with Mozart still blaring in my ears. More people are getting on and blocking the windows. Soon I won't be able to see the hills anymore.

Before we watched *Doctor Zhivago*, Tressa played *Peter and the Wolf*. After the violins strummed two or three times, my attention went flying right out the window, just like it does in class, but all of a sudden Tressa started going on and on about how her Russian grandma, Babsha, used to play *Peter and the Wolf* for her. That's when Tressa got up, stretched her left leg from floor to ceiling and held it behind her head as she spun slowly on the ball of her right foot.

It was glorious. She gave me a private performance—a *private* performance. After she stopped spinning, she rolled us two smokes from a pack of Drums that she had on her stereo console. She lit one, leaned back on her scarlet sheets, and soaked up the third movement of *Peter and the Wolf* (or maybe it was the fourth or the fifth, I'm not sure how to track that shit). She said, "Tchaikovsky always sounds like *work* to me. Know what I mean? People with threshers in the field. Serfs and work. That's what it sounds like! Yeah! Serfs and work." She took a big drag off her Drum, I guess celebrating her newest insight. I thought, holy fuck, this chick's cultured. And she stood back up, put her Drum in an ashtray, pulled down her dagger-print skirt, and we fucked a second time...or tried to.

After we did it, or tried doing it, that second time, we watched *Doctor Zhivago*. Me and her got under one of the afghans that Babsha wove by hand, something Babsha learned to do from her own mother before the Ruskies shipped her mother to the Gulag. Tressa snuggled up close, but, y'know, I couldn't...y'know, like, *hold* her. She's not my girlfriend. She's not. But she was up close. And she had her hand on my thigh. But she had class. She didn't try running her palm up my crotch or anything, so that's good. But we watched *Doctor Zhivago* and, when we got to tape two, Agatha and Aubrey came in. I jumped back to the other side of the couch, but Tressa laughed and said, "Um, it's alright, Seamus. Come back." She pulled me back to her and kept me there. And Agatha and Aubrey giggled. Aubrey put his arm around Agatha. "Puppy love," he cooed. I squirmed. I couldn't help it. It's, it's just…not fuckin' like that with me and Tressa.

Later, Tressa told me she told her folks all about what we did in their bathtub the week before and they all had a huge roar over it. All they cared about was whether Tressa was keeping up with her pills and her studies. She told them she aced a physics exam on Friday and popped a pill at 10 a.m., Saturday. That was good enough for them. Her folks are so fucking cool. Aubrey's Dad's from London, his name's Aubrey too. Sometimes I think I'm asking too many questions, but they at least act like they're happy to tell me everything they know. I'm always asking what England's like. Aubrey lived there with Agatha for a while. Agatha and Aubrey even told me to call them by their first names. No adults let me do that. Brody wouldn't if I wasn't his brother, but I'm done talking to his yuppie ass anyway. I'd give anything for Aubrey to be my dad. Anything.

During the movie, Aubrey and Agatha got under another one of Babsha's afghans and watched with us. They said they saw *Doctor Zhivago* on their second date at Amherst. That's where Tressa says she might go next year after she gets back from Switzerland. Guess I'll be all out of friends when she does.

Sure as hell didn't have any when I first saw her. I kept trying to make friends on Belmont and at Wax Trax but couldn't. It seemed like you always had to have friends going in if you wanted more later on. Fuckin' catch-22. And you had to look like you knew what the fuck you were doing at all times, which I didn't, I just… didn't. Shit, I'm from Jarvis Park—the uncoolest neighborhood in all Chicago. How the fuck could I? When I first started going to Wax Trax, I'd walk in and the guy behind the counter with the tar black hair and purple and blood-red dreadlocks would hiss a python hiss and spit some venom word like "poseur" at me. He couldn't get away with saying that shit to any customer Brody's age, but me, man—I was, like, fourteen years old last year, nothing more than pennies in my pockets, didn't know how to dress like the renegades by the twelve-inch singles and imports—my belly was red fuckin' meat for those fangs he probably goes home and sharpens every day after work.

I used to walk past the counter in a million shades of shame. There's almost no light in Wax Trax, except a few lava lamps and low-watt bulbs under purple, beaded gypsy lampshades. In the display case by the register they got all these vibrators, nipple clamps, cock rings, and every color of Manic Panic hair dye. (I didn't know what any of that shit was till Tressa told me.) Used to be bongs, bowls, and roach clips in there too until they couldn't afford to keep bribing the Chicago cops to let them keep running a nice, clean head shop. I've never smoked pot, so I didn't miss all the paraphernalia when they took it out. They still got sex gadgets in there, though, and, every time I pass the counter, I still get scared of getting stuck in a cock ring.

But man, oh fuckin' man, the first time I ever heard the music pounding off the speakers at Wax Trax! It was all Rotten-level rage with scrap-metal beats and serial-killer synths gang-raping the room. But the chaos never fazed none of the punks in the store, who probably just rolled right off their cold-turkey-stained mattresses late that afternoon, vowing to hit the methadone clinic, er, maybe some time that week. All them might've been smacked out of their gourds, but all them—and I mean *all* them—were conscious enough to dig through all the right rows of records. Once they were done stocking up, they'd all head to the counter with stacks and stacks of LPs from bands nobody outside their little cliques ever head of—Pailhead, G.G. Allin and the AIDS Brigade, Revolting Cocks, Crucifucks, Fetus, Skinny Puppy, Fear, Einstreizen de Neubauten, Social Distortion, Naked Raygun, The Cramps, Minor Threat, Tones on Tail, Leibach. And they'd all stand there jawing with the guys behind the counter. Everybody knew everybody else—which everybody went to such great big motherfuckin' pains to show. How the fuck did they all meet each other anyway? Before Tressa, I never fuckin' met anyone.

    Didn't take me long at Wax Trax to know I fuckin' knew nothing. My Sex Pistols, my Clash, my Dead Kennedys, my Circle Jerks—that was all bush-league bullshit to them. That's why asshole behind the counter called me poseur. Took one look at my Rotten hair and sensed that Sex Pistols was all I fuckin' knew. But, shit, man, how was I supposed to fuckin' know anything else? Again, it's not like I fuckin' knew anyone. I had to figure out all this shit on my own—which is pretty fuckin' impossible when there's a new band born every minute and no place to look them up. *Rolling Stone* and *Spin* are so fucking out of touch with their U2, Clapton, and Springsteen yuppie shit. They can't even do a decent article on The Cure.

    So, I'd go upstairs to Wax Trax's boutique. They got this book nook up there, next to all the leather jackets, Air Ware, Frye boots, and fetish gear. The bottom shelf holds Xeroxed booklets that punks off the streets make, with all these Mohawks and decapitation sketches on the front and back covers. They got some punk history books upstairs too.

    Before Tressa came around to school me in all this shit, I'd pull up all the books and try reading them cover to cover in the store. There was a fuckin' excellent one called *Punk: A Sordid Saga* by Ian Whitehead. I flipped through it every time I went upstairs. But, for the longest time, I never made it past the chapter on The New York Dolls…and they were, what, '73, '74? Right when I'd get to '77, that British, Siouxsie Sioux bitch upstairs would always stop me while she was hanging up another rack of slut clothes and shout, "Oi! This ain't no library. Buy it or beat it. Your choice." And I'd just close the book thinking, "Bitch, I wouldn't have to be up here studying if you assholes would just come down off your fucking high horses and talk to me: tell me what I should be doing, what I should be listening to. But, no, it's all your own gutter-snob-clique secret. Cunt." But you just can't say that shit and save face, so I'd close the book like nothing ever bothered me and leave the store. *And then*...I'd come back the next week! Part of it was her accent. A real live British bitch in Chicago.

But one day—it must've been the one day a month she's off the rag—she took pity on my square ass and let me put *Punk: A Sordid Saga* on layaway the way most people do clothes. It was about forty bucks, so it took for-fuckin'-ever to pay off, but now it's lying dog-eared, underlined, and scribble-margined next to my bed. I'd carry it everywhere if I didn't have to lug all my fuckin' textbooks around. But thanks to the 85A making me late so many mornings, and thanks to my unbridled daydreaming, it looks like I won't have to lug this shit around much longer.

One Saturday last year, I bought PiL's *Happy?* at Wax Trax. A couple weeks before that, I heard all the gutter snob clique talking about how the new PiL was coming out. Well, I got it the fucking day of the release, probably before any of them. Who's the fuckin' poseur now, poseurs?

After buying *Happy?*, I took the L from Fullerton to Washington and transferred to the O'Hare train to go back up to Jefferson Park. I was wearing Dad's purple-and-black checkered flannel shirt (since I don't have any passable ones of my own), my black Lee jeans (since I can't afford Levis), and some used combats, a size and a half too big for me, that I bought for $12.79 at Belmont Army Navy Surplus (since I can't afford Docs). (How the fuck do kids on Belmont afford this shit? I mean, how the fuck? They wear 8-hole, 10-hole, 12-hole Docs—imported from England, don't you fuckin' know. They're all decked out in leather jackets, painted collar to hem with shock-band names nobody but them's ever heard of. Man, back before Tressa, I remember thinking, do they paint this shit themselves? Or is there some shop they can get some ex-con to do it? Or do you gotta have friends who know how to paint? And where the fuck do these people find all these fuckin' friends?) There I sat on the northbound L, my stomach twisting into sour knots at the thought of the Jefferson Park escalator, my transfer to the 85A, and my return home to Mom and Dad.

And there she was. Standing up after the L sped into the West Town Tunnel. Tressa. Only I didn't know her as Tressa. No, she was this bald black chick in a Charged GBH T-shirt where a baby with a green Mohawk sits next to a garbage pail under the spray-paint title, "City Baby's Revenge." A black chick, wearing a GBH shirt? I mean, fuck, don't they jam out to Salt N' Peppa, Rob Bass, or, if they like the rough stuff, don't they crank up Ice-T or N.W.A.? But, no, there's this black chick in a fuckin' GBH T-shirt! G-B-fuckin'-H! Grievous Bodily Harm! And she was wearing a ripped-up kilt with a chain-wrapped black leather belt and these chauffeur boots almost as long as her legs. She had pewter rings on all her fingers and a green army bag strapped across her body. And she looked older. I mean, way older than sixteen. I'd put her as old as…shit, twenty! And I looked at her across the L car—a sight I'd been scouting for all my life. She broke all molds, shattered all stereotypes, stood in defiance of this whole fuckin' world, right there on the northbound L to Jefferson Park. A black chick into GBH.

Only she didn't get off with me at Jefferson Park. She got off about five stops before at Logan Square. *Logan Square*, where all the Mexicans live. "She lives *there*?" I thought, "Hispanics don't like blacks. That's what I hear. Can't imagine they like punks either. They're all into that salsa shit they blast from Pintos at Forest Preserve picnics. Drive up ten to a car…" Man, the way I saw shit back before Tressa.

But I wasn't worried about her that day. Wasn't worried about her getting raped on the way home. No, I thought, look how much ass she's kicking already. A black chick into GB-fuckin'-H! This was all before Tressa played me black punk bands like Bad Brains. I didn't know blacks were in on this shit. It was fuckin' brilliant! I thought gangs'd be sorry to fuck with her ass.

Tressa caught me looking at her as I wondered all this shit about her before she stepped off the L. She tilted her head down and gazed at me with that ice-cold sensuality, like those Paris runway models you see on TV sometimes, right before they walk upstage away from all the flashing cameras. Where was she going anyway? Her apartment? Does she have her own apartment? Does she have roommates? Are they punks too? Or, um, artists? How does she afford it? Are they starving artists, seven to one room? Does she have a job? Where does she work? Where does she hang out? Is she an artist too? What kind? Tressa walked off the L and onto the escalator at Logan Square, just like one of those Parisian runway models.

When I reminisce about that day these days, Tressa says that she doesn't remember any of the shit I'm saying. But I do. A black punk Parisian model in chauffeur boots. I'll never fucking forget it.

The L ride home that day went from a nightmare to the sweetest of dreams. Being back home wasn't even that bad either. Even if Payne had been right across the street at McCaskey's shouting faggot at me, it wouldn't've made any fuckin' difference. I walked right on past Mom too while she watched the *MacNeil/Lehrer News Hour* and ate her usual peas, carrots, and cauliflower, still steaming from when she'd defrosted them in the microwave. Mom said something whiney and complain-y to me about some shit, I don't even know what—maybe I got grounded that week for swearing or first quarter grades or some shit that I just fucking forgot about when I decided to go to Wax Trax instead. Anyhow, her words were in vain. I was too euphoric, walking on clouds all the way up to my room where I ripped the wrapper off *Happy?* I held a little ceremony and bowed to my Johnny Rotten poster before I put *Happy?* on my turntable. Man, it was the best fucking album since *Never Mind the Bollocks*, and I thought of Tressa every track. She was defiance itself. A black chick into GBH.

CHAPTER VIII

Punkin' Donuts

I didn't actually meet Tressa until a little later, the night the skinheads jumped me on Belmont. Man, I don't care what people say. They cut skinheads all this fuckin' slack. Say most on Belmont ain't Nazis, they're anti-Nazi. Some are even black, some are Jews, and some of the whites even walk around with T-shirts on under their bomber jackets that got ban signs over swastikas. That don't mean dick. Nazi, anti-Nazi: one's just as bad as the other. Some of the Anti-Nazi skins wear pink laces in their ox-blood Docs, meaning they killed a queer—maybe one of the queens walking around Halsted Street, just about a block over from Punkin' Donuts. Skinheads are fuckin' scumbags—Nazi or not—and, if I didn't believe in anarchy, I'd petition for a law to lock them all up for life.

One night, fall quarter 1987, I went to Medusa's wearing the 1940s-style black porkpie hat I bought at Wax Trax. The one I saw Colby wearing. Man, I'll never fucking forget seeing him in it. I saved up for months to buy one for myself. I stood alone on a box on Medusa's main floor and lost myself trance-bogeying to house music, which the video-room snobs say only trendies and poseurs do, but who gives a fuck? Go upstairs to the video room, the cool crowd just sits around smoking cloves, cliquing up, slamming to kill-kill music, and sneering at you. I went in thinking I was going to do my usual thing of shuttling my ass, all alone, up and down the stairs between the main floor and video room, wishing I had someone to talk to, wishing I knew people, but I said no. That night, I just wanted to trance out on the main floor.

Once I'd sweated all the water out of my body, I straightened my hat, buttoned my black overcoat, and walked down the stairs, out to Sheffield Street. As usual, I came to Medusa's alone and left Medusa's alone. It was about ten o'clock and I had to be all the way back home for my 11:30 curfew. Shit, none of the punks in the video room have fuckin' curfews. Their parents don't make them go to Mass on Sunday mornings either. If I believed in God, I'd swear he's hell-bent on keeping me uncool. But I still had about half an hour to kill. I lit my second to last Marlboro and walked over to Punkin' Donuts at Belmont and Clark.

That's all I did on Saturday nights before Tressa. I'd end a lonely night at Medusa's with a cigarette, a raspberry jelly donut, and a medium black tea at Dunkin' Donuts. They always got punks in there or in the parking lot. They don't call it Punkin' Donuts for nothin'. I'd sit at the counter and watch crowds of punks swarming inside and outside the store, never minding the Pakistani donut pushers chewing their asses out every five seconds for acting up and being assholes.

That night, of all the weak-ass musak that could possibly be playing on the Lite Station that Punkin' Donuts pipes in, "How Deep Is Your Love" was playing. I sat at the counter, listening to disco disaster, watching all this anarchy and, for some fucked-up reason, thinking, maybe I'll have friends here someday. Or maybe I'll know punks in England. They don't even have to be punks. Just people. Regular people. In England. And I smoked and stared out the window and sometimes at the smoke curling off my cigarette and wondered what I could do to make a living in England—maybe I could be a shrink like Dr. Strykeroth (that crossed my mind a lot) or an actor on the BBC like I always wanted to be or maybe I'd write books—and I tried cooking up ways I could immigrate legally too. I drifted away, dreaming up all these possible futures as the Lite Station moved on to Barbara Streisand, of all bitches, belting out "Send in the Clowns."

In my daze, I felt someone come up behind me and take the 1940s hat off my head. I swung around on my stool and saw it was a fuckin' skinhead. He had these scary motherfucker red and steel-blue eyes and a face that some mad sculptor must've chiseled out on a bender—all these sharp-ass, severe-ass angles. He cocked an eyebrow, opened his gob slowly like a carp, and blew a mouthful of cigarette smoke he'd been holding straight into my face. His band of nick-headed Neanderthals all hooted and howled and flipped me off. I didn't say a fucking word. (Shit, would you with eight motherfuckin' skinheads staring you down?) They all turned around and walked right into a forest of other punks and skins, some of them grabbing chicks who looked like they were itching for a grabbing. They decamped to make their rounds round the block. Fucker still had my hat on when he walked out with his arms hanging on his two buddies' shoulders. Never fuckin' knew how to walk alone, I guess.

But, see, there's this shit I do every time somebody disses me like that. Even used to do it with fuckin' Andy Payne. For about five minutes, I try convincing myself they didn't mean what they just fuckin' said or did. They meant something else. Maybe this guy thought I *was* someone else. And that's what I dumb-ass did after the skinheads left. Said to myself, Oh, it's crowded in here. He was talking to a lot of people. Maybe he just forgot to give my hat back before he left. If I see him again and ask real nice, he'll give it back. Maybe we'll even hang out next time. Maybe he'll introduce me to his friends. Maybe I'll end up shaving my head too and hanging with them. But I can't tonight. I got curfew. That's what I fuckin' said to myself!

And I went on thinking about England. And I went on thinking about Dr. Stryeroth, how tight and tan his skin is, how lucky I am to get together with him every week. And I thought about Colby. Wondered what he's doing, if I'd ever see him again. I remembered how Colby had steel-blue eyes too, but they weren't all schizoid and broken capillaries like that skinhead's. And I recalled how Colby's features weren't craggy like that skinhead motherfucker's either. They were soft, delicate. His cheekbones were high and they sloped down in such a gentle curve. His lips were like plump little cherries and just as red. I lost myself, thinking about England and Dr. S and Colby.

After a while, out of the corner of my eye, I saw someone hovering over me. I was so caught up daydreaming, I didn't even notice anyone sitting next to me. I turned my head. No, no one was sitting there. Dude wasn't *sitting* at all. He was standing, hovering, some scruffed-up, fucked-up, scrawny-ass drunk, maybe forty years old. I got a better look at him. He was wearing a tight mellow-yellow undershirt under a blue ski coat with a fur-lined hood. He made this crazy-ass belt out of a bunch of different colored bandanas—red, dark blue, black, yellow, baby blue—that he'd tied together and let hang from a loose knot at the crotch of his faded Levis. He put his left hand on his left hip and jutted his right hip out to me. He smiled, looking down at me, tapping the toe of his tan construction boot on the brick footrest and taking a long drag off a Virginia Slim. (I saw the pack on the counter, under his pink Bic lighter. It was fuckin' Virginia Slims.) He exhaled a long, lingering stream of smoke. His breath reeked of menthol cigarettes and bottles and bottles of hard liquor, I don't know what kind, as he leaned up close and heaved a long, heavy "Hah-iii" into my face. He puckered up, looked deep into my eyes, and, losing and finding his balance again, blew me a kiss. I flinched and leaned way the fuck away from his mouth.

All the punks around me were falling all over themselves, whoopin' up a fuckin' storm. Some skinbird with a bleached fringe cut was on the other side of the counter from me, holding a cigarette in a hand tattooed with the cheapest India ink she could shoplift. She smacked a smooch my way and said, "First time, princess? Feelin' a little tight back there?" Her friends clustered around her, laughing at both me and the molester like we were made for each other—and like they were gonna kill us any second for it.

The drunk kept mooning over me. How'd this perv even get through the doors with all the skins and scary motherfuckers skulking around? How'd he escape getting his gumpy ass beat? He's lucky he didn't get killed for just walking within a block of Punkin' Donuts. I didn't finish my black tea. Didn't want that flit feeling me up or vomiting on me. I hit the streets. As I left the parking lot, I kept looking back, hoping he wasn't stumbling after me. For a second, I could even see why skins would be proud to wear pink laces.

I walked back to Sheffield on Belmont. Passed a bunch of Jesus freaks, holding candles and singing "Amazing Grace"; one of them handed me a leaflet. I was still in shock from the drunken fairy, so I took it. The front page looked like some of those Xeroxed booklets they got in Wax Trax's boutique, except there were no sex-and-violence graphics and the punks on the front cover were wearing crosses on their leather jackets and slogans like "Jesus Rules" and ban signs over the number 666. I crumpled the leaflet and pitched it in the gutter. I lit my last Marlboro, crumpled the pack, and tossed that in the gutter too. Not fifteen minutes earlier, Belmont was crawling with people. I don't know what happened, but it was almost empty now. When I got to walking under the L tracks, I saw a group of burly guys heading my way in the night shadows. As I walked closer, I got a better look at them: skinheads, the ones from Punkin' Donuts, the ones who flipped me off and laughed at me.

I saw the one wearing my hat. I walked up to him and said, "Can I have my hat back?"

He got up in my face, "What? What?"

I said, "Just, my hat. Just…can I—?"

He pushed me over into the alley off to the side of the tracks with his chest, "What? What?" He backed me into the brick wall on the side of Belmont Pawn Shop. His gang surrounded me. "What?" he bellowed. "You sayin' I stole it? You sayin' I *stole* your hat? Is that what you're fuckin' sayin'?"

I looked at their faces. The skinhead next to the thief was a black guy, about an inch shorter than me and built like a fuckin' glacier; the guy next to him looked Mexican but his knuckles were white and his breath and eyes were set for attack. Five or six others, black and white, stood in back of them. All I could do was freeze.

"Huh?" the skinhead shoved me back into the bricks again, "Answer me, you little faggot."

I gulped and muttered, "Well, in Dunkin'—" He punched me hard in the fuckin' gut. One of the black skins hollered, "Got any proof, you lil' carrot-top faggot?" and clocked me in the face. They whipped me to the ground. My forehead scraped against a spread of rocks, pebbles, and some glass when they turned me over. They plunged kick after kick into my stomach and a few more into my back. I could feel every hit, but it was like part of me, the part that couldn't feel pain, had left my body and was watching all this shit go down from some kind of aerial view. I thought, oh shit, I heard of shit like this. This is it. This is fuckin' it. The white light's coming and some Imperial Wizard Skinhead's gonna award these animals some pink fuckin' laces for what they're about to do to me.

I heard a voice scream, "Sonny!" It was a chick's voice, "Sonny!" I saw her, this black chick in fishnets, jungle boots, and a black biker jacket with band buttons and handcuffs hanging off the belt. She walked right in and broke it up. It was unbe-fuckin'-lievable. She weighed all of a hundred pounds and she just walked right in and all them just backed up. All of 'em! The minute the black guy who took the first swing at my face saw her, he jumped back about four feet. The guy who stole my hat, she pushed him in the chest and he backed up all the way to the wall, like some hungry-ass bear was coming at him; so did the rest. As I lay there, hurting and bleeding, the black chick spun around, screaming, "What! What'd he fuckin' do?"

Thief said, "He's accusing me of shit."

She walked right up to his face, "What? What's he accusing you of, A.J?"

He put my hat back on and said, "Stealin' his hat." He cracked up and the other skins cracked up with him. She grabbed my hat off his head and slapped him—hard. One of the black skins, the one who called me a carrot-top faggot, he wrapped his arms around her waist, swayed his crotch into her ass, kissed her neck, and said, "Come on, Tressa baby. Don't get loud."

"I ain't your baby, Sonny," she elbowed him in the stomach, pushed all 200 and some odd pounds of him off her. "Don't you ever put your hands on me again! Don't you ever! Want me tellin' parole you in on this? Do you?"

Sonny looked at her. He smiled slow and wide. He kept that slow, wide smile on her, I guess thinking he could make her melt and smile back. Her face did not move. I watched her and that's when it hit me: she was the chick on the L! Sonny stood with his smile on her about ten, fifteen more seconds. Soon as he got it that her face wasn't about to flinch for him any time this century, he motioned for the rest of his crew to follow him out of the alley and they all walked right back to wherever they were going before they all stopped to pound me.

Other people started showing up. I could see their bodies but not their faces, and I didn't feel safe looking anyone in the eye. The girl who saved my ass bent down, "You okay, baby? Can you breathe all right? Here, try breathing deep from here." She patted the spot right below her belly, a little ways above her privates. It took a few tries. I still hyperventilated, but, after a little while, my breath went back to normal. "Oh, shit," she said, "Look at your forehead."

I shook, "What? What's wrong with it?"

She brushed my hand away, "There's a gash. Did you land on your head, honey? Think it's a concussion?"

I shook my head, "No, I don't feel it."

"Good," she said, brushing back my hair. I counted about four or five people around her. I don't know how soon they came after the skinheads left. One guy helped me to my feet and put his hand on my back. "You alright, little buddy? Need me to call an ambulance?" I shook my head no and tried smiling, but I didn't have a smile in me.

I turned to the girl who saved my ass and said, "Thanks." She put her arm around my back and said, "Come on, baby. Let's go to a phone." She thanked the other strangers, told them she had it under control, and they walked back into the night. I left my hat where she set it down in the alley before she came to look after me and I ain't seen it since.

I started going to the phone at the corner inside Muskie's, but she said, no, we should try walking about a block and a half west, get away from everyone and everything, if I could manage. My back started throbbing and I was doubling over, but her arm on my back somehow gave me the strength to keep moving. She took me to the payphone outside Violet's Flowers on Seminary. I dug a quarter out of my pocket.

"You don't need a quarter to call 911," she said.

I put it in the phone, "I'm not calling 911."

"Why not?" she asked. "I'll give you names."

"I'm in enough trouble with them."

"I'll be a witness. I'll tell them I helped you report 'em."

"They'll kill you."

"They won't do shit to me, baby. Nuh-uh. Sonny's in

LOVE with me. But, shit, if he was the last man alive, I'd still go fuck every monkey in the jungle. I'm telling you, though, even if I got his ass dragged to the electric chair, last words'd come out of his mouth'd be my first and last name. And, don't worry, honey, they'll all back off you too, if I tell them. Just like I just did. Just like they just did."

"No," I said. "Thanks, though."

"Who you calling then?"

"My dad." She leaned up against the side of the payphone dome and watched me ring him up. Dad answered. I said, "Dad, I got…" The tears called up, started flooding out of my eyes. I kept hyena-gasping.

"What the hell's a matter with you?" he crowed. "Why are you simpering like a little ninny this time of night?"

"Fuck you, asshole!" I screamed. "I just got jumped! I'm bleeding from my fucking skull!"

"Don't you ever talk that way to me, mister."

"Oh, fuck. Look, I got more important shit to do than argue with you about my fuckin' mouth. I'm bleeding!"

"I mean it, you little punk—"

"I'm bleeding!" I screamed and started bashing the receiver against the top of the metal payphone dome. "I'm fucking bleeeeding, motherfucker!" I let the phone drop and swing from its cord as I spun around on the sidewalk. "FUCK YOU!" I kept screaming over and over on the pavement, spit bubbling out both sides of my mouth, humiliation tears waterfalling out of my eyes. "FUCK YOU!"

Tressa walked up, took my hand, told me to cool down and tried calming me down while I cried. She got on the phone. Dad was still on. I only heard her end of the conversation: "Hello, my name is Tressa. Your son was assaulted. He needs a ride…He was beat up…Yes, beat up by some skinheads…Yes, that's right. Skinheads…Yes, they did beat him up, sir…Well, how could he fight back, sir? But what's important is he's okay. He's just got some blood on his forehead. And I'm sure by morning he'll have bruises on his face and his back and his stomach…No, I think he can get by without a hospital, but he needs a ride…Sir, I'm not interested in your epithets. He's your son. He needs a ride…We're at Belmont and Seminary…My name's Tressa. What's your son's name?…Seamus. Okay." She got off the phone. "Alright, now, Seamus. He's on his way."

I said, "I'll take the bus."

Tressa smiled and kissed my cheek. "Good idea. Dad seems like a real asshole. Hope you don't mind me saying so. Hmmm, doesn't look like you do."

"No."

"Is he in the army? Was he?"

"Marines," I said, wiping my nose off on my sleeve, "made it to captain."

"Hmmph, even better," she replied. She rubbed my shoulder, "Sure you don't want to call, tell him you're taking the bus?" I shook my head no. "What's your number?" she asked, "Want me to call him?" I shook my head no. She wrote something on a slip of paper and handed it to me. "Well, this is my number. My name's Tressa. I want you to call me tomorrow, Seamus, tell me you're okay, okay?"

I sobbed. Tressa held me. Was this the only way I could make a fuckin' friend? She waited for the 77 Belmont with me until it came. "Use some iodine solution on that gash!" she called out as I got on the 77 and paid my fare. "And call me," she said, holding her hand like a phone cradle to her ear as the doors closed. I waved and mouthed, "Thank you." As the bus pulled away, I saw her walking back toward Punkin' Donuts.

I must've been a bloody sight. Everybody on the bus looked fuckin' horrified as I walked down the aisle toward the back where I grabbed a seat. The 77 seemed to hit every fucking red light on the way to the O'Hare Line at Belmont and Kimball. It was already 12:30, an hour after I was supposed to be home. My head fuckin' hurt, my legs fuckin' hurt, my back fuckin' hurt—my stomach, my pride, it all fuckin' hurt. But at least I got to meet that black Parisian model chick who got off at Logan Square many Saturdays before. She even gave me her number. That's one better than Colby did after I saw him on the L.

Right when the bus pulled up by the expressway, I saw Dad's Corsica coming down the southbound ramp onto Belmont. Part of me wanted to get off the bus and wave him down so he wouldn't waste a trip. But I didn't. I sat still and stayed on for two more blocks to take the L to Jefferson Park. I saw his Corsica turn left. He didn't see me.

The L came right when I got down the stairs to the tunnel. I knew I'd already missed the last 85A. I had to walk about three miles home with my whole body aching like one big fuckin' sore. Those were three loooong motherfucking miles.

By the time I finished walking all the way home through the Forest Preserve from Jefferson Park, it was almost 2 a.m. Whole way home, I kept remembering shit like *Salem's Lot* and *Children of the Corn* and all those bedtime stories from the Black Forest, where goblins lurk behind fir trees, ready to gobble up any passing traveler. Not a bone in my body bristled, though. In fact, I would've given that goblin my last dollar if he'd just do the fuckin' job and finish me off so I wouldn't have to do it myself. Couldn't count on the kids at the Black Masses deep in the woods to do it. I mean, y'know, if they're even there in the fuckin' first place. Rumor had it that those Taft High School twerps would slice open screaming cats by a bonfire at an altar where a high priest would say the "Our Father" backward in front of an upside-down cross. Rumor also had it they were always on the lookout for a human sacrifice. Really, the worst those pussies ever did was wear Slayer T-shirts, smoke grass at picnic tables, and shake up spray-paint cans in the underpass.

When I opened our front door, I saw Mom was waiting up at the kitchen table in her green flannel nightgown, clutching her silver rosary in her right hand. "Jesus, Mary, and Joseph!" she gasped, "What happened to you, Seamus? What happened?" She took my face in her hands, but I shook out of them. I fuckin' hate it when she touches me, even when it's just by accident, like if we brush against each other going to different parts of the kitchen. Eeeewww! Fuckin'…creeps me out. She reeked of Oil of Olay and night moisturizer. She wanted to treat me with iodine and grabbed at my clothes, trying to see the rest of me. I jumped back like she was the fuckin' plague incarnate. I'm not strippin' for her, ever!

Dad's Corsica pulled into the driveway. The car door banged shut and he barged into the house. "There you are, you little punk!" He charged at me, but I had my fists up and ready for him, so he just fuckin' stopped, stood on a dime, seething, his fat gut sagging. He knew what happened last time he tried puttin' 'em up with me. He pounded me all the time since I was little, but, when he came at me a couple months before, I laid him out cold with a right hook. Jumped on him, went fucking savage with my fists. Would've killed him too, remembering how many beatings he gave me when I was weaker than him, but I decided just to spit on his fat ass and move on. He's not worth going to fuckin' juvey for. Since then, he just fuckin' mouths off and makes it look like he's coming for me. But if he ever, ever lays a finger on me again, I swear I'll put him in his motherfucking grave. "You little puke!" he bellowed. "I was driving around the whole north side looking for you!"

Mom squealed, "Phil, he's hurt."

"I'm not surprised," Dad said. "It's about time someone put him in his place. If he talks to anyone else the way he talks to me…"

I stomped past Mom, "Both of you, just mind your business. I'm washing up and going to bed."

"The hell you are!" Dad gnashed his teeth. "And you're grounded until further notice, mister. Much further notice. You'll be in dentures and Depends before we're letting you out of here."

I rolled my eyes, like his groundings ever meant dick squat to me. Mom held one hand up to Dad, "One thing at a time, Phil. Seamus, tell us what happened."

I sighed, "I was in Dunkin' Donuts. A skinhead took my hat—"

Dad put his cute-lil-motherfucker mock smile on, "Oh, you mean that goofy hat you walk around in?" He pushed his glasses up on his nose and began mock-nodding his head, fast, like he always does when he's asking to get killed.

Mom's eyes were tearing up, though, so I ignored him, but, man, he's so fuckin' lucky I didn't tear the meat right off his bones. Mom held her rosary beads to her heart like she was staring into the face of Satan. I blocked Dad out and stared straight at Mom as I gave a pat, *Hill Street Blues* blow-by-blow: "A skinhead took my hat. He left Dunkin' Donuts with his friends. I walked out to take the 77. I was trying to get home on time. I saw him on my way to the bus stop. I asked if I could have my hat back. Next thing I know, him and his friends were having a free-for-all on me." After all that matter-of-factness, some valve in my heart opened up and I started crying again—something you never want to fuckin' do in front of Dad. Mom tried putting her arms around me, but I didn't want it. I wriggled away and turned my back.

"A black kid takes your hat and you ask for it back." Dad tapped the side of his head, mock-nodding some more. "Now that's what I call using your noggin."

"It wasn't a black kid! It was a white—" and I almost said fuckin', but I didn't want that fat fuck telling me to watch my language, so I just stuck to my point, "skinhead. The guy was white and, by the way, a black girl came up and got 'em all off me."

Dad smirked, his head going up and down again like a kewpie doll, "Oh, that's swell. So now you got girls fighting your fights for you." He nodded, jowls jiggling, smirk frozen on his face.

Mom was a shuddering mess, so I didn't smack the shit out of him like I should've. Mom said, "Well, you're never going there again."

I didn't respond. I knew damn well I'd be back on Belmont the next week, if only to do teatime with Tressa. I was grounded for foul language, "insubordination," and violating curfew, but Mom's fifty-eight and Dad's fifty-nine and they had me too late in life for either of them to enforce house rules.

When I went to Dr. Strykeroth's office on Michigan Avenue the next Monday, he also took my face in his hands. His eyes were pooling with tears like Mom's. None dropped, though. I didn't mind him holding my face. I got cozy in his hands. "Seamus," he said, "who did this to you?"

"I don't know," I answered. "Some white guy named A.J. Some black guy named Sonny. There were some other guys there too. Skinheads. Never met 'em before. Got good news, though. I finally made a fuckin' friend on Belmont."

He brushed back my hair, ran his fingertips down the side of my neck, and kissed my bruises and the scar on my forehead.

CHAPTER IX
Colby at Irving Park Station

There's this lavender-scented sex hormone—a crotch-teasing, unisex Spanish fly—they pump from all the ceilings on all the floors at Medusa's. It fills your nostrils, fills your pores. It makes your blood beat, your body burst into flame. Mix that with all the cigarette smoke and sweat, you got yourself a two-story teenage cathouse—three stories if you count the stairs going up to Granny, the bouncer.

And that's *before* you hear the drum machines and heavy bass. The owners are probably drumming up business for the local abortion clinic: "Send us your teens! No fetus can beat us!" If so, that clinic must be doing one hell of a business. On every other stair up to the top floor, there's another funny-haired guy knocking back another funny-haired girl's tonsils and pressing her tits so hard and spazzy, you'd think he's making an emergency batch of biscuits out of them. And the only lights on the staircases are the little cartridges set in the walls that only give off about as much light as bike reflectors on an empty street with no lampposts. The hallway walls come in lots of colors. The coal-black walls stay coal-black, but they swirl the blood red and sky blue walls with cloud white. They all glow in dim neon till close. Not that I'm ever there to see them turn the neon off. I got a fuckin' curfew, remember?

They can't serve booze at Medusa's. It's a juice bar for minors. It's against the law for them to tank us all up, so you gotta go out back by the dumpsters and guzzle out of a paper bag before going in. Even Medusa's is forced to prohibit some vices. That's why they got Granny frisking you for firearms and drugs before she lights another cancer stick and dropkicks another rabble-rouser out onto Sheffield Street.

Beyond that, you're free to let your dick hang out and your body get beat in a mosh pit. The bouncers are required by law, though, to break up any brawl they see involving less than three people—that's word for word what I heard Granny telling a new bouncer she was training one night. In the pit, though, it's nothing but consensual punk rock. There are a few signs up saying that they're not responsible for any injuries or lost or stolen items, but I'm not sure that stands up in court. Course, if anyone's stupid enough to sue, they'll probably have motherfuckin' Al Capone at their door before a judge can even sign a subpoena.

As for dicks hanging out, maybe you see it once in a while, but I don't think guys in the video room got too much to show for themselves there. And their teeny-weeny weenies were just what I was thinking about as I walked around the top floor after seeing Colby get busted. True, Colby did keep his hands up while Narc searched his pockets, didn't kick him into the train while it was moving. Doesn't mean he don't got balls. Means he's got brains. Nobody gets away with shit in this country unless they're in the White House—or my neighborhood's whitey households. Colby knows when it's in his best interest to cooperate. But just his naturalness—that hair he refuses to fuck up—it shows he's got more going on in his jock than any of those sneering, snooty, funny-haired freaks who run from jocks and futz with their hair every fuckin' five minutes. When I think of Colby, it makes me want to stop fuckin' up my hair too. But I'm not ready to give that shit up just yet.

The L's pulling up to Irving Park and Pulaski now, far, far away from Medusa's. This is where courtyard apartment buildings make their first appearance on the O'Hare line, left and right of the train. The building to my right has gray-painted wooden staircases, running at sharp angles down to the alley where dumpsters sit brimming with garbage bags. Not a lot of nightlife here. Some dive bars, some greasy spoons, not a lot of trendy restaurants, and no clubs. No one ever talks about it. Never gets mentioned in *The Reader*, which I pick up every Thursday to look up shows and sex ads. Every morning, this L platform is crammed pillar to post. Unlike Jefferson Park, Irving Park station doesn't have a lot of buses coming in from all over Chicago. Must mean people boarding here live here. Yeah, I could see that. There are lots of apartment buildings around; you can pack a lot of people into a neighborhood that way.

The apartment buildings are big too. On my way back from school once, I overheard an architect trying to impress his girlfriend by calling all the buildings around here "Tudor." Whatever the fuck that means. To me, they just look like a bunch of big Joe-Mama gingerbread houses. Every time I pass, I feel like I'm in a fairy tale. Tempts me to get off the L and walk into one of the courtyards. I keep thinking I'll get sucked into some time warp, like in *The Time Machine*. I'll be transported to some fairy tale, like *Hansel and Gretel* or Mozart's *Magic Flute*, only I'll be the main character. Finally get a shot at a life worth living.

But could I get that here, at Irving Park and Pulaski? It's not Piccadilly Circus. It's not even Belmont and Clark. The people getting on—a lot of the men—look and smell like big Bluto bohunks. Don't know what kind of jobs they're headed to. Maybe they're on their way to construction sites or factories—but wouldn't they be starting their shifts a lot earlier in the morning? The women, a lot of them look like Polish cleaning ladies, except others look dressed for the office. Maybe they're secretaries. Must be the ones who learned English and took typing classes at community centers. Good for them. Not all of them do. Some of 'em been here forty years, never learned a lick of English. Give them all the credit in the world, though. Must be fuckin' hard as hell, making your way after moving halfway around the world with nothing.

The ones who do learn English a lot of times wind up way the fuck ahead of any of us who were born here; the Chinese almost always do. But I bet the Polacks send most everything they earn back home. Wonder if their money orders ever make it past the guards at the Iron Curtain. But why are their families back home so fucking poor? Aren't they all guaranteed jobs under communism? That's what the guy who passes out *The Socialist Worker* under the Belmont L says. So why the fuck do they want to come here? Probably swallowed a shitload of American propaganda, just like Americans have.

No, Irving Park-Pulaski isn't the coolest hood on earth, but I always scan the station anyway, hoping to see Colby. Why the fuck did he get on here? I mean, here, of all places? I don't know, but I keep thinking I'll see him getting on again and, when I do, I'll walk up and say, "Hey, weren't you the guy who got busted for packing a marker?"

Yeah, that happened on the L one Saturday night— months before the first time I saw Tressa get off at Logan Square. Out of nowhere, this legion of leather-clad kids got on at Irving Park and Pulaski. My eyes got big, round, hypnotized. I had to clench my jaw to keep it from hitting the floor. You gotta understand, these were ultra-vivid Brit punks, not no bland, fuckin' eunuch Americans. No, we're talking, they had...oh, man...charisma...their presence, it just *radiated* throughout the car like nothing I ever saw on Belmont—only like what I'd seen in photos in *Punk: A Sordid Saga*, like the ones of Siouxsie Sioux on stage in '78, wearing a black trash bag and a Nazi armband. And they didn't even have English accents when they talked. But they couldn't've been from fuckin' Chicago. I mean, they sounded like they were, but fuckin' no one knows how to dress that cool here, except maybe Tressa.

And they all got on here, at fuckin' Irving Park and Pulaski! Four of them—two girls, two guys. One of the guys had this blond Billy Idol hair. No, but it was better, much fuckin' better than fuckin' Billy Idol. What he did was, he spiked it all around to look like Sid—a blond Sid Vicious, it was fuckin' brilliant! He had this tight-fitting black peacoat. Looked like he tore it up and then put it all back together with all these safety pins and sewn-on calico swatches. And the guy wasn't wearing combats like the rest of the fuckin' world. No, he wore black motorcycle boots with a red bandana tied to one of them. First time I ever saw that. His skin was deep bronze. He had this one chick hanging on him. She had a tar-black bob, shaved close to the skin on the sides and back, the rest dangling in fringes from the crown of her head to her chin, and her eyes were lined Cleopatra-style. She fuckin' flaunted that fifteen-year-old hooker look—leopard-print coat; shredded, sheer nylons; go-go boots; and this sizzling hot-pink mini. The other chick was this blonde with long, curly hair. Her body was wrapped tight in a knee-length, black leather coat, her big bust busting out of it. Don't know if she had anything else on besides her sheer scarlet stockings and black fuck-me pumps. She was sitting next to the kid I heard them call Colby. Her arm was in his, she was damn near in his lap. He had his hand on her thigh. Saw him move it over to her other thigh too and a little ways under the hem of her leather coat. She acted natural and let him do it right there on the L. But I couldn't tell whether, when he tried going up her skirt, he actually found a skirt.

What I wouldn't've fuckin' given to be Blondie right then and there in that seat. Oh, Colby. Like I said, he had that 1940s black porkpie hat on. It had a bow, like a bowtie, on the right side. Used to see those hats on sale at Wax Trax, but they looked fuckin' ridiculous, sitting like clumsy clods on the racks. I'd look at that pile of hats and think, who the fuck could pull off a look that's worth it in that? But Colby was as good an answer as I could ever ask for. At one point, he took off his hat. He had black hair and a simple, short haircut. Didn't do anything hardcore to it—no parts shaved, wasn't bone-close or fuzzy like a skinhead's either. He just let it be the way it was, nothing to prove. Now that's guts. His eyes, I could fuckin' drown in them—the deep blue sea with moonlight lapping in the waves. His skin looked like it could tan like Dr. Strykeroth's, but he kept it white as porcelain. He wore a black biker jacket with the Murphy's Law logo painted in green on the right sleeve—yet another band I never heard before Tressa. He wore a gray collared shirt and black Levis cuffed over black, 8-hole Docs, like he was about to throw a fuckin' Molotov cocktail at Buckingham Palace.

But, no, there was something a little too precious for violence in him. Maybe he was a little like Siouxsie Sioux—a gutter punk gone sensitive artist. His lips were so rose-red, they could've dissolved into wine and I would've been on my knees lapping up every last drop. But his hand was up some succubus' thigh. What I wouldn't fuckin' give to be that succubus with that thigh.

Colby and his friends were all laughing together. Looked like they'd all known each other a long time. Maybe they all grew up around the block from each other. He's so fucking lucky to grow up in a neighborhood where kids are doing the same shit he is. Who do I have? Fuckin' Andy Payne? I had to do all this shit on my own, and pricks on Lehigh are driving up and screaming faggot and freak at me for it. I couldn't hear what Colby and his friends were laughing about. Maybe I was too stunned to listen. Maybe I was so caught up in all the fun they were all having together, their talk just faded into white noise.

I kept my head down and made like I was looking out the window. Dr. Strykeroth would've given me a noogie if he saw that and said, "Why don't you go up and try mingling, knucklehead?" Dr. S says I should have every reason to feel confident. He says

I'm beautiful. But, no, not like Colby. Didn't even feel fit to look at him; couldn't stop looking at him either, though. It was like standing before God. Every now and then, I'd scope out my own gear. Sex Pistols *God Save the Queen* T-shirt; red hair, loosely fucked-up, shaved on the sides and back; a moth-eaten long black funeral coat that I found in our crawl space and that Dad's always trying to stuff in the Tuesday garbage; scuffed-up combats, too fuckin' big for me. I had nothing on these cats and I knew it. If Colby didn't have me so spellbound, I would've walked out between the L cars and dropped myself like a sad sack under the speeding wheels.

Sid Vicious/Billy Idol took flat balloons out of his inside coat pocket and started blowing them up. He passed the first one, a red balloon, to Colby. Colby took a black Magic Marker out of his Murphy's Law jacket's right pocket. Blondie hung on his arm and watched with a red-lipstick smile as he started scribbling eyes, ears, a nose, a goofy-ass mouth, and all these fucked-up curls on the balloon. When he was done, he let the red balloon fall and bounce at his feet. Sid Vicious/Billy Idol blew up another balloon, a purple one, and passed it to Colby who lost no time marking it up. I didn't get a look at what he was drawing but they were all howling up such a fucking storm at how fucked-up it all looked, they got me laughing too, but I caught myself before they could catch me and quick-looked out the window at the oil towers and bungalows coming up on Addison.

A few stops later, as Colby sketched more shit on to the second balloon, some fashion-disaster redneck with Andy Travis hair, a lumberjack shirt, tan corduroys, and gray New Balance gym shoes got out of his seat and clopped over to Colby and his friends like Boss Hog. "Excuse me," said the redneck. The whole posse looked up. Redneck said, "Get off with me at the next stop please." Colby and his friends looked at each other and back up at him, 'huh?' scribbled all over their faces. Redneck dug out his wallet and flashed a badge, "Get off with me at the next stop." He was a fuckin' narc.

Narc waved down the black guy who worked the train doors. Black L Guy nodded back. The L pulled up to California and Fullerton. Black L Guy got on his walkie-talkie, mumbled something to the conductor, and got on the PA, announcing, "We'll be standing in the station momentarily." Narc said to Colby and his friends, "C'mon. Off the train. Now. Empty your pockets." They all filed out on to the California Street platform in the setting sun, not knowing which fuckin' way was up.

Narc started frisking Colby, who stood with his hands in the air. I got out of my seat and called out the car, "What? What the fuck you harassing him for?" Narc turned around, but Black L Guy closed the doors before Narc could make a grab at me. The L pulled out of California Station, taking me miles and miles away from Colby and his friends. Black L Guy said, "Lucky he didn't drag you out for mouthin' off." I threw my hands up, "They're all fascists, man. Cops are all fucking fascists. Anyone who looks different, man. Anyone who looks different." Black L Guy looked down, shook his head and chuckled to himself.

I didn't see the humor. I sat back down, fuckin' fuming. What the fuck was asshole Narc bustin' Colby and his friends for? Drawing on balloons? Littering, when the first balloon bounced? Guess there were no murderers or serial rapists to go out and hassle that night. At least Colby didn't write "DIE FAG" or some shit like that with his Magic Marker like Payne, who never gets busted for any of the shit he does.

Part of me wished Narc *did* hustle me out to the platform. Man, I thought, I could be in a jail cell with them tonight. Beats the shit out of going to Medusa's. We could play poker on the cement floor and talk Johnny and Jello Biafra and Malcolm McLaren all the way till we make bail. Would've been the start of something beautiful. But, no, Black L Guy had to close the fuckin' doors. Probably for the best, though. Wouldn't want Colby and his posse seeing fuckin' Mom or fuckin' Dad or fuckin' both. I mean, shit, who else could I call to post bond? Brody? And I sure as fuck wouldn't want any of them hearing the stupid shit Mom and Dad would say in front of everyone in the pokey: Mom's shrill, condemning religious vomit; Dad's bull's-eye putdowns; their genius for making me want to crawl into a hole and die. So maybe Black L Guy did me a favor.

Still, on the way to Washington and Dearborn, Colby's all I could think about. Even walking the Washington tunnel to the Howard Line, I just kept turning his image over and over in my mind. I started thinking I should go back to Wax Trax and take another look at those hats. I should get one. Then Colby and me could walk down the streets together. I'd wear the hat and the biker jacket just like him and I'd get something painted on my sleeve too. Maybe a Union Jack with a circle around it and maybe there'd be another circle in that circle too, one that wraps around a jagged A, the first letter to the words, "Anarchy in the UK," all those letters sketched out all-cool-n'-shit on the inner perimeter of the larger circle that's around the Union Jack.

Maybe I'll even get Colby to paint it for me, I thought. I liked what he drew on the red balloon. He's probably a good artist. I imagined somehow getting the money together for the hat and the jacket. I'd wear black Levis too, rolled up and cuffed just like his. Except I wouldn't have Docs. No, I'd have fuckin' motorcycle boots with a red bandana tied around one of them, just like his friend's. Now that would be an original look! Colby and me could be a two-man gang. We could laugh together, walking down the street, just like Sid and Johnny used to down Kings Road, screaming, "We don't fucking care!" I'd throw my arm around his shoulder like I'd later see that fuckin' skinhead throw his arms around his friends' shoulders, only we'd be real friends, not just a couple reverse-conformist thugs.

And it could be at Irving Park-Pulaski. I don't fuckin'

care. Not everything's gotta go down on Belmont. Maybe we could go back to his house, I said to myself. Maybe he lives in an apartment and his Mom's never there; she's always at work or with her boyfriend—y'know, typical broken home-type shit. We could play fuckin' Dead Kennedys, 7 Seconds, Crass, and whatever else he's got in his room. Bet Colby's got all the albums anybody'd ever fuckin' want. We could light cigarettes in his room. Play music on Saturday afternoons. Spend hours in there together, just the two of us. Then we could hit Medusa's.

As I walked up the stairs to the Howard L at Washington, I thought, I'll conscript Colby into my London Plan. Fuck knows I've been mapping it out since I was 11; now I'll just add him. The Plan's pretty straightforward. Right when we turn sixteen, we'll get jobs at a supermarket or something, a Jewel or a Dominick's—maybe even one around Irving Park and Pulaski, who knows? If something more glamorous turns up, well, so much the better, but anything'll do at this point. We'll save up a couple years and leave the day whichever one of us is younger turns eighteen. I'm sure Colby was only fourteen, like I was last year. He doesn't look any older than me. He's just got his shit more together than I do. That'll all change, though, once I build a bigger life in London. All this might mean we can't go to Medusa's or Wax Trax as much as we do now...not if we're saving up and shit...but whoop-dee-fuckin'-doo! Those places suck ass anyway. Instead we can hang at his place, smoke cigarettes, blast 7 Seconds, Sex Pistols, fuckin' PiL.

As the northbound L came, I told myself, I'll tell Colby we'll fly from O'Hare to London. Last I checked in the Sunday *Trib*, the cheapest fares run about $600—and that's roundtrip. We only need one-way, so it'll be a lot cheaper. We'll get to Heathrow (that's the airport there). We'll get on the Tube (that's what they call the L in London, and, in quids [that's what they call bucks], it shouldn't be any more expensive than the L). We'll find a squat (that's an abandoned building where you can stay till you have enough quids to pay rent on an apartment; lots of punks live in them) somewhere in Brixton (that's where David Bowie grew up but it's mostly Rastafarians now; they got blacks in England too, with British accents, it's mental!). We'll find some punks at the squat, ones we can trust to look after our shit. We'll get back on the Tube and go apply for jobs at some West End pubs (that's what the Brits call bars). Almost all of them pay you what they call "under the table" (that means you don't have to worry about being an illegal alien).

We'll start making money and get our own apartment. And then, who knows, maybe I will go to fuckin' college. Maybe it'll feel right by then. I'll forge my high school transcripts and get into some college in England. Maybe Oxford. They won't deport me if I have a student visa. I won't have to work under the table anymore either. I'll kick ass at Oxford and become a shrink like Dr. Stykeroth—but I'll practice in England, not here. Fuck no, not here.

Or maybe I'll follow my real dream of being a BBC actor. I hear they've got a lot of actors in the West End. Maybe I can meet 'em if I'm working in a pub where lots of them go after shows. They can tell me where to audition, how to get started in British show biz. I'll get parts in plays. They don't have to be big parts. They can be bit parts. But the more I act, the more attention I'll attract. BBC agents'll see me in small theaters and, pretty soon, all of England will see me on the BBC and *Masterpiece Theatre* and shit. That's all it takes.

And I'll tell Colby he can do whatever the fuck he wants, whatever he fuckin' dreams of doing! I'll encourage him. Maybe his mom never encouraged him, maybe his dad walked out on his mom before he even got a chance to give Colby a shred of encouragement, but I'll fuckin' encourage Colby. Maybe Colby wants to own a club, a much cooler club than fuckin' Medusa's. I'll say, go ahead, do it. Maybe we can run it together, just as long as I don't have to do any fuckin' math. It can happen. All this shit can happen. You just gotta believe it.

I got off the Howard Line at Belmont and walked to Medusa's, hoping Colby'd be out of the clink soon so we could make friends and get moving on our London Plans. Once inside the door at Medusa's, I stood in line—or in the queue, as they call it in England—on the pitch-black stairwell heading up to the main floor, where Granny, the chain-smoking old lady, pats you down. She might be older than God's own granny and bonier than a skinned fish, but I've seen Granny bounce skinheads the size of fuckin' Appalachia on to the curb. Dudes who'll mosh with Godzilla know better than to fuck with her. I stood among hordes of punks, skaters, New Wavers, housers, skinheads, trendies, poseurs of all stripes—every one of them pulling out every fuckin' stop to show off how many people they all fuckin' know. I stood all alone, this time thinking, I'd rather be alone than be friends with these assholes.

It took me fifteen minutes in the queue to make it up the stairs, which gave me ample time to look the whole Medusa mob scene up and down. What can I say, it looked fuckin' pathetic! Most of them probably piled into cars and drove in from the fuckin' suburbs, where they all play punk the same way little girls play dress-up with dollies. Not a one of them came anywhere close to Colby in coolness. It's like, on the L at Irving Park, I had a vision of perfection that ruined me for anything I'd ever see again (until I'd see Tressa, that is, and maybe until I see London up close and personal). Granny slid her hands into my pockets and down my sides and legs and let me move on. I paid five bucks admission, looked back down the stairs and sighed so all those fucks could hear it as I walked up to the video room.

For about an hour, I wove through the *Rosemary's Baby* meets *Teen Steam* orgies in the neon rooms, where they blast lavender-scented Spanish fly and Meat Beat Manifesto videos. It was like, all at once, I was walking across two planes of reality. One was the lower plane, where all those freaks are into all that show-off shit, playing up to each other, acting like they all fuckin' know it all, not letting anyone into their little cliques unless the majority of their clique approves. Then there was another plane. Call it fuckin' Mount Olympus, where the gods get together. Colby lives on high there. As I walked through the video room, I imagined his friends must live up on Olympus too, or else why would he be hanging out with them?

Mount Olympus, it's where people are above all the poses video-room fops strike. It's where people like Colby got bigger plans for their futures than fucking up their hair and buying twelve inches and test-pressings from bands only a few fucks know about. I thought, Colby and people like him…they do shit like move to other countries and make art and write books and make music, the kind that's got lots of range and puts lots of styles together, not just this monotonous industrial shit. At least, that's what I imagine they do. They express their true selves. You can see it on Colby's face. Not a blemish on it. There's just that glow rising from his soul. He's lit from within. He doesn't feel the need to fuck up his hair. Him and his friends—they're fuckin' self-styled. Lots of people wear leather jackets and boots, but, I dunno, not like them. I can't explain. There was…fuckin'…something about it. I dunno. It was that…fuckin'…Mount Olympus experience. All at once, or, at least in my mind, I was on Mount Olympus and the lower plane, the neon rooms. And I wanted to be way up in the land of the gods and away from that fuckin' lower plane, the fuckin' neon rooms.

That's why I walked out of the video room. From the third floor at Medusa's, there are no stairs to Olympus—though I hear that, if you blow the DJ, he'll take you up to the roof and cut you some lines of coke. I figured I'd cut my losses on the five bucks admission and walk back out, past the old lady with her cigarette and the bouncers following her lead. I didn't expect I'd ever be back, though I also didn't expect there was any other place for a fuckin' freak like me to go.

As I stepped into the hallway toward the Exit sign on the main floor, I looked at the new queue of people waiting to pay up and get frisked. Right at the front of the queue, I saw a leopard-print coat. I saw a long, curly mass of blonde hair hanging down a knee-length black leather coat. I saw blond Sid Vicious hair. In front of all them, I saw a fuckin' 1940s black porkpie hat. I froze. It was like, I couldn't go to Mount Olympus, so Mount Olympus fuckin' came to me! But last I checked, wasn't Mount Olympus getting hauled into the slammer? What'd they do, break out? Mustn't be the cleverest group of punk-rock gods and goddesses if they decided to go on the lam in Medusa's. Where the fuck'd they think the cops'd go looking for their divine little asses first?

What should I do? I thought. Go talk to them? Find out what happened? Find out if they got sprung or if they fuckin' sprung themselves? I'm not good at that shit—going up and introducing myself. I used to try that shit at Xavier when I first got there. I'd go up to kids at school; I'd say, I'm Seamus; they'd look at me; I'd stand there. I'd ask what they're into, who their favorite bands are. More standing there. I'd say my favorite bands, say what I'm into. More standing there, sometimes some laughter sputtering out of them. After a while, they'd take one last look at me and walk off. And I'd still be fuckin' standing there. I don't know what it is about me. I don't know why the kids at Xavier walked off. I don't know why they laughed at me later if they never bothered talking to me first. I told myself I'd never invite that experience again. I decided, if I wanted to know somebody, I'd wait for them to introduce themselves to me first. Only, nobody ever came up and introduced themselves—so I never met anybody, not till Tressa. I had to do everything by my fuckin' self, go everywhere by my fuckin' self, learn all this shit by my fuckin' self. Rejection just hurt too fucking much to keep trying to talk to people, but Dr. Strykeroth's still trying to get me to risk it anyway.

But I wasn't up to it that night. I had Plans, real big fuckin' London Plans for me and Colby, but I just couldn't bring myself to walk up and introduce myself. I looked at what I was wearing. I looked at where I'm from. I kept my head down and decided to brush past Colby on my way out the building, even though I knew that later I'd regret being such a chicken shit.

But, on my way to the last set of stairs, Colby walked right up to me. Right fuckin' up to *me*! He said, "Hey, weren't you on the L when we got pulled off?" I stopped, froze like a fuckin' corpse in a morgue. My dream was fucking forcing itself to come true right before my fuckin' eyes. I had no fucking idea what to say. I fumbled around my coat for a cigarette. Colby looked puzzled when, instead of answering him, I took a long pause to fish out and light up a Marlboro. Finally, I squeaked out the definitive answer Colby'd been waiting for: "Yeah."

His friends gathered around me in a group. I thought I'd fuckin' faint! Fuckin'…sensory overload! The chick in the leopard-print coat clutched on to her Billy Idol/Sid Vicious boyfriend and said, "We were arrested."

"What?" I said.

Sid Vicious/Billy Idol said, "They called a squad car and took us to the station."

"They fuckin' cuff you?" I asked.

"Of course," he said, "They have to by law."

I didn't know how the fuck I was gonna manage the rest of this exchange. It all came on so—*phew!* —fuckin'…all of a sudden. There's no way I'm cool enough to keep this going, I thought. I gotta be, like, 100,000 times cooler than I am right now to measure up to what they're all used to up on Olympus. I decided now was as good a time as any to put on the voice I always wished I had—a cockney fuckin' British accent. Why not? It's my life. I should be able to sound whatever fuckin' way I want. I should be able to be whoever I fuckin' wanna be, even it means I gotta make some shit up about who I am and where I'm from.

Right then and there, in Medusa's lobby, I transformed from Seamus from the Northwest Side to Seamus from the motherfuckin' East End of London. A whole spiel—all the basics I could tell people—started forming in my head. After all, I'd be meeting a lot more people now that I was the fabulous Seamus from the East End of London. I'd say, "Hello, I'm Seamus from the East End of London:

1. I drink tea.
2. My dad's the British ambassador to America.
3. 'is job shipped 'im to Chicago. I 'ad to accompany 'im.
4. I miss London.
5. I'm goin' off me fuckin' trolley with boredom 'ere.
6. I plan on goin' back to London. It's so much fuckin' better that side of the pond."

This was a stroke of fucking genius! This would be my life story from now on! It'd be like living in England without living in England yet! My new voice, my new persona would charm the fuckin' shit out of Colby. We'd take tea at teatime. We'd talk on the phone. He'd tell me how his day went. We'd plan to take tea-and-sympathy again, real fucking soon. There'd be lots of tea. Lots and lots of fuckin' tea.

I'd tell him how *outrageous* London is. I'd study up on it in the encyclopedia and all the travel booklets you can get for free from Caldwell Travel Agency. I'd talk like a fuckin' insider. There's no way he could find out the shit-truth about me: that I'm Phil and Mary O'Grady's son and I've lived on the Northwest Side all my life. He'd never meet Mom and Dad. I'd make bloody fuckin' sure of that. And it's not like I know anybody'd he'd know. It's not like we'd run into anyone from my neighborhood, not around here. It's not like I'd have to worry about anyone from St. Xavier busting me out if we ran into them; they'd never fuckin' deign to speak to me in the first place. If Colby'd call my house and Mom'd answer, I'd just tell him my parents are using American accents to fit in ("What can I say? Wanker mum and wanker Dad is into fittin' in."). I'd never have to be Seamus from the fucking Northwest Side again. Now I'm Seamus from the East End of London. And soon I'll tell Colby he could move back to London with me. This was a stroke of fucking genius!

All these thoughts flashed through my head in the time it took to take another drag off my Marlboro. Colby said, "They had us in custody for almost half an hour."

My first word in my new voice was, "Ay? Why?"

Colby twitched down an eyebrow, "Well, you saw. I had a marker on me."

"Righ', Righ'," I said. "The balloons."

"Yeah," Colby replied, raising and then twitching his eyebrow back down again, "the balloons. You saw that guy get up and walk over to us, right? He was an undercover cop."

"Righ'," I said, nodding, smoking and talking all at once, like I once saw Johnny Marr do on *120 Minutes*. "Fuckin' narc. Fuckin' wanker."

Dead silence, thick as midnight. I'd spent years practicing a cockney accent in my bedroom and I thought I was doing a pretty fuckin' good job, considering the short notice. But not a word of it washed with Blondie, Colby's leather-succubus girlfriend. Fuckin' Blondie. She let go of Colby's arm and fixed me a glare that said I was the fakest fuckin' fraud she'd ever fuckin' laid eyes on. She even spun around and laughed at me in front of all the freaks traipsing down the hallway and bounding up to the third floor.

Colby was nicer than Blondie. He just went on with what he was saying, "Anyway, I told the cop I wasn't using my marker to tag graffiti. I was just drawing on some balloons. They couldn't find any evidence against us, so they confiscated the marker and let us go."

I took a mean drag off my Marlboro, let it out in a long exhale and laid down the law, "Tell you wha', mate, them fascists is wankas. Fuckin' wankas. Oughta declare a state a fuckin' anarchy and say fuck off with the lotta 'em." More morgue silence. Blondie snickered one last time and walked right on past me up to the video room. Leopard Print followed and so did Sid Vicious/Billy Idol, both of them chiming in on Blondie's laughter.

I realized I was the stupidest fuckin' twat alive. Mount Olympus was a fuckin' golden bird, laying golden eggs in my hands and I dropped the eggs and let that fucker fly away. What about living in foreign countries? What about making art with all them? What about the books I'd write while we're all sitting around cafes at teatime and going to the gigs they play (if any of them are in bands, that is)? What about the friendships we could make with each other, the kinds people make movies and write biographies about years later? Did I fuckin' blow it like I'm blowing my chances of staying at Xavier?

Since I couldn't take looking at Colby's flawless face anymore, I let my eyes drop to the dark hallway floor. My eyes fell in motherfucking defeat to Colby's boots as he started marching away with his friends. I wanted to take the cigarette I was smoking and stab it a thousand times through my left hand. Gone were all hopes, dreams, and best-laid London Plans with Colby… and there was no one to blame but my fuckin' self. Before that moment, I never met a mirror I liked and it didn't look like I ever fucking would.

As I was taking another drag off my cigarette and was about to incinerate my flesh, I felt a gentle grip on my shoulder. I looked over. It was Colby. "See you around, man," he said. "Take care of yourself." He took a look back at me. To look me in the eye. To see me. It was a look of understanding, like he understood how hard it must be standing there, wanting to burn myself alive. Did he ever feel that way himself? I can't imagine. He's so fucking beautiful and cool. He got me, though. Caught me fronting with that stupid fuckin' cockney accent. He fuckin' got me and cast no look of hate when he did. His look seemed like love, actually. But, no, I wouldn't go that far. He still followed his friends and kept his back to me the whole way up the stairs to the video room.

Guess he wasn't expecting me to follow. I wasn't expecting to either. But, after he went upstairs and I took a couple more drags off my smoke, which I didn't end up stabbing through my hand after all, I took a pen out of my coat pocket and scratched my name and number on the piece of paper I always keep for emergencies like this. I walked back into the video room, the lower plane, where I saw Colby making the rounds through a fuckin' blue million neon video-room denizens, getting hugged and kissed and clasped and loved a blue million fuckin' times over—the ambassador from Olympus that Dad never was from England. I stood back a couple minutes and watched.

A Thrill Kill Kult video was raging on all the screens. It made me bold. I nerved up the nutsack to tap Colby's shoulder. He didn't feel it at first. Sid Vicious/Billy Idol and Blondie were watching me, fucking aghast, as I kept tapping him. Colby turned around, took a step back, and looked at me. I handed him the slip of paper with my name and number on it and said in my plain Chicago voice, loud enough for him to hear over Thrill Kill Kult, "Here. Just in case you need a witness for what happened on the L." He smiled and said, "Thanks." I smiled back and walked out of the dark neon rooms, past Leopard Print, Blondie, and Sid Vicious/Billy Idol. I thought of asking Colby for his number, but I already fucked up once in the main-floor hallway. I wasn't gonna fuck up again. I walked off Mount Olympus for the night. But now its king, this teenage Zeus in a 1940s porkpie hat, heard my plea. Maybe he'd call me later to welcome me on to his pantheon.

But what would he gain by calling me or being my friend? He's already got friends. By the looks of it, he had the whole fuckin' video room. What did I have to offer, except my London Plans? And I could have a life in London without him, I know that. It'd just be a lot fuckin' lonelier, that's all. At least Colby's always right there in my mind, though. That's what I thought to myself as I made my last exit to Sheffield Street: "Colby will always be on my mind. Even if he never calls, even if we never take tea, he will always be on my mind."

It's been well over a year now. Colby still hasn't called. Not that I'm waiting by the phone anymore. And I haven't seen him around since that night either, not even at the fuckin' Murphy's Law concert, where my eyes were peeled out of their fuckin' sockets for him. And I've been back to the video room time and again and he never turned up. He wasn't even at Medusa's when Ministry played. Fuckin' everyone who's anyone was there! Not him, though. Who knows, maybe he moved. God, I fuckin' hope not. I so want to see him again.

I never told Tressa about the night I met Colby. Never told her what happened with Narc. Never told her about my attempts at a cockney accent and a new story. But I did ask her if the name Colby rang a bell. She said it didn't and asked me why I asked. I said somebody told me some story about somebody on Belmont named Colby but I couldn't remember how it went. I could tell she could tell I was lying. I remembered the story. Knew it fuckin' chapter and verse. I was its author. "Colby's coming with me to London": I nursed the story all last year. I nurse it now, but not so much now that a year has gone by and the phone hasn't rung. Yet my London Plans still stand if he ever wants to hear my pitch, if I ever see him on the L again, if we ever become friends. I'll keep watching out for him at Irving Park station. But I won't do a cockney accent next time. That was just fuckin' stupid.

PART TWO:

WEST TOWN STORIES

"All about the Personality Crisis

You got it while it was hot

But now frustration and heartache is what you've got..."

New York Dolls, "Personality Crisis"

CHAPTER X

How It's Done in West Town

The bus is on fire. It's got bloodlust Ozzy Osbourne eyes, Jaws' razor teeth, and a face like the Soul Train on *Soul Train*. There's a white guy in a Gestapo uniform. His eyes are bulging. His tongue is wagging. He's sticking his finger in the blue bus' ass. There's a *Red Dawn* explosion behind him, a nuclear holocaust. There's a black hooker painted space-invader green. She's standing on top of the burning bus with a great big fuckin' fro, a tight-as-fuck pink mini, ten-stack platform shoes, fists clenched and pinned to her hips.

Too bad you can't paint that shit on buildings without a permit. It's cool as fuck. Takes a shitload of talent too. Man, I wish I could paint, but I can't even doodle out a damn circle. No wonder I'm flunking geometry. If we were in a state of anarchy like we should be, we could paint whatever the fuck we want, wherever the fuck we want. Just listen to Mozart. Did he have to wait till he had a permit to make music?—Well I guess maybe he did. There was that scene in *Amadeus* where he had a bitch of a time getting approved by the imperial court to do a harem opera. But...whatever, man...it shouldn't fuckin' be that way.

But, I gotta admit, some of the murals the city does dole out permits for are pretty fuckin' impressive too. I mean, lots of times they use rubbish Day-Glo colors and a lot of times they paint a lot of corny-ass get-high-on-life, school-is-cool themes, but you can tell the painters put their heart in that shit. Lots of times they get little neighborhood kids to help out and they teach them to paint and let their imaginations roam. And, even though I think we should all have the right to paint whatever the fuck want, wherever the fuck we want, I gotta admit, it does bother me when gangs spray graffiti on murals little kids helped paint.

I don't think Raul's ever defaced a kid's mural, but Tressa says the cops are on the scent of whoever put graffiti art like the nuclear-holocaust bus up around Logan Square and West Town. Apparently the Nazi finger-fucking the bus' anus isn't Raul's only brainchild. Just his most famous. He sprayed it on the back wall of the roof where, from March to November, pitbulls wheel around a parked Harley-Davidson and crumpled Miller cans. Raul tags under the name Snipsta, and he's tight with the dude who owns the pitbulls and Harley. I don't know what that bandito's story is, but I always wonder how the fuck he maneuvered a Harley all the way up to his roof. Did he drag it up the fire escape or hang pulleys down to the alley? Who knows? Drug lords can arrange anything, at least that's what I hear.

I've met Raul a couple times at Tressa's house on Logan Boulevard. Skinny kid, brown as a colt, kind of sits around a lot with his head down, groovin' to EPMD, making macho street gestures in time to the beat. He's friends with Tressa's brother Joshua. Raul's in some gang; I don't know which; I didn't ask and I won't. Agatha is afraid Joshua might be in a gang too. Joshua got busted for graffiti twice. He's twelve years old and on parole. I'm sure he's just fuckin' around with his friends. I don't think he's in any real kind of gang. He's too sweet a kid to ever hurt anybody. He always gives me a hug good-bye whenever I leave their house. He gets lots of As in an IB program like Tressa and he's learning Russian so he can talk to Babsha better now that she's slipping and thinks she's still back in Stalingrad. Joshua's not Raul, he just dresses like him—a gangsta wearing jeans that are, like, twelve sizes too big for his scrawny ass, and, when Agatha's not looking, Joshua puts a blue bandana on his head. But he's no more in the Folks or People than the fuckin' metalheads in Jarvis

Park are Satanists or Gaylords. But even sweet kids get killed out here, especially if the wrong assholes see that sweetie pie tagging the wrong name on a wall.

I worry right along with Agatha and Aubrey about Joshua being on the streets. He's the little brother I never had. And there are all sorts of stories out there about how gang leaders threaten to kill kids who won't join up and do drug runs for them. But, then again, I don't think Mexican gangs in Logan Square and West Town are gonna go out of their way to recruit a black kid. That shit just doesn't happen.

The L's already out of Logan Square station and the West Town tunnel. Tressa didn't get on this morning. Not surprising, we're almost never on at the same time. She doesn't have class first period at Lincoln Park, so she usually doesn't leave this early. When she does step on the L, though, her patchouli precedes her.

For the longest time, all I knew about West Town was what I saw out the L window. Riding above the neighborhood, you look out and see blocks and blocks of tenements. Most of it's not public housing, though. The buildings look a lot better than they do in Cabrini Green or the Abla Homes near St. Xavier. They're not caged in at the backstairs and there are almost as many gorgeous buildings mixed in with the uglies. Got lots of turn-of-the-century graystones and whitestones too, like Tressa's house, where gargoyles still perch on ledges and people still grow bountiful gardens behind filigree gates.

But when you look at the alleys and rooftops: fuckin' graffiti everywhere. And not every graffiti artist out here is a gifted artist like Raul. Some of this shit goes way back to the disco days—balloon letters in hot pink, blueberry Bubbalicious blue, and Squirt yellow—shit straight out of *The Warriors*, shit they just left up there, never took down with turpentine. I mean, shit, if you're gonna keep graffiti up, at least keep it in the same decade as now.

Lots of the other scrawl on those brick walls will spook

your shit if you stare at it too long. See the lynched skeletons and rolling skulls painted on the buildings? See the names tagged next to them? Joshua tells me they're all on the Folk Nation's hit list and that, when you see a line sprayed through a name, it means the Folks made another hit and are making their way down to the next name, the next hit. Look at all those fuckin' crossed-out names! Not an inch left on the walls. And I hear some of the names belong to El Rukns, Chicago's biggest street gang, the one on trial now for accepting money from Muammar al-Gaddafi to blow up the country. Man, I'd rather have fuckin' George Herbert Walker Bush running the country than the El Rukns—and, coming from me, that's saying some shit.

Other hit-list names belong to that white supremacist gang, the Gaylords. The metalheads in Jarvis Park keep tagging the Gaylords' name in the underpass, even though none of those pussies ever met a real live Gaylord. But, if they're gonna scam a name, it figures they'd pick the KKK gang. Wonder if those racist fucks ever noticed there's a "gay" in "Gaylords." Bet they wouldn't be so quick to say, "I'm a *Gay*lord" then. Gaylord wannabes in my neighborhood think watching *Faces of Death* and *Headbanger's Ball* makes them badass, but they ain't never been within ten miles of a drive-by.

Gangs in Logan Square and West Town don't play. They're not Satanists like the metalheads near me try to be, but the pitchforks they spray in the alleys are satanic in their own way—their own motherfuckin' psycho way. Gangbangers here think nothing of massacring whole warehouses full of rival gangs. If the metalheads in my neighborhood only knew the shit that goes down on this side of town, they'd piss their Metallica-Megadeth pants sopping wet and plant their asses on the 85A back home, pronto. There's a whole lot of killin' going on in these parts. You can see Agatha's got cause for concern. I mean, that non-permit, finger-fuck mural that Raul put on that pitbulls-beer-cans-and-

Harley roof is tame compared to the pitchforks, skeletons, severed heads, and crossed-out names on the backs of the buildings right down the alley.

But last year, I noticed something else happening at the West Town stops: whites getting on. That's right, whites. Hot ones too. The guys, man, lots of them had this shoulder-length hair, but not at all like the dumb-fuck metalheads. No, this was classical-looking long hair—refined; in Mozart's time, people got wigs custom made to look like them. Except these guys were also wearing the kinds of moth-eaten coats and clothes that people clean out of their attics and give to the poor.

Some white guys wore their hair short, though. They kind of looked like Nelson Algren, the guy who wrote *The Man with the Golden Arm*. Tressa made me read it and quizzed me and I got an A! It's about a smack junkie. Algren used to live around here. Anyway, yeah, some of the white guys looked like Algren— rough, hardscrabble, kind of like Bogie in Sam Spade movies. Some wore glasses too—like they strained their eyes reading small-print philosophy, like reading philosophy's all they ever fuckin' did when they weren't sitting around with their friends filling up ashtrays, coughing up their lungs, and discussing the ills of society and the fuckin' fate of humanity.

The white chicks had the same vibe going and wore the same sort of rags as the Algren guys, except, like, in spring and summer, when they didn't have to wear sleeves. That's when the chick vibe got a little different from the guy vibe. A lot of the chicks were swashed in tattoos from their wrists to their shoulders, some of them wouldn't shave their pits either. But, I dunno, these weren't punk chicks, exactly. It was something deeper. Something more…thought-out. They were all fuckin'…sexy fringe-society. Fringe-society rebel chicks. Rebel-bohemian chicks, yeah, that's what they were, rebel-bohemian chicks. Not punk exactly. They were doing something smarter than straight-up punk, something more along the lines of what Rotten's doing with Public Image Ltd. Something more varied and artsy than purist punk.

But the rebel-bohemian chicks were adults. I wondered how they managed to keep this look going past high school or college. Was that all part of the plan? Did they dress this way so they could flunk job interviews, drop out of society, and live off the dole like London punks? But, no, these chicks had to have jobs. They weren't sleeping in. They got on the L early enough for me to think they must be on their way to work and they weren't dressed down enough to panhandle. But who'd hire them looking like that?

Watching them, a big-ass monologue used to race through my head:

Do these chicks change in public washrooms before they go to work? Do they have real straight, nine-to-five jobs like everybody else? Are they secretaries? Do they look like secretaries once they come out of public washrooms? Do they cover their tattoos in chintz blouses? Do they put on puffy wigs, horn-rim glasses, and Easy Spirit pumps? Do they tell their bosses, "Right away, sir," and rush off to brew another pot of coffee in the office kitchen where they stand around thinking up the plot to a dirty novel they might write or the score to some future mosh-pit favorite? Do they each go out to lunch with the other secretaries and act like one of the girls? At lunch, do they keep their shirt cuffs high on their wrists so they don't slip down, exposing their tattoos, their double lives, as they raise their salad forks to their mouths? At 5:01 p.m., do they sneak back into public washrooms and rip those secretary costumes right off their rebel bodies? Do they strut out of public washrooms at night, wearing swashbuckler tattoos and Road Warrior *rags?*

Or maybe they got cool, chill bosses who let them wear whatever the fuck they want. But are there cool bosses like that around? I mean, besides the guys who own Wax Trax *and* The Alley *and places like that?*

But these chicks gotta have jobs. They got rent to pay, I'm sure.

But they look like they're doing something else with their look, making some other kind of statement. Making art, maybe? Maybe that's what they go home and do at night? Sculpture, painting, film, maybe writing? Maybe they would've all hung out with Andy Warhol back in the sixties? Maybe they're reviving Warhol? Maybe they're even on Mount Olympus. Maybe they know Colby. Do they have all that going on under their puffy wigs and horn-rims at work?

Sometimes these guys and dolls come on with canvass or leather cases, spattered with paint and stocked with paintings. A lot of the Belmont/Wax Trax look boards too: fucked-up hair, hardcore band names and other kinds of rebel slogans and insignia painted on leather jackets. But the leather paint jobs are fuckin' top-notch this side of town, like they spend fuckin' hours and days doing nothing but painting their jackets, like they plan on hanging them in museums once they get sick of wearing them.

I don't have to travel all the way east toward the lake to see this shit on Belmont anymore! This shit's happening right here in Logan Square and West Town. Right off the L the 85A takes me to! Who fuckin' knew? This blew my fuckin' mind when I first saw it. Who were these white people and what the fuck were they doing here? In these Hispanic neighborhoods? Were they *living* here? Could that possibly be? They're white.

Early freshman year, on the L home from school, I saw this white anorexic artist chick. She had a green-dragon tattoo on her left forearm, a scaly turquoise rattlesnake on her right arm, and these bold fuckin' blond-green dreadlocks. She was talking to a white anorexic guy—one of those shorthaired philosopher dudes who smokes too much. He said to her, "It's been a long time. Where are you living now?"

She said, "Damen and North."

"Ah!" he exclaimed, "do you like it?"

"It's cool. Cheap. I mean, not a lot of heat. Winters suck. But can't complain about the kind of space we're getting for the rent." My ears were pricked up like a hard-on as this anti-Xavier chick went on, "We made a little studio on the back porch. We're all getting *tons* of use out of it. I just finished a new series."

"Ah-so?" he bowed his head forward a little. "What's your subject?"

She answered, "The series is called: 'Unshackled: the Line between Art and Porn.'"

"Hmmm...last I checked, you didn't believe in that line."

She raised her shoulders, "Still don't. That's my point. I'm putting up a whole wall of new work—collages, photos, a couple paintings—just to contradict what I think is a *false* and puritanical dichotomy. A couple pieces are close-ups of Yours Truly's cooch."

"You don't say," the philosophy reader said, almost slobbering over his shirt, "Who snapped those shots?"

"I just laid down and slid a camera up there. It's all part of my quest to piss off prudes and femi-nazis alike." An eavesdropping old granny shuddered. The anorexic artist chick went on, "Oh! Cindy'll be doing some performance art. She's got this one act, 'The Sword-Swallower and the Shimmy.'"

"Where can I see this?" the guy asked, panting.

"It'll be on at Stone Park for two weeks next month. Cindy'll be doing her show from Thursday to Saturday, both weeks. You know Stone Park? The gallery that just opened on Evergreen, right across from Wicker Park." He nodded. The L pulled up to Damen. "Whoa!" she said, "this is my stop. Listen, are you still at the same number?" He nodded. She gave him a quick hug, kissed him on the lips, and said, "I'll call and give you our new address. You can come by."

"Yes, I'd be delighted," he answered. "Perhaps I could watch Cindy rehearse for the Sword-Swallower number. Sounds most...insalubrious."

"Yeah, you can ask her," she said, standing between

the open doors. "It's a demanding piece, though. I don't know if they're letting anyone watch rehearsals." He sighed. She got off and waved one last good-bye on her way from the Damen platform to the stairs.

The philosophy reader got off at the next stop, Western and Armitage. I saw him take a keychain out of his pocket and pick out a key as he reached the station stairs. Something inside me yelped, "That's the key to his apartment! He's fucking living here! Just like that fuckin' dreadlock chick! I mean, she even said it. She's living at Damen and North, she said it! They're fucking *living* here!"

I looked over at the empty seat across the aisle. Someone'd folded up the arts section of the *Trib* and left it there. I fixed on the headline: "Move Over Greenwich Village: West Town's Got You *Beat*." A blurb in the center of the article read:

> The cheap rents, raw talent, and density of cafes and galleries in this primarily lower-income, Hispanic community distinguish West Town as one of the world's foremost multiracial artist enclaves.

The gods must've been smiling on my ass. I felt like the guy who sailed in right *after* Columbus docked on the New World, whoever that chump was. I made a grab at the article, but before I could get my hands on it, some asshole came along, claimed the seat and stuck the whole arts section in the crook of his arm. Bastard probably just went home and threw it in the trash. But at least I found out it was true: this was an "artist enclave"; the white guy who wanted to jack off next to the Sword Swallower was living in West Town! Actually fucking living here like so many other artists in "one of the world's foremost artist enclaves."

To make confirmation in eighth grade—Mom and Dad

made me fuckin' make it—we had to do two nights at Our Mother of Guadalupe's soup kitchen, which is, I dunno, somewhere around here. The soup kitchen's cafeteria was standing room only. To seat everybody, we had to haul extra folding chairs and card tables into the sooty hallway. Swollen bellies as far as the eye could see, all rumbling over the sound of tomato soup falling into bowls. There were hardly any whites, except a scattering of poor white trash who'd never drunk anything finer than powdered milk or ripple wine their whole lives. Everyone else was looking glum or cackling in Spanish.

On the streets were lots of souped-up, rust-bucket cars blaring mariachi and salsa music. Saw squads of kids dirt-biking on broken-up sidewalks, popping these huge, fuckin' sky-high wheelies that'd make my neighborhood's moms fuckin' faint. I remember this big fat sweaty hombre in a wifebeater undershirt leaning out a third-floor window, playing Too Short and looking out over Sacramento Avenue; one floor below, two large Latinas shrieked and ear-pierce-belly-laughed over Schlitz cans as they sat on stools, talking Spanglish on the front fire escape. Sombreros hung out front of some restaurants. Push-cart vendors in cowboy hats rang little tricycle bells and pushed corn-on-the-cob, popsicles, ice-cream sandwiches, pretzels, and powdered twister bread on all the many loiterers.

All us little gringo boys and girls—just out of doing our good (and mandatory) deed in the soup kitchen before becoming confirmed little Catholic dorks—bunched up in a tight circle around Richie Matanko's Dad and Father Schultz as they escorted us to their cars. Richie Vrba, this loudmouth from the year before ours, spread some shit about how gangs around here come out of the woodwork, stick you up with switchblades, and slice your pockets open to steal whatever dimes and quarters drop out so they can go buy cerveza fría and marijuana. Worst shit that happened, though, was some Mexican guy, hanging out on his building's front stoop and smoking a Lucky, looked at Tom Jacobs and said, "What up, homes?" That was enough to send most of my eighth-grade class running for fucking cover to Mr. Matanko and Father Schultz's cars.

A year later, I started going to Xavier and had to take the L through West Town every day and see all the gang graffiti on the alley walls and roofs. Now the paper's tellin' me this is a fuckin' "artist enclave"—with *white* artists! Some are fuckin' punks too! I never heard of shit like this before. I was...*thrilled!*

CHAPTER XI
Cassandra and Orestes Wash Away Pigeon Shit

They walked down the boulevards in smocks and berets, cradling paint palettes—those starving *artistes* in Paris long ago. You hear legends about crotchety landlords and mustachio chefs chasing deadbeat poets and painters with butcher knives. You see old movies and musicals about big-name suicide artists beating checks at cafés. The whole time they're laughing up their smocks—laughing even while running from butcher knives, laughing long before they get big and famous, long before their art starts selling, long before they look back and smile on how cold the little attic they lived in was, how little food they had and how the wine, whores, and absinthe flowed even when the cash didn't.

But that was Paris and that was a fuckin' long time ago. First time I saw all this shit going down in West Town, it was Chicago, 1987, and these *artistes* were in salsa gangland. This is the only upside I can see to going to Xavier. I get to see this shit every day! All this shit going down right on my way to school!

Kept asking myself how this new breed lives. Well, on the cheap, obviously. I kept imagining buildings full of white artists and Mexican families, living in apartments right next door to each other. Ay-yay-yay! What's it like living in a cheap-rent building full of artists and Mexicans? Sounded one hundred fucking percent better than living in a doorman building on Michigan Avenue or Lakeshore Drive. That's where Brody burns up all his loot. I kept trying to imagine what West Town apartments look like inside. In my mind's eye, I saw the ceilings caving in, dripping like Chinese water torture. Fuck, what I wouldn't fuckin' give to move out and get tortured by some of that Chinese ceiling water!

Long after Grampa Liam died, Grandma Margaret kept living in the West Side tenement Dad grew up in. The building looked a lot like the tenements in Logan Square and West Town. Mom and Dad kept riding Grandma's ass to move out, but Grandma Margaret flat-out fuckin' refused to leave the West Side when the neighborhood was what Mom and Dad call "changing." Grandma came down with Alzheimer's after a while, though, and Mom and Dad had her legally committed to Saint Martha's Rest Home in Inverness. I guess it's for the best, though. It was right around the time Grandma Margaret started pissing in her refrigerator's vegetable drawers. She could've electrocuted herself. The staff won't let her do that at Saint Martha's, but it doesn't stop her from trying.

From the L, I picked out one apartment in particular on the third floor of a building I pass every day at the corner of Milwaukee and Cortland, a few blocks north of North Avenue. I was reading *Agamemnon* at the time, so I spun a daydream about a guy named Orestes living in sin there with his girlfriend Cassandra. The whole scene reeled in my head like an old black-and-white movie. Up until about six months ago, I was playing out the scene for Dr. S every time I went to his office. "Your ever fertile imagination, Seamus!" he'd say.

The whole scenario went down in black and white. Just like George and Mary Bailey, squatting the house on Sycamore Street in *It's a Wonderful Life*, Cassandra and Orestes have to keep slapping newspaper pages and ad posters all over wall cracks to keep the rain from pouring in. It's hot and muggy, inside and outside the apartment. Cassandra's smoking a black Sobranie cigarette, the kind Tressa buys with French novels at Europa Books on Clark. Cassandra's sitting on a window seat, watching silent rain. She's reading a used book, a collection of Greek tragedies. She's wearing a form-fitting black dress and a garter belt, but she's thrown her stockings on a Murphy bed, just like the one Grandma Margaret and Grampa Liam used to pull out of their tenement apartment wall. Cassandra: she looks like pictures of Henry Miller's ex-wife—tall, blonde hair crinkled into a bobby-pinned bob—I somehow knew the look before Tressa even gave me *Tropic of Cancer*. And just like Henry Miller's wife, Cassandra invites women over and slow-dances with them to scratchy Billie Holiday albums when Orestes isn't home. After a while, they tumble into bed for lesbian sex fests. There's a tarp over her painting, which sits on an easel at the east wall. She's taking a break from her new painting. She's worried about Orestes, her writer boyfriend.

Orestes looks like the anorexic philosophy dude who talked to the dreadlocked anorexic chick on the L, except with a much more forties Nelson Algren look. Instead of wearing tight Am Vets sweaters, he's got on brown tweed pants and white-collared shirt with sleeves rolled up and a white wifebeater tank top peeking out of it. He's trying to crank out a novel on a manual typewriter, but he keeps going fuckin' ape-shit on it like Jack Nicholson in *The Shining*. "It's not coming together!" he's always fuckin' screaming. "It's not fucking coming together!" He screams that shit all the time. He's even slammed the manual typewriter on the floor a few times and threw the last one through the window. And he had to save up months for this new one, which he still throws on the floor; Cassandra had to board up the window pane with cardboard just like I did with my bedroom window on Jack Daniel's Vandalism Day, last Thursday.

Cassandra fears for Orestes as she sits in the window seat, smoking a Sobranie, watching Orestes pound his typewriter and slug back cold black coffee. He cashes out another smoke and pitches more typing paper he can barely afford into the trash. He's past thirty and hasn't pumped out a book yet (just like Henry

CASSANDRA AND ORESTES WASH AWAY PIGEON SHIT

Miller; I fuckin' love Miller, that crazy cock). At this rate, it doesn't look like he ever fuckin' will either. They're listening to Dixieland over the old-style, World War II radio. When Cassandra looks out their front-room windows, she sees rain and the Coyote Building and, past that, the whole downtown skyline, all in grainy black and white. She doesn't know how long she can take this shit. She had to have some idea what she was getting her ass into, though, when she shacked up with a writer. They're known for their fuckin' moods. They can't *not* have them if they're gonna write any shit that's worth a goddamn. She's flush with fuckin' moods herself. See the tranquilizers in her falling-apart purse? See the hypodermic needle and tourniquet in the dark drawer?

Man, all last year, I lived on fantasies about Orestes and Cassandra—turned them over all day, every day once I found out West Town was a fuckin' artist enclave. Dr. S fuckin' loved it when I'd have him lay back on the couch and hear all my new Cassandra and Orestes tales. I made all those stories up in algebra class every day at fifth period.

Mrs. Pischke would be up there chalking up numbers and symbols that never made any fuckin' sense to me and I'd avert my eyes and mind just like I do whenever I see pigeons shitting all over statues. All her algebra equations looked just like pigeon shit to me—white, putrid, chalky clumps dripping down Mrs. Pischke's blackboard. What fuckin' killed me was that all the other kids were right on top of that pigeon shit! Right fuckin' on top of it! Like the pigeon shit was some sort of sphinx that'd give them the world if they could just solve its riddles. If they didn't solve the riddles quick, though, the pigeon shit would annihilate their every shot at a future. But all the kids in class looked like they could hold their own with the pigeon shit—all except dummy me, who flunked the entrance exam and is just about to flunk out of Xavier now. After answering the riddles the pigeon-shit sphinx posed in class, all the other kids would go home, raring to do homework and solve more pigeon shit.

Even when I'd feel fuckin' motivated to solve some pigeon shit myself, though, Cassandra and Orestes would pop right back into mind. I'd be in my bedroom with the *Fundamentals of Algebra* book open on my desk and I'd start sketching out numbers and symbols with no clue about what knots to twist them into next. I'd try bullshitting out some algebraic-looking answer, but my equations made no more sense to Mrs. Pischke than pig Latin does to a pig. After twisting up algebra symbols and numbers for as long as I could stand, I'd end up ripping into my textbook pages with the tip of my pen and shoving that shit off my desk.

In no time, Cassandra and Orestes would hijack my brain and I'd kill the lights, crank up something like Bauhaus' *The Sky's Gone Out,* and fall fast asleep on my bed, dreaming about their life together in the apartment on Milwaukee Avenue and Cortland Street—the Sobranie cigarette, the World War II radio, the Coyote Building, the garter belt, Henry Miller's wife, the Murphy bed. My mind would drift into its own fuckin' element and I'd say, fuck school! Why should I let school limit my fuckin' education? The West Town crowd knows its shit so much fuckin' better than Mrs. Pischke—and I'm not talkin' no fuckin' pigeon shit. I'm talking shit that matters.

Nobody at St. Xavier or in Jarvis Park would ever understand why I'd savor an image like Cassandra and Orestes' apartment, why I'd ever want to befriend freaks, heroin addicts, abject writers. Well, shit, at least fuckin' freaks have fuckin' lives to write about…or sing about or draw or paint about. At least they got stories to tell. What stories will the Plain Janes around me tell about their lives? "I did what everybody else did. The End."?

Between Cassandra, Orestes, and Colby, I had all the imaginary friends I'd ever fuckin' need. Still, I fantasized about making more—real ones, I mean. I'd sit on the L imagining all the partying that West Town freaks must do. What would one of Cassandra and Orestes' parties look like? Would their deep artist and punk friends stop by with weed and wine? Would the Mexican families come upstairs with enchiladas? Would it turn into a lavish fuckin' fiesta with salsa, Dixieland, and hardcore bands playing all at once? That's what it looked like in my head, and I'd be right there with them: me, Tressa, Colby, and everybody else—on the night before me and Colby'd take off for London. Little by little last year, all my dreams of London started fusing with my dreams of West Town. I started thinking that hanging out in West Town till I could move overseas might not be the worst thing in the world. I mean, shit, there was life in West Town. Maybe not as much as London. But it was a great fuckin' start.

But I wondered, these visions of West Town: Was there anything real about them? Or was I just imagining shit? Did these visions only make sense in this sick head of mine? Was this still the same West Town that Nelson Algren lived in right after the war? The more I rode the L, the more I saw my ideas were... black-and-white movies. I mean, c'mon, manual typewriters? Orestes and Cassandra living like George and Mary Bailey? What the fuck! Couldn't there be a more modern spin on this ball?

One morning, while I was riding the L past Damen and North, watching the Mexican mammas below wrangling their niños on the way back from the supermercados and *panaderías* on Milwaukee Avenue, I spotted this one white guy sunning himself on a hot tar roof. I saw him only a split second, but that one quick flash will stay with me my whole life long. The guy was blond. He looked dark and German like Dr. S, and, like Dr. S, he had a washboard belly. But his body was better than Dr. Strykeroth's— younger, firmer, all-out finer—a fuckin' golden Apollo, someone who'd probably be the rage in California. He didn't look anything like an Algren-type artist. Folks graffiti and non-permit mini-murals surrounded him, but clearly, with a white surfer god like him laying out on a tar roof, West Town was getting real fuckin' sexy, real fuckin' fast. Later, I heard Al Jourgenson lives one block south of the Damen stop and Ministry records in a studio about a block away from his apartment.

So, yeah, maybe my silver-screen take on this place was what Tressa says my take on a lot of shit is: "passé." Tressa fuckin' loves summing me up with that one little French putdown, so I went to the fourth floor library at Xavier and looked *passé* up in a French-English dictionary to see what the fuck she was talking about. I hate like hell that she's right. All this cutting-edge shit going down and my passé ass is thinking George and Mary Bailey.

So, I decided to do some detective work, sleuth this whole fuckin' scene out, and see whether West Town leaves Belmont rolling around in its own passé slop. I figured I took enough Spanish since fifth grade to get by with whatever store signs and street signs weren't in English. I knew I'd better act fast, though. Now that the *Trib* article leaked out, the yuppies would be right on the gringo artists' heels, buying up and knocking down all the Mexican families' homes.

One day after school, I got off the L at Damen. I gotta admit, I hoped the other passengers would admire me. I hoped they would wonder the same shit about me that I wondered about the tattooed Cassandras and chain-smoking Oresteses. I hoped they'd be sitting there thinking, "What's he doing getting off here? Is he fucking deranged?" I stepped onto the platform, squared my shoulders, plumed my tail, and strutted in front of the packed train like I was headed to my own personal drug den. I trotted through the turnstiles and crossed over to Milwaukee Avenue with the sole goal of walking, exploring, doing some Louis and Clark or Kojak shit.

My eyes were big as every street I walked down, but I still couldn't see signs of gringo artist life. All I saw were tire shops, a Salvation Army thrift shop, a McDonald's, a Walgreen's, a Cut-Rate Appliance store, and a couple Dollar Stores whose front windows were crammed with a hodgepodge of everything from imitation Nerf balls, hula hoops, and wiffle bats to Day-Glo paintings of Santa Maria and red candles in glass bottles decked with stickers of Saint Jude and Saint Joseph. There were also *panaderías* filled with powdered breads and jelly sticks. I counted at least six bums too, a few of them passed out over paper bags stuffed with forty-ouncers. The mud lots under the L tracks looked like fuckin' landfills, piled high with every imaginable piece of rancid trash. The sidewalks were jagged and littered with shit like Quarter Pounder wrappers, greasy french fry holders, last week's stomped-on newspaper pages, rusty bicycle chains, a Speed Racer action figure that some kid must've dropped from his stroller, shit and piss from stray dogs, and a mud-caked little pink teddy bear on the curb, wearing a little white T-shirt with a Valentine heart on it. Peering into the Lavenderia windows, I still didn't see artists doing laundry. I just saw large, dark mujeres schlepping armfuls of wet clothes from washer to dryer while packs of kids hung from their necks and skirt hems. On Le Moyne Street, there was a line of beggars waiting for the food pantry to open at the redbrick St. Stanislaus Catholic Church.

I walked the side streets. A lot of the houses had iron bars on the windows. Mucachos sat on car hoods, drinking cerveza and blasting rap. The multi-family buildings looked sturdy but dirty. The lawns were unkempt and clogged with everything from dirty diapers to beer cans to tiny cellophane packets. Lots of families had saints' pictures in their windows that look just like the ones on display in the Dollar Store windows. The alleys were covered in graffiti. Jehovah's Witnesses huddled together in their Sunday best on a Thursday afternoon, ringing apartment buzzers and doorbells, trying to push *The Watchtower* on anybody who wouldn't slam doors in their faces. I saw them skitter away from a few houses that had signs saying, "Nosotros somos Catolicos." Saw lots of kids hanging in the street, throwing footballs, showing off their back-flips off chain-link fences. Others were just clowning or shooting the shit with their homeys.

No one messed with me, except two white guys, wearing Church of Jesus Christ of Latter Day Saints badges. They fuckin' circled me, said, "Excuse me. Would you like to come to church?" I tried walking away but they circled me, fuckin' hot-boxed me. "Come on," one of them said, "come with us. It'll do your soul good." I said, "Fuck no!" and shrugged past their freaked-out faces. By the time I made it to the corner, I sensed they were still standing right where I pushed them off me. One shouted, "Don't let the devil eat you alive, kid. Turn back before it's too late!" I kept my back to them and stuck my middle finger up until I turned the corner at North Avenue.

By now, I'd walked about a mile and a half around West Town and was about to give up my search for Cassandra and Orestes and head back to the Damen L. But about twenty yards away, I saw a white woman with fire-engine red hair and a black vinyl coat walking out of a building at North and Hermitage. I saw a guy in his twenties or thirties brush past her, heading the opposite way. He had wavy Christ hair and was wearing green wool cargo pants, black 8-hole Docs, and the kind of black-and-green checkered overcoat that old men in fedoras wear. He walked into the building the lady in vinyl just came out of.

I sped up to see what was going on in there. I passed a black woman standing under a streetlight in an aqua Saran Wrap miniskirt, black pantyhose, white pumps, and the furriest fuckin' rabbit coat you ever did see. She took the cigarette out of her mouth, gave me a wave with her pinky and third finger and said, "Hey, little lamb. Lost your flock n' lookin' for trouble?" I picked up my pace and turned my head away. She howl-laughed, "C'mon, baby doll. It'll be the best milk money y'ever spent."

When I reached the building at Hermitage Street, I spied

a wooden sign creaking off a cast-iron pole. Painted in blood-red on a tar-black board were the words "Café de Sade" and beneath them, the words, "Coffee, Tea, Iniquity." My heart quivered. So did my legs and stomach. I could just imagine Mom's reaction to me being right under that sign. An image of the cross above St. Aloysius' altar even flashed across my mind. I couldn't let that shit stop me, though. I cut the ole apron strings and soldiered through the glass door.

CHAPTER XII
Café de Sade

Once inside the building, I had to go up a short flight of stairs. My pounding heart bruised my ribcage. I expected some psycho-deviate in a leather mask to greet me. Kept thinking I'd see a seething dungeon behind him; flaming torches; *Hustler* bitches chained to stone walls; topless waiters in dog collars, crawling with tea sets tied to their backs, a French maid flogging their fannies. But when I opened the door to Café de Sade (Coffee, Tea, Iniquity), all I saw was sunlight.

Whatever sun there was on that gray afternoon poured into all the café windows—six jumbo ones in all, half as high as the walls. I took several steps in and spied a huge loft space with brown hardwood floors running all the way up to a white-tiled washroom and a gray concrete storage room with stacks of empty red plastic milk crates on the floor. The walls were no-frills, stark white actually, except for some pretty fuckin' distorted, surreal nude paintings that were hanging up for sale. I wanted to sneak a closer peek, but my eyes got hooked on the books and fliers on the south wall.

The bulletin board had one flier lobbed on to another, mostly ads scrawled in black marker for roommates and apartments for rent. It's a wonder each thumbtack could stand the weight of all that paper. I didn't know all the street names yet, but the addresses on the fliers looked to be about as far north or west as Café de Sade, so I figured they were advertising in the neighborhood. Other fliers were up for bands I didn't know, playing at bars with addresses that also looked to be somewhere in West Town. Ads for plays were up too. There was even one for, *Medea* on Milwaukee Avenue! I took down the number so I could call the theater manager and beg him to let me in free.

Right under all the notices were a couple magazine stands, a couple feet apart. Just like at Wax Trax, Xeroxed rags were scattered on the bottom shelf, but instead of being filled with hardcore cartoons and execution scenes, the pages had city-life photos and sketches—skyscrapers, parks with oak trees, faces of all colors, pictures of abandoned buildings with busted and boarded-up windows—with poems twisting around the objects.

They had fresh stacks of *New City*, *The Chicago Reader*, something for queers called *Windy City Times*, and something for actors called *Perform Ink* that had a blurb, "Chock-Full of New Auditions, Look Inside!" I wondered if there's a little rag like that in London. Could really fuckin' use it if there is. They had a rack of glossy mags for the fine arts crowds too, but none of that tony shit looked like it was selling.

There were bookstalls too—one for fiction, one for non, another for poetry, another for drama. The book spines were new and shiny with lots of Euro-trash names. I walked over to the drama section and recognized some of the writers from English class—Shakespeare, Euripides, Oscar Wilde, Thorton Wilder—but I didn't know any of the others. This is where I found Brecht for the first time. He was the *spitting* image of my West Town Orestes! Same smoker's face, same scabby Algren edge—it's like I was daydreaming about Brecht all along and didn't fuckin' know it!

I flipped the book open to the middle. I didn't get to read a lot of it just standing there, but I liked what I read so far and, if I'd had the money, I would've bought the book on the spot, but all I could afford to do besides shoplift was vow to go find it at the library the next day. Shoplifting from a glorified soup kitchen like Café de Sade seemed about as low as knocking over an old lady for butterscotch, so the Chicago Public Library it'd have to be. I kept reading this Brecht guy's words. They were so full of poetry. I felt I was studying lines for some show I'll be in some day on London's West End—not too fuckin' far-off into the future if I have any shit to say about it.

Even more than the writing, though, I liked *Three Penny Opera*'s layout. It wasn't much different from any other play I ever picked up before—acts, scenes, lines, stage directions—but I took to it more than anything I'd picked up before and I still can't say why. I thought I might even write something like *Three Penny Opera* myself someday. I swore right then and there that I'd read the whole thing as soon as I could.

After getting drunk on Brecht for a while, I looked up and took in the breeze of coffee and cigarettes wafting through this de Sade place. I'd always liked cigarettes but not coffee. I never even liked the smell. Suddenly it was sweeter than fuckin' roses. Was this the gods' way of telling me to wake up? "Wake the fuck up, Seamus! Smell the fucking java! This is your promised land!" I straightened my spine and took the gods' call. After I put Brecht back on the shelf, I made a little bow to him like I do to my Johnny Rotten poster and I turned to face the smoke-filled dull roar of dishes clanking and people philosophizing in Café de Sade's table area.

All but one or two tables were full. And Jesus fuckin' jackpot! A lot of the same portfolio-bearing freaks I used to moon over on the L were in here too! Including some of bohemian-rebel chicks, who, I guessed, had probably changed out of their office wigs and clothes in some public washroom before coming. Then I saw it wasn't five o'clock yet, so I figured maybe they played hooky from work that day. The guys at the tables were kind of a hybrid of my new friend Brecht and Belmont gutter punks. Rough, unwashed, but civil enough not to vandalize the place. Blacks and whites were hanging at the same tables, dreadlocks on both. I don't see much of that every day. At Xavier, most of the black kids go sit on one side of the cafeteria, freezing out any white kid who tries sitting with them. Not at Café de Sade. And besides me, there wasn't an un-tatooed body in the house.

The waitstaff looked as badass as the badasses they were waiting on. They were even playing fuckin' Joy Division behind the bar. Fuckin' Joy Division! Fuckin' perfect taste, man. But the waiters and waitresses didn't seem like London dole queue punks. They were working their asses off, slinging coffee and taking down orders and bussing tables and shit. And the people at the tables—lots of them had used-looking Euro-trash books laying out in front of them as they smoked, talked and drank coffee and espresso drinks with their friends, who all had intellectual looks on their faces and seemed like they were talking about…I dunno…whatever shit intellectuals talk about.

Facing the café on a barstool by a window ledge was a Large Marge with short spiky orange hair. She was dressed all second or third-hand in a beige man's suit, brown men's wingtips and a red polka-dot clown tie. She was buried in a book by Marquis de Sade that was longer than the fuckin' Chicago Yellow Pages. I guessed Marquis de Sade was the guy they named the café after. Later, Tressa read me some shit from his book *Juliette*, which Aubrey has in his library. It's from the eighteenth century and fuckin' filthier than any shit that's *ever* come out of Johnny Rotten's mouth and anything GG Allin's ever done on stage. Two hundred years before punk, just like Mozart!

Café de Sade was living proof you didn't have to be some dumb-ass Belmont punk or skin to make a statement. There are more intelligent ways to nonconform. Fuck, I wanted in on this shit.

I went and sat on a stool at the counter and ordered a cup of Earl Grey from the muscle-head Italian guy in the sleeveless dungarees. We got a whole cabinet of Earl Grey at home for some reason, and I drink about two pots a day out of Haverford tea cups as practice for England. The Italian dude gave me a hard, what-the-fuck-you-doing-here-little-shit look. My whole life I've gotten that look. It doesn't fuckin' work on me anymore. And I didn't even care that, when he finally got around to bringing me my fuckin' Earl Grey and I said thank you, he didn't even fuckin' say you're welcome or anything. He just fuckin' glared at me. But deep inside, I knew then like I know now that the day will come when I'll be old enough for him and everybody else to treat me with respect. And when that day comes, I'll be long gone in London and he'll still be brewing beans back in Chicago. And, besides, I was too busy looking around, smoking Marlboros, and acting natural to brood over him being an asshole.

Looking around Café de Sade, I asked myself the same shit I used to ask myself when I had no one to talk to at the Dunkin' Donuts counter: By the time I'm old enough to be one of them, what will I be? A writer? An actor? A shrink like Dr. Strykeroth? But, at Café de Sade, I had better role models than the scum, thugs, and poseurs who hang on Belmont. A writer, an actor, or a shrink? Maybe all three! Was anybody in de Sade doing all three? Or were they all *just* painters or *just* writers or *just* in bands or *just*…doing whatever the fuck they just do? Well, I told myself I wouldn't limit myself to justs. I've always known that, somewhere in me, I got a lot of talent to be a lot of things, all at once. And somewhere in time, all that talent will come out in a flood that keeps on flooding—and it'll happen in London, where I'm bound to feel a lot fuckin' freer than I do even in West Town.

CHAPTER XIII
Debriefing

I unbuttoned Dr. Strykeroth's oxford shirt cuff. It was the last button I had to undo before we'd move on to the massage portion of our weekly session, the Monday after I first set foot in de Sade. He gave me a wide smile as I went to slip him out of his shirt. "So," he said, "Anything new happen this week?" He leaned forward in his armchair, moving to one side to lift his arm out of one sleeve and tilting to the other side to help me get him out of the other sleeve. I lifted the shirt off his back and draped it over the glass coffee table to his right. He asked me to draw the blinds a little tighter. They looked closed enough to me, but he's always so fuckin' paranoid that someone high up in the Standard Oil Building offices is gonna look down and see what we're up to.

"I've found a whole new scene," I told him as I knelt down next to his feet. "A *whole* new scene."

"For your play?"

"Maybe," I said, "but, I mean, I found a whole new scene to hang out in."

His eyes lit up and his smile broadened, "Oh, yeah?"

I tapped his right leg and he lifted it up a little for me as I placed it on my thigh and unlaced his black wing-tipped shoe, "Ever heard of Café de Sade?"

He nodded, "Oh, sure."

I removed his shoe. He was wearing long, elegant, black dress socks that felt like silk as I ran my fingers over the top and sole of his foot. "So, you've heard of it!" I exulted as I started

135

massaging his foot.

"Well, yeah," he laughed. "You think that place is new?"

"Well," I said, undoing the laces on his other shoe, "I didn't know white people hung out on that side of town. Sure as fuck didn't think there'd be cafes there." I shifted over to his left leg and he put it up on my thigh. I took off his left shoe.

"Well…of course," he told me. "There've always been whites there. White writers especially. Writers have always lived there…ever since *I* was a kid."

"Really?"

"Yes," he nodded. "Lots of painters and sculptors and all that too. They started moving there after the writers."

I started manipulating his toes. "When did that shit start happening?"

"A long time ago," he said. "A *long* time ago."

"So, you ever been inside Café de Sade?" I asked, kneading the muscles of his left leg and moving up to his bare chest.

"Yes," he answered.

"Really?"

"Ye-e-s," he laughed. "I might not be the bon-vivant-raconteur-man-about-town you are, Seamus, but I've gotten around a bit in my day too. And I'll tell you something else. Ready to hear it?"

"Yeah, I'm ready."

His grin grew, "They have orgies at Café de Sade."

"Orgies?" I gasped, getting up to work the muscles on his neck.

"Yep. Every Wednesday at midnight."

"What d'they fuckin' do there?"

He looked like he was about to answer, but said, "You'll have to ask someone else, Seamus."

"Wait," I spun around the chair to face him, "you know somebody who's fuckin' been there? For orgies?"

He nodded, "Let's just say, I've at least heard *tell* of them."

The corners of my mouth damn near reached my smiling eyes, "You been to them, right? You fuckin' been there!"

"I'm not telling you," he said.

"C'mon!"

His smile fell away, "When I say I'm not telling you, Seamus, I mean, I'm not telling you." His smiling eyes scaled down to slits. I looked at him. He fixed me a cold-ass glower. Everything went quiet. He patted my arm. His face went back to normal.

I continued massaging him. "Well...I guess I'll never know what goes down at midnight on...what day? Wednesdays?"

"Well," he replied, "Not till you're eighteen. After that, the party's all yours."

I started undoing his belt. "It'll be too late by then. I'll be in London."

"Well, you should keep going to Café de Sade," Dr. Strykeroth said as he arched up his back to help me remove his belt. "They have poetry readings there, you know. I've been to those—that much I *will* tell you."

"Who reads poetry there?"

"Anybody. They have what they call 'open mics.' They open up the microphone to whoever wants to read anything they've written. You should read at them. Start making your name now. It's never too early and you have so much to give. You've got a lot of gifts, Seamus. A lot of gifts."

And so I started going to the open mics and reading my play in public between improv jazz acts. The weirdo who takes tickets and claims to be psychic said, "I see that your play will be on stage." I asked him when and he looked me up and down and said, "In your early 20s." Early 20s? I can't fuckin' wait *that* long!

PART THREE:

THE REST OF THE RIDE

"There is a time for departure,
even when there is no certain place to go."
Tennesee Williams

CHAPTER XIV
Huck, Jim, and Kirik

Chicago Avenue is such a dank tunnel. The walls are black as pitch, like there should be chimney sweeps hanging off them. It's so *Oliver Twist*. Except here, it's Hispanics, not orphans, getting on in rags. Every now and then, some white artists get on in rags too. Guess the scene's moving south of West Town now.

It's 7:55. Shit! Class starts at 8:05 and we're only at Chicago Avenue. Fuck! That's it, I'm late! I'm late! Fucking 85A made me late *again*!

Three years. Three years and I'll be overseas. But high school might be over way sooner than that, the way my grades are going.

But I did get a B on the *Huckleberry Finn* test in Mr. Banaszak's class last week. I didn't like the book. I mean, I didn't *hate* it. But the dialogue, man: when was the last time a black guy said, "Well *dawg* my cats"? They don't fuckin' talk that way, Twain. And why the fuck did Huck give the judge his gold? Couldn't he spend that shit up the Mississippi? And why the fuck did he give two shits what Miss Watson and Aunt Polly think? He practically shits himself, imagining they'll tell him he's going to hell for conducting a one-man underground railroad...and he *believes* them!

But Huck was a black sheep. I like that. It's the main reason that, back and forth from school on the L, I didn't break out Henry Miller and chuck Twain on the third rail. I like how Jim keeps calling Huck "honey." Makes me wonder what else went

141

down on that raft. Huck staged his own death with boar's blood. That's so *Carrie*, so GG Allin! He aided and abetted a runaway slave. Dig that too. I mean, I'd do it in a heartbeat. In the mid-1800s, this great nation of ours counted a black man as three-fifths human. In my neighborhood today, he's worth even less than that. Even so, Huck was willing to risk body and soul to save a black man on a bride-ship raft. All that in mind, I went ahead and read the book. Me, reading required reading! Twain deserves points just for getting my ass to do that.

I'm surprised Xavier even teaches *Huck Finn*. I mean, they banned *Slaughterhouse Five* and *A Clockwork Orange*. Even liberal schools ban *Huck* for how Huck says "nigger" all the time, but we got a lot of black kids in class who say they're not offended: "You have to look at it in the context of the times"; "Huck admired Jim more than anybody"; "Hey, at least Twain wasn't in the Klan!" Plus, when *Huck* first came out, most states banned it for making Huck and Jim seem like heroes, not criminals—shit, back then, people probably thought Huck didn't say "nigger" enough!

After answering all the multiple-choice questions right on the test, I got to the essay question: "In your own opinion, was Huck a hero? Why or why not?" I wrote four lines:

Absolutely Huck was a hero. Do cowards and conformists learn from outlaws and outcasts? Do they flout conventions? No, but Huck did and that makes him a hero in Twain's book and mine.

Mr. Banaszak wrote in the margin "Inadequately argued! I asked you to write an essay, not an anthem!" I got 100 percent on the multiple choice, but Banaszak only gave me 50 percent on the essay section, which brought me down a whole letter grade. But, shit, I made my point, plain and simple, loud and clear. Why more did he want? Asshole!

I could've brought my grade back up by answering the

extra credit question: "If you planned to run away, how would you do it?" Well, fuck, I can dive right into this answer, I thought. My pen ripped across the worksheet:

I'd pack my bags in the middle of the night, leave through the den door, and hop the fence into the Czernovski's backyard. I'll go downtown and...

My pen came to a screeching halt. Some voice inside me said, "Don't answer. Cross out all the shit you just wrote...*now!*" I scratched everything out and turned in my test. If I went ahead and answered the extra credit question, I would've gotten an A. I needed nothing less than an A to pass English—(and that's if I also get an A on the final exam in two weeks)—but I didn't want to give away anything that could catch up with me.

But, shit, why didn't I just take a page out of Kirik's life? His story kicks Huck's honky ass. It was in a *Time* magazine that Mom threw out with a pile of *McCalls*. The article was called "This Is Our Homeless Youth." I keep it folded up in my rucksack. Kirik, a freak with a freak name. His mom died. His dad drank. He had a Dresden doll, angel face, so the hillbilly kids at his school in Oklahoma kept calling him faggot and beating him with baseball bats. Dad would slug mugs of beer at the bar, black out, and go home and slug Kirik. Said it'd make a man of his sissy son, especially since the school kept calling him at the aluminum factory to say little Kirik was getting teased so bad he stopped showing up to school in the mornings.

Kirik passed a lot of playing-hookie time back at home, listening to the old soul and blues albums his dead uncle left behind. Kirik sang and danced to the albums for months on end and, one winter night, he jumped right out on to Route 66 with no money and hitched all the way north and east to the city all the songs kept singing about— New York City. Now, it's not London, but it's no slouch either, I hear. Kirik got money from God Squadders who kept picking him up, talking Jesus, and leaving him with the addresses to their churches. He even turned the tables on one codger cunt in a trenchcoat who pulled over in a West Virginia forest after picking Kirik up in Pennsylvania and tried diving down his pants. He grabbed the gun the codger cunt stuck to his throat, pistol-whipped him, shot his kneecap out and made off with his wallet too. Kirik got to New York in twelve days.

He was only fourteen, and, sure, he had to sell his ass on the street for a while, but some social workers came along and took him to a halfway house called Oliver's House that sets street kids up with jobs or good schools, whichever they wanted. They got him into a hard-to-get-into *Fame*-type performing arts high school, and now he's a big deal actor on Broadway and he's even playing leads in London.

I wrote Kirik a letter once, addressed "c/o" the *Time* reporter, Ken Bailey. I said, "Dear Kirik, You're my hero." I told him all about Andy Payne and Dad and school and Johnny Rotten and how I want to act and write. I didn't think Ken Bailey would pass my fan letter on, but about six months later, I got a postcard back. It had the Empire State and a bunch of other New York buildings on it. All it said was: "Seamus, Thanks for your letter! It meant the world to me. Let your dreams be your guide. Kirik."

He didn't give a return address, but I don't care. I got his story. If only I'd fuckin' used it for extra credit on the Huck test! Shit!

CHAPTER XV
ST. XAVIER

There it is. The statue. St. Francis Xavier, patron saint of missionaries, standing snug in the billion-dollar niche of a trillion-dollar school. He's wearing black Spaniard robes, a rope belt, a gold cross with rubies, and bird shit on the crown of his bald, monk-cut head. His hands spread out wide above the housing projects and crack pipes on Blue Island Avenue, like he's letting the seeds of hope and miracles fall onto broken concrete where they'll never, ever take root or grow.

They tell us that in the 1500s, Father Francis Xavier went to India and sent some letters to the Vatican saying he'd looked all over the fuckin' place but couldn't find one goddamn Christian. Well, the Pope took care of that right quick: sent in the Inquisition, slaughtered tens of thousands of Hindus, crushed temples until most of the Indians in the area were all too ready to give up their gods and swallow wine and wafers. That's how Father Francis Xavier became *Saint* Francis Xavier and they built colleges and high schools in his name like mine here on the south side of Chicago.

His statue is as safe as my school, which has heat-packing cops working security around it twenty-four hours, seven days a week. There's a forcefield defending St. Xavier from all the local gangs. How does this one school get so much protection? St. Xavier must let protection pennies fall from heaven on the first of every month. Or maybe Father Mahoney's been paying the cops off by dipping into the tuition payments that are putting so many parents in the poorhouse. But, hey, no one's forcing the kids' folks to pay. Other way around might be true: parents might force their kids to go, but the kids sure as hell aren't holding knives to their parents' throats 'til they sign tuition checks.

I see the maroon bricks, the Kremlin-like gold onion turrets, golden awnings, and the frozen marble fountain, encased in a fiberglass dome, just waiting for the janitors to turn on the waterworks in spring. I see where Dad's money and everyone else's is going. I see the sprawling additions the construction workers are putting onto the school. I look to the side. I see the Jes Res, where the Jesuits live in luxury suites with Mercedes and Cadillacs in their garages. They share it all, none of it's private property—a comfy loophole they found in their vow of poverty. I see the plaques on the side of the building, where the names of alumni donors are carved in stone, going all the way back to 1851. At assemblies, Father Mahoney's always bragging about how St. Xavier was one of the few buildings to escape the Chicago Fire in 1870-something-or-other. The Chicago Fire saw Xavier's statue and backed the fuck off, just like the skinheads did when they saw Tressa coming to my rescue on Belmont last year. Only, St. Xavier isn't here to save my ass now like Tressa did that night.

It's 8:33. I'm twenty-eight minutes late. I look up to the second-story windows under the sandstone arches and see the backs of classrooms full of kids. The teachers are teaching. The kids are wearing cheery wool sweaters, some yellow, some orange, some red, which they usually accessorize with penny loafers or docksiders. Before they come inside, they're out there wearing galoshes or snowboots, but by the time they get to their lockers, they're shedding that shit and stepping into their fuckin' *Sweet Valley High* shoes. Everyone's paying attention in the second-story classroom, you can tell. They're chomping straight through the pens and pencils in their mouths, trying to show off how seriously they're taking all this shit. So seriously, in fact, they're risking lead and ink poisoning to suck up as best they can.

Glass is rising in my arm again.

Funny how I don't mind catching my death when I'm just outside school, but I fuckin' loathe it when I'm waiting for the 85A. If I got to school on time, I'd be fast fuckin' asleep in biology by now. Standing in the snow, I feel clear-headed, like I don't have to fill my head with anything but howling wind and hissing tires. I should set up a little table right here on the sidewalk, get a little inkwell, and compose haikus or something.

There's Dean Russell in the commons. Shit, he's waving. But what am I so fucking scared of? It's not like Russell hasn't put my ass in JUG a zillion times now. I'll take it on the chin, head to my locker and walk into biology with a late slip. Dean Russell stands, eyes wide open with mock delight as I walk in. He says his usual, "Glad you could join us today, Mr. O'Grady!" takes out his ledger and checks another mark in the tardy column next to my name. "One more and you're expelled."

I stop, "*One* more?" He smiles and gives a long nod. "Just one?" I ask. "I thought I had two."

He clicks his tongue against the roof of his mouth, "According to my records, you only have one."

I shake my head, "No, no…I've been keeping track."

"Oh, so have I, Mr. O'Grady!" Dean Russell laughs. "So have I."

"There must be some kind—"

He clicks his tongue again, shaking his head slowly, "No, Mr. O'Grady. No mistake. My records are never wrong. I keep them in the *strictest* order. Now, you can contest my claim…but I don't advise it. You're looking at the one judge and jury for your case. Go see Ms. Hayes, get your late slip, and get to class. I'll see you in JUG this afternoon."

I stand in silence. His eyes bear down quizzically, "May I ask why you're not on your way to Ms. Hayes, Mr. O'Grady?"

I shudder, "The 85A was late."

"Ah yes," he says, "the Eighteee-Fiive A. That trusty, rusty bus of yours. The one that's responsible for all your troubles."

"Well, not all, but, yeah, some. I can't help that it's late."

"The 85A can't help you, Mr. O'Grady, and neither can I," he says, clapping his ledger shut. "Nor can you help yourself, apparently. So, with that, I'll see you in JUG."

"Dean Russell, I can't go this afternoon." His eyebrow goes up again and his head goes back as he makes like he's standing a hundred feet higher than me. I say, "I can make it tomorrow, though. Can I go tomorrow instead?"

"Tell me, Seamus," he puts his fingers to his chin, "why can't you go this afternoon? Tell me. I'm all ears."

"I have a doctor's appointment."

He chortles, "Well, it looks like you'll have to cancel, won't you? Make a call from the cafeteria at lunch. Ask your doctor if he—or she—can sneak you in, say, in the first week of February. I assure you, in two weeks, you'll have all the time in the world to keep your appointment."

"Why?"

"You won't have school."

I squint, "You mean, we don't have school in two weeks?"

"No, Mr. O'Grady," Dean Russell shakes his head again, "*You* don't have school. Next week is final exams. I've spoken with your teachers. By the end of this week or early next, I'll be speaking *personally* to your parents. Even in the most unlikely event that you'd get solid As on all your exams, it would still require nothing short of a miracle for you to pass enough classes to stay at St. Xavier. Now stop wasting my time and yours. Go learn something in class while you still can. I'll see you in JUG. We'll call it your *bon voyage* party, yes?"

My blood bottoms out, my legs knock together, my world dissolves. Just to keep from vomiting on Russell's Florsheims, I turn and walk away. Not that he doesn't deserve my vomit, but I've embarrassed myself too much already. I feel Russell's eyes burning in my back. I want to do something. I want to walk up to the third floor and hurl myself out the boys' bathroom window. There are way too many fuckin' stairs up to there, though, and my legs can't do the climb just now. I'll have to do it little by little. Or maybe I'll just give Russell the fuck finger and storm back out the doors.

But where would I go? I gotta talk to Dr. Strykeroth and he won't be at his office until after school.

I take the brick staircase to the first floor and pull the oak door's gold handle. Every time the bell rings at the end of each class, the janitor opens this door like a fuckin' royal guard and all the kids pour through. When the bell rings to start the next class period, the janitor closes the oak door and goes back to his peon duties. They got him trained like an accordionist's monkey. That's how you get to stay here. You learn the regimen, just like the janitor and the honors students do. As for me, a squeezebox player would make fuckin' monkey meat out of me. If there's one thing I don't know how to do, it's follow orders.

The door swings shut behind me and I walk across wall-to-wall oriental carpeting. It's a mini-Vatican I'm walking through as I hang a right to the dean's office where Ms. Hayes sits perched. I look at the lacquered walls. They even got candleabra on the walls; the plastic candlesticks have glass containers on top with electric lights flickering inside like manic tongues of flames. There's a huge fucking painting of the Virgin Mary being lifted to heaven by a choir of angels. I guess there's gotta be some reminder of religion in this Jesuit Falcon Crest. The housewife docents go on and on about how the Assumption painting was done by one of those big-deal Spanish painters from centuries ago: "It's featured *prominently* in the finest art history books." I've heard that phrase dropped around here more times than quarters in the 85A's coin slot. Every now and then, down the hall, there's a cross with a muscle-bound body on it, 'cuz you know Jesus hit the gym every day right up 'til they crucified him.

I stand before Ms. Hayes' desk. "We need more efficient service," Ms. Hayes tells whoever's on the phone, "and we expect it no later than two o'clock tomorrow afternoon." She slams the phone down. Hayes chomps her Big Red and looks up at me through a mane of white fuckin' poodle hair. Her bangs droop in fringes across her megafocals. She's wearing a fuzzy Shetland wool sweater that has a fuckin' white terrier stitched onto it. She's got a framed photo of her own 80-year-old pet terrier on her desk too. "Oh, it's you, O'Grady," she says. I stare at her like a laser-eyed male Medusa for calling me by my last fucking name, but Hayes don't turn to stone for nobody except maybe the dean or Father Mahoney. "Need a late slip?" she sighs and I nod. Ms. Hayes rips a late slip off a paper pad and signs it with one of those fancy fuckin' secret signatures that the dean's office changes day by day so they can catch forgeries. It's a fuckin' police state, this!

"You know, O'Grady," she says, contemplating the late slip, "life's got a way of coming down hard on kids like you when you get older." She holds out my late slip. I take it…but she won't let go. I look into her eyes. That's what she wants—for me to look her in the eye. She makes a bitch face for a few seconds before unhanding the slip and letting me exit police-state headquarters.

CHAPTER XVI
Fetal Pig

Today's lab menu features fetal pigs cut up and strung up on tin trays. I get to look forward to leaning over an unborn pig, tied spread eagle over a tin pan as the formaldehyde wafting from its open stomach evacuates my sinuses and pulls the mucus right out of my head cold. Since last week, I've just been looking over its carcass, thinking, "You lucked out, kid. They killed you before you were born."

I walk down another carpeted hallway. The hallowed halls as the Jesuits call them, not to toot their own fuckin' horns. Before going into lab, I stop at my locker and open it to see Johnny Rotten's face looming off my "God Save the Queen" sticker. I look in front of me, I look behind me, I kiss my Johnny Rotten sticker. I put my coat and scarf in the locker, grab my biology textbook and workbook off the top shelf and turn left into lab.

Everyone's wearing protective masks over their noses and mouths. Mr. Grielford is helping Emily Yu put a pig back together from all its torn-out parts. Emily Yu is bound to be an Ivy League superstar. Last week in lab, I heard her chitchatting with Stephanie Virtuno as Grielford went around the lab dropping off aborted pigs at everyone's stations. Emily kept ticking off names of schools she'll be applying to at the beginning of senior year. She rattles them off like they're fuckin' nothing as she stares all lazy at the ceiling, "Um...Yale, Harvard, Dartmouth, Stanford, Princeton..." All the while, my substandard stomach's wrenching like the last spasms of death. I could just hear Dad's voice, "That could be you, saying what that China girl's saying, if you weren't such a goddamned dunce!"

I can read Henry Miller, D.H. Lawrence, Brecht, Algren, Euripides all day and all night, but my eyes and attention can't adjust to any of the words in my schoolbooks—not even my English book—no matter how hard I try. And I can't understand any of the shit Mr. Grielford says in biology. So, for months now, I've just stopped trying. And every now and then, there's retribution. The worst retribution: hearing Emily Yu drop names like Harvard, Yale, Stanford, and Princeton when I'll be good as gone from St. Xavier by February, Russell says.

But even Emily Yu needs help. Look: Grielford's fuckin' helping her now, even as I walk to my chair. They both got their eyes on a microscope and their faces sucked into the pig's stomach. But Emily knows how to meet Grielford halfway. She gets him on his level. They actually have intelligent conversations about the shit they're staring at. Me, I just hand him my late slip and he gives me that *you*-again look.

I walk back to my lab partner, Jerry Gilhooly. Another Irish kid. Normal, normal, normal. Even in the fuckin' dead of winter, he's wearing the same white, collared Polo short sleeve he wears every day. A white, collared, short-sleeved Polo shirt; dingy blue corduroys; white sweat socks and docksiders. What a magnificent ensemble! And he lives by fucking Belmont! You'd think he'd take a cue from all the Mohawks and Manic Panic by his parents' apartment, or at least the fuckin' Le Chateau store. Not that I like Le Chateau's shit, but at least it's something! But clothes and cool's not Gilhooly's bag. Yale is.

I don't know why we even have fuckin' lab partners. Grielford doesn't grade us as a team. He grades on what we're doing on separate sides of our pig. Our pig's snout is rumpled. Its eyes are so startled, you'd think it'd actually been alive long enough to see what a fuckin' horrible world this is.

While I'm fixed on what a fucked-up world this is, Gilhooly's fixed on the work at hand. I look over at his petri dish. Everything's set out so meticulously. He looks through a microscope. He looks to the ceiling. He ponders. What he's pondering, I don't fucking know, but he's pondering all right. He nods his understanding to the air like he's signaling to fuckin' Hermes, god of science. And he scribbles some answer into his workbook fucking furiously, like he just got a lock on some big-ass truth that his memory had better fuckin' catch before it flies the fuck away. After the new revelation is in his notebook, he moves on to some new part of our pig. And I stand around, and my workbook is empty as ever. Question #3 asks, "Is there evidence of diffusion in the subject's muscle tissues?" How the fuck should I know? The pig's dead! No, it was never born! Why the fuck are we still staring at it? Some more useless college weed-out shit that'll get Gilhooly into Yale and Emily Yu into everything Ivy League.

Mr. Grielford comes by. He goes to my microscope and looks at the pig's breakfast I've made of my pig's innards. Mr. Grielford bends his bushy, crescent eyebrows down at me. He's got owl glasses on and his gray hair twists into a cone off the side of his head. He's patterning his life after Dr. Strangelove, I'm convinced. He peers through the microscope again and looks back up, his eyes going hard on their target, otherwise known as my face. "You're not *getting* it, Mr. O'Grady," he grits his teeth, "After how many times?" My adrenaline rushes in, as usual, but strangely not as quick this time. I already know I'm walking the final stretch of my Green Mile. I've been closing in on it ever since my mind first wandered away from my schoolwork, way back in first grade.

I come clean, "You're right, Mr. Grielford. I don't get it." Gilhooly has his head turned away, but even he can't help sneaking peeks.

Mr. Grielford says to me, "Well, do you think you can *get*

it by just fumbling around on this plate and hoping for the best?"

I opt for honesty, "Yes, that was my plan."

His pupils slit to show the tips of bloody spears. His lips curl back, "Come with me, Mr. O'Grady." He turns, his white lab coat crumpling over his slumped shoulders as he lumbers to his desk. I follow a few paces behind as Mr. Grielford walks behind his desk and bends over his grade book. With a crooked finger, he motions me over: "I'm not supposed to do this, Seamus, but I want you to take a look at this column. It's your classmates' marks from last semester. I'll start down here…at 'M.' Muldoon, A. Nan, A-. Neiberg, B+. Norbert, A. Nyles, B-. Not great, but not bad. O'Connor, A. And here we go, O'Grady. Now take a look at that and read me what your grade was last semester."

I look away. "I don't have to read it. I can tell you. D-. "

Mr. Grielford continues reading, "Opat, A. O'Shaugnesy, C. Not outstanding but not abysmal, just average. I could read up and down this list and you won't find one other D, much less a D-. And that was last semester, when you did *better* than you're doing now." His eyes have turned to granite. I can focus on nothing else. This is where the vampire licks his chops before impaling a neck. Did he wake up this morning feeling like a stupid prick and now is all too happy to pass that complex off on someone else?

I break the spell, "What do you want? What do you want me to say? Or do you want me to say anything? Do you want me to just stand here, sweating? Is that your plan? Just to browbeat and belittle me?"

"'Browbeat' and 'belittle,'" he laughs, "That's quite an impressive vocabulary you've amassed, Mr. O'Grady. I suppose that's how you compensate for your overall idiocy."

"You're right about me 'not getting it.' I don't get a thing you're teaching. Maybe you should teach better."

"The others seem to catch on just fine, Mr. O'Grady. Their grades prove that. Do I have to detain their learning just so you can catch up? From a thousand yards behind?"

"You don't have to detain anybody," I say, "but, yes, you do have to help me catch up. That's your job."

"Don't tell me what my job is, Mr. O'Grady," he slams his grade book shut. "Get back to your pig." His eyes go cold again, as if to tell me to wipe that smirk off my face. But my smirk is my last dignity. I wouldn't dare wipe it off.

I go back to the pig. I see the entrails on my petri dish. It looks worse than the pigeon shit on the blackboard in math. I grab my stool. I see the pig's kidney glistening under the lab's fluorescent lights. I could do a damn good job with a pig's innards if we weren't in science class. Like, I could do a good job with them if this was one of those ancient islands they talk about in Greek tragedies, the ones where the augur casts the guts of an animal on the ground and reads the future. Reads everyone's lives. Tells the deepest and darkest about their lives today and their destinies tomorrow.

The other students are all talk-talk-talking all at once. I can't make out any of the words they're saying and I don't care. I like it this way. I hear their scalpels clank as they set them down on the tin supply tray. I hear their slides rattle as they set them under their microscopes. They're shuffling around. They're writing out long answers in their workbooks. I've got nothing written in mine today. I take out my notebook and write a poem, a little longer than a haiku, the one I wanted to write right before I saw Dean Russell pacing in the commons:

I need only fill my head with the sound
Of cold wind howling and traffic hissing
And puddles splashing
On Blue Island Avenue
To know there's no such thing as failure
If teachers aren't around to fail you.

Mr. Grielford sees I'm not doing my work and he breathes heavy. I have no expression on my face at all. He drops his stare and turns away. He knows I'm the prophet from the cave with the pig's entrails before him.

CHAPTER XVII
Hallowed Halls

The bell rings and kids burst out of class. Girls are giggling and gossiping about some shit, I don't know what. Guys are walking together with a lot of grunt and swagger, talking the way guys talk, walking the way guys walk. Guys sometimes strut up to me, mocking my usual gait, making me out to be some pansy floozy fruit. And how the fuck did they figure out how a real guy walks? They must've had some nose for it, right from their first baby steps. And they don't gesticulate like I do, not even the Italian guys, and they mock me for it. They're guys through and through.

I never made a guy friend here at Xavier. Even the Xavier guys who go to Belmont and Wax Trax with their skateboards, who shave parts of their head and let their bangs hang in their faces, they don't even want to be seen talking to me. When I first got to Xavier, I wanted people thinking I was hot shit. I knew my Sex Pistols backward and forward. For some fucked-up reason, I thought everyone saw *Sid & Nancy* too. I thought everyone here would know every line like I did. So I started quoting Sid, saying, "I was so bored once, I fucked a dog!" I said it more than once. I said it a bunch of times. I thought people would know I was quoting a movie, I thought people would know I was joking, I thought people'd think it was cool. No, now they just know me as the kid who fucks my dog. I've never even had a dog, much less fucked one! I've never been in a bathroom stall at Xavier, but I hear some assholes are scratching shit into the stall walls about me being a faggot who fucks his dog. I'm sure whoever's writing that shit never fuckin' talked to me even once, but they still think they got me pegged.

I walk down the hall. Everyone's slapping each other five. I gotta admit, sometimes I'm jealous. It's gotta feel nice to be included. In lieu of friends, I've just worked on my look, kept my red hair fucked-up, wore lots of chains on my right wrist and safety pins and a PiL button on the blazer I wear most days. The pride of the fuckin' pariah!

All my friends used to be imaginary. Now I've got Tressa. She's real and she's always with me, even when she's not here. But soon she won't be here at all. She'll be in Switzerland and I'll still be dreaming about England. I'll still be dreaming about knowing people there who'll walk with me the way guys at Xavier walk with each other, who'll call out to me like kids call out to each other in the hallowed halls.

And now I'm heading to Mr. Banaszak's English and American Lit class, where we study writers—creative types that Xavier all but takes to the gallows in real life but praises to the stars once they die and stand the test of time. And the assholes who want to get into Notre Dame, just like Brody did, sit back and wonder why the fuck they gotta learn a bunch of shit that a bunch of unemployed fags in pantyhose and pirate shirts wrote. But they suck it up and study it anyway, knowing it'll get them where they want to go.

With me, it's the opposite. Outside of class, I read great authors all night and day, but in class I'm zoning out. Listening to Mr. Banaszak's weaselly, punk-hating voice read Byron is like watching a Revolting Cocks cover band do a benefit concert for the Young Republicans. It's fuckin' blasphemy, and the only kind of blasphemy I don't applaud. So instead I cringe. I tried and tried to kick my habit of cringing, thinking it might be nice to see an A on my report card for once in my life. For a while, I even tried pretending Mr. Banaszak—with his four eyes, comb-over, and peach-colored corduroy suit coat—was Ian Curtis with his deep voice, suicide rants, and electric stage presence. I tried imagining I was seeing Ian Curtis up in front of class, trilling depressing lyrics and transmitting ecstasy to the crowd. But, even in my vivid imagination, Ian Curtis' voice couldn't boom past Banazak's, which often comes accompanied by hacking phlegm, brought on by a pockmarked nose that I've caught him picking on more than one occasion.

So here I enter room 305. Class starts in two minutes. There's a framed picture of Shakespeare on the sidewall. His collar is starched, it stands in stiff crinkles all the way up to his jaw. He has a jeweled broach pinned at his collar's throat. There's a fuckin' earring in Shakespeare's right ear and he's wearing an upholstered velvet jacket with puffy, padded shoulders. I take my seat and look around at the class. The football jocks are low-riding into their seats as they hold their pens, casual-like, impressing the little sluts on all sides of them with their macho-man acts. The little sluts let their knee-length skirts ride up in their chairs.

CHAPTER XVIII
Twain's Contemporary

Banaszak's feet are up on his desk. He ignores the class and reads something by John Updike that's got rabbits running across the cover. He's wearing the same tacky-ass beige suede shoes he wears every day. Why do English teachers have to look so fuckin' sexless? Why do they send these fuddy-duddies in to open the world of poems and novels to us? Makes me want to fuckin' run screaming to an early grave. And maybe if I was dead and buried, I could go direct to the spirit world and meet the actual poets we're studying.

The bell rings. Banaszak shuts his Updike and opens the *Macclesfield Treasury of English and American Literature* to a bookmarked page. "Open your text to page, um, 254," he announces, "Where we will cross the great Atlantic to Great Britain to meet Mark Twain's contemporary, Charles Dickens."

Charles Dickens. An image fills my brain till the pen-streaked door three seats in front of me begins to fade. I stare at that door all the time when I'm bored. It's had Supertramp scrawled on to it ever since the seventies (I'm guessing). Someone scribbled CUNT into the door, maybe even as far back as the seventies, and someone else scribbled out the U. This shit happens to me all the time. The room falls away and a daydream takes over. Right now, Dickens' England is growing larger than life. I'm seeing sooty stone walls appear above cobblestone streets, little kids in dirty little scarves and dusty little overcoats cough up tuberculosis and hold out their hands for spare change.

Banaszak's shouts out, "Kuklinski!" half snapping me out of my little reverie, though I stay in a daze. Tim Kuklinski stops chatting up Sonia Maddox, who slips a long string of curly hair behind her ear and looks back down at her Macclesfield textbook. "Yes, *SIR!*" Kuklinski shouts back, half-joking, in his husky jock huff. All the football fucks laugh on cue.

Mr. Banaszak gives Kuklinski a snide look of warning, "Was England fighting a civil war at the same time as the United States?"

Kuklinski pauses, "Um, I don't believe so, *SIR!*" His football friends back him up with laughs.

Banaszak scratches his bald dandruff head, "Very good, Mr. Kuklinski. Now, when Lincoln was fighting slavery, was England also at war over slavery?"

Kuklinski answers, "Um, not that I know of, *SIR!*"

"You're wrong, Mr. Kuklinski," Banaszak says. "Can you believe it? You, Tim Kuklinski, are wrong! Now why is it you're wrong?"

"'Cuz I'm an idiot, *SIR.*" Everyone picks up the cue to laugh, except me. I'm still busy hallucinating cobblestones, soot, and tuberculosis.

"Truer words were never spoken, Mr. Kuklinski," Mr. Banaszak cracks back, "but there's an even deeper reason for your mistakenness, and that is that England *was* fighting slavery. Not the sort of slavery that was taking place in the American South, but another kind of slavery. It was a slavery of the spirit. Labor abuse, child exploitation, whole families locked up in debtor's prison. Even...*sexual* slavery."

The cool kids put on mock-shock faces and say, "Oooo." A few jocks woof, "Oh, yeaaah..." Now I'm seeing cobblestone, soot, tuberculosis, *and* a dominatrix in a lacey teddy and SS cap. She's tap-dancing on a chimney sweep's chest as I hear Banaszak talking to the class from somewhere outside my dreaming as the images in my mind are projected on to the Supertramp, C-scribbled-U-N-T door. The dominatrix is stomping and stomping, and the chimey sweep's panting and panting like I'm sure they do at the Café de Sade orgies and…

Oh, shit! I was staring at the door at first and my eye wandered off. Now I'm staring at Kuklinski. Kuklinski's looking at me looking at him. Shit, he thinks I'm having fucking fag-fantasies about him. He's recoiling in fucking horror. Fuck. I turn away. My days of him not pushing me around are fucking over now.

This is the kind of shit that happens to me when my mind drifts. Kuklinski's signaling to Chris Salzman, who's a first-string linesman or tight end or whatever other fuckin' distinctions they lay on these muscleheads. Kuklinski's jerking his head and thumb my way. Salzman grunts a jock grunt to Kuklinski and they both turn around and face me head-on. I pretend not to notice, but they notice I notice—and they know I know why they're looking at me.

I scan the room for Asian kids. I want to pick up some Asian-kid energy—Chinese, Filipino, Japanese, Korean, I don't fuckin' care which! Just gimme anything Asian! Just make me a fuckin' Asian kid now! Asian kids are always under the fuckin' radar. They're never in trouble. People write 'em off as nerds and let 'em go off and be geniuses. They never seem to want for anything. I always feel calmer when I look at Asian kids. Maybe I'd be calmer if I was one.

There's Sandy Yim. Sweet little Sandy Yim has no dark side. There's nothing suspect about her. She's just a studious little Chinese girl in a pink sweater and gray corduroys. Nobody notices her, nobody bothers her. She knows what's expected of her and she doesn't question those expectations, not as far as I can tell. Her life's all the better for it—for walking the straight and narrow, like Adam and Eve before the serpent slithered up and told them to fuck authority. Once you start fucking authority, you can't stop. Believe me, I know; your ass gets cast out of innocence and straight into experience. Maybe there's a way for me to go back to the days before I started fucking authority. Maybe there's still time for me to be the prodigal son and come home. Maybe I can take on Sandy Yim's identity. Maybe I can become invisible like her and escape Tim Kuklisnki and everybody else's wrath.

But I can't work that kind of magic right here in Mr. Banaszak's class. Kuklinski gives me a fearsome fuckin' glare.

I wandered lonely as a cloud
That floats on high o'er vales and hills...

Who wrote that? Was it me? No, it was one of the Romantics. It's in the library book I kept reading over Christmas break. Maybe Coleridge? No, it wasn't Coleridge. I think it was Wordsworth.

"Mr. O'Grady! Mr. O'Grady!" He's somewhere outside still, a faint voice and finger-snap somewhere outside my daze. "MR. O'GRADY!" He snaps me out of my trance. Banaszak walks over to my desk, "Are you still with us?" Shit! It's happened again. How fucking long have I been drifting off? He says it again, annunciating every word, "Are You Still With Us?" I pause. "Well, are you?" he asks.

"No, he's ogling Kuklinski," Chris Salzman quips. The whole class rips with laughter. My face and body flush hot with blood. I turn my head toward the window, away from the class.

Mr. Banaszak looks at Salzman, "Well, Mr. Salzman, just for that, be sure to tell Coach Johnson that you'll be serving football practice in JUG today."

My face rolls back to the rest of the class. Sandy Yim is the only one among them who's not smirking. She has her head down, her usual low profile. Salzman shoots me silent death threats from out the corner of his eye. I turn back to the window. I feel more glass piercing my arm from inside.

"But getting back to Mr. O'Grady," Mr. Banaszak says, pointing at me, "Seamus, I'm wondering where you've been this whole time—while the rest of us have been dutifully learning about the charitable efforts of one Mr. Charles Dickens."

I say to Mr. Banaszak, "I'm sorry. My mind was…off somewhere."

"That's all too common an occurrence, Mr. O'Grady. Where was your mind today, may I ask?" I say nothing. "It must have settled upon a fascinating subject of meditation. You've been absent for most of the period."

Faces are relentless with their staring. I roll my neck to the right and feel tears welling up from deep inside.

"Mr. O'Grady, would you at least be good enough to read from the top of the page?" Mr. Banaszak says.

"Sure," I say, clearing my throat. I look at the title on page 254. "'Charles Dickens and the Chartist Movement.'"

"No, Mr. O'Grady," he shouts back with thunder and ire, "we left that page ages ago."

"Oh," I say, looking to my left to see what page Tim Kuklinski is on. Before I can spot the page number, Kuklinski blocks it with his arm.

"Don't show him, Mr. Kuklinski!" Banaszak says.

"Yeah, don't worry," Kuklinski says back.

Banaszak comes up to my desk and stands over me with the shadow of a wolf over a henhouse, "Now we're discussing one of Dickens' primary influences. He's a poet…one who spoke to the Great Man's soul. Do you know who that might be?" I look down at my desk and shake my head no. A tear races out the corner of my eye. "He wrote a short poem. Its title…well… remember the impromptu essay I had all of you write on the first day of class?" I hide my face and nod. "In that assignment, you mentioned wanting to make a certain city your home. I must say I was *fas*cinated. And, you said in that essay that you wanted to be a famous writer, is that true?" I nod again. "Good Lord!" Banaszak says, "Could you imagine the state of literature?" The class laughs. Banaszak continues, "Where do you want to be a writer? What city?" The class' eyes pound down like a flock of fuckin' vultures over a field mouse.

"London," I whimper.

"Well, then, have you heard of a little poem called, 'London'?"

I say, "Yes." He stumbles back and gasps with his usual twat sarcasm, "Really? And who might have written it?"

I say, "William Blake."

"Did you sneak a peek at someone's textbook? Is that how you know?"

"No," I say. "I know 'London.' It's one of my favorite poems. I know it by heart."

Mr. Banaszak takes a long step forward and closes his Maccelsfield text. He looks down at me, a strand of greasy hair falling from the bald spot it once made such a desperate attempt to cover. "Really?" he asks.

"Really," I nod.

"I'm sure you're aware what the penalty for audacity is in this classroom, Mr. O'Grady. It's almost as bad as the penalty for lying. You're going to have to stand up in front of class and recite every single line of this treasured poem, which you claim to know by heart." I look up at Banaszk again, sheepish and unwilling. "If you do, it'll be your get-out-of-JUG-free card," Banaszak says, in front of everyone in class, everyone who'd hate like hell to be me right now. "If you cannot accomplish this Herculean feat, you'll not only be sent to JUG but you will have scarred yourself for life in front of all your classmates.

"Go on," he says.

On my way up to the front of the class, a paper ball smacks the back of my head and bounces on to Mary Muldoon's desk. More laughter rolls in. I turn around, fire in my eyes, ready to kill whoever fuckin' threw the paper ball. Even as I dread getting my ass beat by the whole fag-bashing football team, I'm ready to take them all on. Mr. Banaszak takes a seat in my seat. He says, "Mr. O'Grady, stand in front of my desk. And this had better be good." He takes a JUG slip off a pad of paper, signs it and waves the possible penalty in the air for one and all to see.

I see a sea of kids snickering and I say:

I wander thro' each charter'd street,

Near where the charter'd Thames does flow,

And mark in every face I meet,

Marks of weakness, marks of woe.

Mr. Banaszak's mouth is open like a steel trap. I say to him, "Shall I continue?" He slaps himself, as if to awaken from shock. Everybody laughs. He says, "By all means, go on."

I flash back to video clips of Bowie and Jagger showboating on stage back in the seventies. If that's faggotry, then count me in with the faggots! I strut in front of class, ever so subtly showing off how *catlike* my tight ass moves, just like the tiger from another Blake poem I could recite—*verbatim*, no less. But, for now, I'm sticking to the next stanza of "London":

In every cry of every Man,

In every Infant's cry of fear,

In every voice, in every ban,

The mind-forg'd manacles I hear:

Mr. Banaszak jumps in, "Mr. O'Grady, what are manacles?"

"Why, they're handcuffs," I wink. "I thought you of all people would know that, Mr. B."

He looks at me with a frozen face, "I thought your whole objective was to get *out* of JUG, Mr. O'Grady. Don't test me."

I bow slightly and walk in the same pedantic-ass way he does, imitating his weasel voice: "This next stanza probably held *particular* appeal for a reformer like Dickens:

How the Chimney-sweeper's cry

Every blackening church appalls,

And the hapless Soldier's sigh

Runs in blood down Palace walls."

The class is dumbstruck. I finish up "London" by putting my hand on my hip the way real guys never do and say, "And you wanna talk *sexual slavery*, listen to this:

But most thro' midnight streets I hear

How the youthful Harlot's curse

Blasts the new-born Infant's tear,

And blights with plagues the Marriage hearse."

I take a huge bow. The class applauds, all except for Kuklinski, Salzman, and Banaszak. Even Sandy Yim gets into it, she's clapping away. I start walking back to my seat when Banaszak says: "Wait just a minute, Mr. O'Grady. Stay there, stay there. I just want to know...*how?*"

I say, "How what, *SIR?*" Everyone laughs at my Kuklinski impression.

He says, "How could you know that poem?"

I say, "I love Blake." Some jocks make kissing sounds and a couple say shit like, "Oh, he luvvvs that Blake..."

Banaszak says, "Why?"

I say, "Social protest is my life." Some people clap. I don't know if it's for me or if it's because I just delivered a line worthy of fuckin' Marlon Brando.

Banaszak takes his glasses off and shakes his head in wonder, "Well, I never would've guessed that you of all people..." He holds his head some more, laughs and says, "Seamus O'Grady, Holy Lord!" He laughs some more.

I stop him, "W-w-w-wait. What'd you just say? Me of *all* people?"

He raises his eyebrows and nods, "That's right. I said... you of all people." He smiles and blinks.

I walk right back up to my desk, where he's sitting, and put my knuckles smack down on his Macclesfield textbook. "And what do you think you are, Banaszak? Some kind of fucking god on earth?" His face falls. His smiles falls. I go on, "You're a pathetic little tenth-grade English teacher twat with a bad tie and a big mouth. Do you think you're someone *I* wanna grow up to be?" I lean in closer as he shifts in my seat, "Huh? How does it feel being a four-eyed fuck, Banaszak? How does it feel to be an ugly, bald, arrogant *cunt?*"

Everyone shuffles in their seats. They look to Banaszak. They look at me. I lean down, stick my nose right up against his fuckin' nose and scream, "ME 'OF ALL PEOPLE'? WHO THE FUCK DO *YOU* THINK *YOU* ARE, BANASZAK? Huh? How 'bout you! How 'bout YOU?" He doesn't say a word. He doesn't have to. I can hear his heart crashing against his ribcage harder than the wrecking ball pummeling the crackhouse next door. He leans back farther.

I stand over him, "I bet you can't recite a single *fucking* line from 'London,' Banaszak, not without the help of your little textbook here!" I pick up his Macclesfield and slam it on the floor. "I just got up there and recited every fucking verse...by heart. Could you do that, Banaszak?" I grab the JUG slip out of his hand, "Think I never seen one of these before, Banaszak?" I shred it in his face. "Now pick it all up, tape it back together, and use it to wipe the cum off your fingers next time you're pretending to take a piss in the boys' room."

The class stays silent. My voice was louder than fuckin' bombs. It's still echoing in everybody's ears. A few girls are crying. I look at Salzman and Kuklisnki. They look like two stunned polar bears. Banaszak sits sweating like a block of ice in the sun as I grab my bag from underneath his legs and stomp out the Supertramp-C-scribbled-U-N-T door, slamming it behind me. I can hear Shakespeare's picture frame rattling on the wall.

A few teachers come out of their classrooms and look down the hall. "What's all this commotion?" one says. I don't know which teacher says it, my back is to him. He calls out after me. I don't turn around, but I can hear him open Banaszak's door and call him by his first name, "Stan, is everything okay?" I'm heading to the second floor, I'm heading to my locker.

On the sticker inside my locker door, I see Johnny Rotten again, screaming into his microphone with riot eyes. The Union Jack is torn asunder over his face. I kiss this sticker. I know it's the last I'll be seeing of it. We've had some good mornings together, haven't we, Johnny? I empty my bag onto the floor of my locker. I keep only my Walkman, my copy of *Tropic of Cancer* (another Xavier-banned book), and, of course, the *Time* magazine article on Kirik. Soon I'll have to go home to collect *Punk: A Sordid Saga* and *Three Penny Opera*...Fuck, that's right! I'm gonna have to go home at some point! Fuck! Well, I'll think about that later.

Right now, Mrs. Martin is charging out of her history class. She doesn't know my name, but, just from being around school, I know hers. She stares me down like there's tumbleweed rolling between us and says, "Young man, you're not supposed to be in the hallway when classes are in session. Do you have a note?" Her classroom door is wide open. There are juniors in there, chomping on their pens and looking out at me.

I take one last look at my Johnny Rotten sticker, slam my locker door and click the padlock shut. I look at Mrs. Martin and flip her off with two fingers instead of one, like they do in England. In my best cockney, I say, "Piss off, slag!" and I walk away.

Mrs. Martin follows me down the hall screaming, "Get back here!" but I make my final descent down the coiled, python stairs to the first floor, hoping to break the python's neck on my way down. No more snakepits for me. "What's your name?" she calls down from the top of the stairwell. From inside her classroom, I faintly hear someone calling out, "Seamus O'Grady. He's a sophomore. He thinks he's British." I hear the class laugh. Another yells: "He does things to dogs!" Mrs. Martin turns away from the staircase and I hear her ask whatever juniors have followed her into the hall, "What? What's his name?" She looks back down the stairwell and shouts, "Never mind. I'll find out. You're not hard to describe!"

I put on my gloves and tighten my scarf. As I reach the last stair to the first floor, I see Dean Russell coming out of his office. "Seamus!" he yells. For once, I don't have to say a fucking word to him. The death knell has already tolled and I'm not stickin' around to hear it again. I keep walking to the lobby. "Seamus!" Russell keeps shouting, picking up the pace after me. I don't look back. I pound on St. Xavier's front-door lever and bound up the walkway to Blue Island Avenue. It's below zero outside but I'll take a long, long walk while I figure out what the fuck I'm gonna do now. A long walk oughta warm me up. At the very least, planning my life from here on out will take my mind off the weather.

As I reach the sidewalk, I hear the crunch on the front door lever again. "Seamus!" I hear Dean Russell screaming. Now Russell's on the street. "Get back here!" he yells loud enough for the cops on school patrol to hear. I take off running toward Racine Street. Russell's too old to keep up, but cops got squad cars. But the blizzard's too blinding for the pigs to see me. If I double it over to Ashland Avenue, they shouldn't be able to tell me apart from all the college kids on the UIC campus.

Shit, don't let me slip on the slush! Just get me to Ashland! Get me to Ashland! Maybe I'll get to West Town and meet some kind of Cassandra or Orestes. Maybe one of them will take me in. Maybe I can live with one of them and spend my days writing plays and getting parts...Fuck! What the fuck am I talking about? Even if life fucking worked that way, I still couldn't stay within a hundred miles of Mom and Dad—Orestes or no Orestes, Cassandra or no Cassandra, Colby or no Colby, Tressa or no Tressa—I couldn't stay here after all the shit that's gone down.

What have I done? What have I fucking done? I had to! I fuckin' had to! Better to mutiny than take the whip in galley chains. As I turn the corner at Blue Island and Ashland, I dart in to blend in with the college crowd and the med students going head to head with the cold on the University of Illinois Hospital campus. I stop to hear the howling wind and hissing traffic break on the shores of a brave new world. But, shit, I got no time to set up a haiku stand now. There'll be time enough for that shit at Café de Sade. For now, I got a lot of walking to do between here and West Town.

CHAPTER XIX
ASHLAND

Snow's slamming down like the fucking apocalypse and I got an arctic freeze wringing all the tears out of my eyes. Xavier should've listened to the weather reports and given us a fuckin' snow day. I could've stayed home; could've, I dunno, brooded along to my Bauhaus albums or something. This whole morning never would've happened. But shit was bound to happen some time.

Cars are slip-sliding all over the street, so everyone's standing on their brakes. They don't want to move more than an inch at a time on this ice, so they sit in bumper-car formation, under a slate-gray sky, in this higgledy-piggledy parking lot called Ashland Avenue.

Shit! An old tan Cadillac just crashed headlong into a new blue Volvo by the Lake Street stoplight. Didn't slow down, didn't brake—nothing. His fender just rammed the fuck in and crushed the Volvo's passenger-side door. The Volvo's driver gets out and pounds his roof. But, no, white boy Volvo driver's cutting that shit out right now! Oh fuck! He sees Pimp Daddy in the full-length fox coat setting his size-thirteen Gucci sole on the street; he sees all seven foot one of Pimp Daddy climbing out of the Cadillac. A Volvo's not worth getting slapped all the way into 1990 for. You can see it on his face he agrees. Something tells me Volvo and Cadillac will be settling this one out of court. But even if they don't, I'm not stopping to be a witness. Last thing I need is for some cop to come take my report and ask why I'm not in school.

I shoulder through the cold like a fuckin' linebacker. The

city trucks are shoveling mountains of snow on to the curb. The dirt and slush are starting to slip into the lace holes of my army boots. I just feast my mind's eye on the piping hot apple cider waiting for me way up at de Sade.

La Hacienda Tacos is blasting Mariachi music from the bullhorns wired up above its doors. Whatever mood those bullhorns are supposed to be setting, they sure as hell aren't making anybody believe we're in fuckin' Mexico. They might just as well be cranking from a fuckin' igloo. That south-of-the-border daydreaming shit's got no place in this blizzard. But, shit, look who's busting on daydreamers! If it wasn't for my own dawdling daydreaming, I'd be on the fuckin' honor roll by now.

And I got seven bucks to my name. By the time I'm done drinking hot apple cider at de Sade, I'll be down to four. Where the fuck will I get more? It's obvious I can't stay in Chicago. Can't stay; can't leave; what the fuck can I do? I could set up camp at an Uptown homeless shelter or maybe the one on South Wabash. They might ask for ID. I can say I don't got any. If they interrogate, I'll just keep my mouth shut. What're they gonna do? Turn me away? They're supposed to be good Christians, remember?

I gotta stretch my last seven—well, soon four—bucks all the way to London. Well, that's not gonna be so fuckin' easy, is it? Even if I could get the money from Tressa, they'll ask for my passport and I ain't got one. To travel alone, you gotta be at least eighteen or be accompanied to the gate by a parent or guardian.

But, c'mon, America's no small neighborhood. It's got its share of freaks to hang with. I can hide out all sorts of places till the coast's clear. Too bad this isn't the sixties. Back then, you could just make a call and some hippy would drive up in a VW and drop you off in San Fran. But San Francisco's the wrong coast. It's too sunny. There's no deep, European Cassandra-Orestes energy out there. I gotta find some place much less sunny to match my usual moods. It's too fucking far from London too. And I don't think it's got much going on for actors…and I'm sure as fuck not heading down to LA to get parts. I'm not selling my soul auditioning for bullshit Hollywood flicks.

Looking at this desolate street, I now know what regret feels like. There's still howling wind. There's still hissing traffic. There are still puddles splashing. My boots crunch on the snow, ice, and salt. One foot in front of the other—they say that's the way to go when you got no idea where you're going next.

If I were Bertolt Brecht, I'd write a poem. I'd smoke a cigarette. I'd fuck a whore. I'd get drunk. I'd write a fucking play. And somehow things would magically open up and, like the painter in my own play, I'd be all the rage.

Russell's probably already called Mom and Dad. Their veins are probably pumping fire and brimstone. Who knows, Dad might've even left his office; his eyes are probably scouring the snow-piled streets for me from a taxi right now—running up a bigger and bigger fare just so he can get madder and madder at me. Russell's probably brought one of his disciplinary review boards together, probably made up of him, Father Mahoney, Banaszak, Mrs. Martin, and fuck knows who all else I pissed off.

School's probably already left a message for Dr. Strykeroth! Fuck! I'll leave a message on his answering service, "Don't tell anyone I'm coming to your office." Great! Now I have to spend fifty cents on phone calls—one for Tressa, one for Dr. S. That seven dollars is vanishing already and I've barely left school!

CHAPTER XX
Café De Sade (Reprise)

There it is. The creaking black de Sade sign. Shit, the hours, the days, the months I've spent in there. Gawking at every table. Taking everything in. Filling up notebooks with anything and everything but homework—ever since I first stepped through the looking glass, ever since I first walked into de Sade. I know every inch of it. I know the faces of all the regulars. That Brecht biographer keeps talking about the "habitués and roués" in Brecht's hangouts in Munich and Berlin and none of them sound all that different from the habitués and roués here. I don't know any de Sade habitué or roué personally. I'm still too uncool and unschooled to talk to.

I see the goateed guy in the corner—the one with the full tide of long, wavy black hair who's sketching right now. I always try sitting by him, just to see what's on his sketchpad. A lot of times he's looking out the southwest window and depicting the shit going down by the Flatiron Building at Damen, Milwaukee, and North—chicken-play traffic, drug deals, homelessness; or he's doing portraits of the grizzled old geezers that the cat sometimes drags into de Sade from the AA meeting over on Wabansia Street, or the sexy, fringe rebel chicks with their tattoos and dreadlocks, or artists from Europe and Japan and Africa who've somehow heard of de Sade and stop in to slum.

Once Goatee Guy even sketched me! I didn't let on I saw, but I saw. This was, what, four months ago? I was sitting at the window seat, the one I'm walking to now. I opened the copy of *The Man Who Died* that Tressa gave me. I was halfway through it before I took out my notebook and started pouring my heart out, about what, I don't fuckin' remember, just a lot of shit going on in my head that day, but *The Man Who Died* got me writing up a storm. When I was about two or three pages into it, I looked over to Goatee Guy's sketch page and saw my ratted hair and Roman nose; I saw my crossed legs and long black pants; I saw my black combats and gray Ian Curtis shirt. Goatee Guy was fuckin' drawing me head to foot the whole time I was reading and writing! He wrote next to his sketch, "*Novice*, September 1988." I wonder where that fuckin' sketch is now? Hopefully not just rotting somewhere between 150 other drawings. But, shit, even just being in a sketchbook adds up to fifteen minutes of fame, right?

At the counter, I shell out three bucks for a hot apple cider and ask the waiter to bring it to the window seat while I go make a call. The snow is melting off my boots and I'm tracking puddles all across de Sade's hardwood floors. I call Dr. S's answering service from the payphone and tell him I have to talk to him, it's big. I call Tressa's beeper too and now I gotta wait for her to call back.

I stand by the phone. It's a good place, Café de Sade. I gotta run away to somewhere that's got something like it. Shit, then, the only other place is New York. I'll go straight to Oliver's House. They could get me a job...I could work at a sandwich shop! Yeah, do something like that. I could get a job at a fuckin' sandwich shop in Alphabet City or something—somewhere close to Oliver's House so I won't have to pay bus fare and shit like I do now. I can save up, just like I was planning to do with Colby— before I blew it all to hell with counterfeit cockney.

New York will be my prep course for London. There'll be lots of shit out there to write about—and maybe I can do what Kirik did and start on Broadway before heading to London.

CAFÉ DE SADE (REPRISE)

And I'll apply for my passport way before my eighteenth birthday, which'll be my last day in New York. Oh, man, this is fucking genius! Wait'll I tell Tressa.

Holy shit, all this shit has to happen tonight! Café de Sade, West Town, Logan Square, the L, the 85A, Mom, Dad, Chicago, Puddles, Xavier, Tressa—it'll all be gone. Gone! Like lightning, like Hiroshima. Tonight.

I wonder what Puddles is doing now. Little Puddles. Little tabby. My little tiger stripe. She's probably huddled up in a ball on my bed right now. Fuck, I'll miss her. I mean, shit, even at, like, third period, any day of the week, I miss her! I can see her little belly inflating and deflating like a little football while she sleeps. Shit, I might not've even lasted this long if it wasn't for Puddles, if it wasn't for getting to cuddle with her after a bad day. Even when Puddles wakes me up in the middle of the night, headbutting and kissing me and wanting a big petting, I don't mind.

This world is so fucking huge and complicated, but not Puddles. She eats. She sleeps. She purrs. She shits in a box. She loves. And she gets plenty of love for it. And maybe it wasn't that way for her when she was a stray, but she's safe and warm now. Life isn't such a big hairy clusterfuck for her anymore. Maybe that's why she's not an asshole like everybody else. If I could find a magic land like in *The Secret Garden*, I'd escape to it with Puddles in a New York minute. There wouldn't be people in the secret garden but there'd be plenty of spirits and enchantment. I'd never leave. I'd stay for-fucking-ever and Puddles would stay for-fucking-ever. But *The Secret Garden* is just a silly old movie about two little limey kids. It's not real. It's just a family flick for little kids who still get to have imaginations, and for their parents, who wish the real world still let them have imaginations.

And let's face it, I'm not heading for any secret garden now. New York don't fuck around and Puddles can't come with me. Even if I could get her all the way to Oliver's House, they'd take her out of my arms and cage her up in a shelter—and who knows the shit that'd happen to her there! Lethal injection, the gas chamber—I can't even fuckin' think about that shit. Just…let her bundle up on my bed where she's safe, let her rest her chin on her little white paws. Mom and Dad will take care of her. They might not pet her. Dad might call her Stupid all the time. But she knows how to break stone hearts, she knows how to blink her eyes and cock her head, so they'll keep her. They'll feed her and she'll keep warm. And maybe there is a God and maybe if I pray, he'll send some spirits to keep Puddles company, so she won't miss me so much. I mean, if there even is such thing as…

Rinnnggg! "Thank God! Tressa! Shit, thank God. It's Seamus…Well, not all that fuckin' great, to tell you the truth. I'm at de Sade…Yeah, I've been here a little while now. I need you to come…Yeah, like, right now…No, love, it *can't* wait."

CHAPTER XXI
Chessboard Table

There isn't enough space at the window seat, so Tressa moves my cider to the tea table next to it, the one with the chessboard painted on top. It always reminds me of the chessboard worlds Alice wandered into. I used to love when Mom would read the Alice books to me.

The waiter brings Tressa the pot of green tea she ordered; he gives her an ear-to-ear grin. And why wouldn't he? She's wearing her thigh-high chauffeur boots, the ones she wore the first time I saw her on the L. She's wearing something long, black, and lacy under her knee-length purple shawl too. I wish I could turn heads like she does. Tressa's dark and exotic. I'm fish-belly white and turn red in the cold. She thanks the waiter and gives him a one-second flash smile. She can't be bothered brokering a free pot of tea today. She's got a bigger fish belly to fry—mine.

Tressa takes the lid off the teapot and the strainer out of the tea. She looks down into the clear water, holds the strainer over it and lets teadrops fall in. She looks up at me. Her face grows a little hard. She clamps the lid back on the pot and says, "It has to steep. It's not ready yet."

They're playing Jane's Addiction's "Ocean Size." One of the anorexic Road Warrior waitresses is mouthing the lyrics as she buses tables in her fuschia camisole and granny heels: "Wish I was Ocean Size/They cannot move you, man, no one tries/No one pulls you back from your hole/Like a tooth aching a jawbone."

I say to Tressa, "Jane's Addiction's so fuckin' cool. One hundred thousand—no million—times cooler than any of the shit the metalheads in my neighborhood listen to."

"Seamus, baby, you gotta get a grip." Tressa's leg is kicking up and down now, up and down. She's shaking. If she catches me lipsynching to "Ocean Size," she'll say I'm not taking shit serious enough. This parting has to be a sweet sorrow, so I keep my trap shut and let the guitars and drums pound down on me like the ocean breaking on an already washed-out shore.

I don't reach for her smokes like I usually do when I want to keep mine from running out. She's already pissed enough. I take one out of my own Marlboro box instead. I won't have many left for New York if I keep on smoking like this. Her elbow's on the table as she presses her forehead with her fingertips, "You know, maybe your parents were right."

"About what?"

"Me being a bad influence."

"What?"

Tressa turns her face back to me, "I keep thinking that if I didn't come around…"

"If you didn't come around, I'd be dead. Remember?" I look deep into her eyes. She's a little wigged-out now, something I've never seen. "There was a mob of skinheads on me, my soul shot out of my fuckin' body. Remember?"

"Okay, okay," she nods, "but I shouldn't've handed you my number."

"Why?"

"That way, you'd be a good little overgrown altar boy, doing all the shit you should be doing."

"And?"

"And you'd be spending your energy on passing tests instead of getting in free to hardcore shows and spending time in places like this."

"And?"

"You wouldn't be getting kicked out of school."

"And?"

"And you wouldn't be following in the footsteps of some hustler who made the cover of *Time*!"

Jane's Addiction is still raging. So are my eyes, which dart straight into hers, "Is selling your ass in a sacristy any better than selling it on the street?"

She puts her hand over her stomach and takes a deep breath, "It's a better ticket to college. You're not going to like me saying this, Seamus, but college *will* get you everywhere you want to go in life. It will. That's why I'm going."

I can't even hold my cigarette anymore. I let the ashtray hold it. "I can't believe I'm hearing this shit," I tell her.

"Look, Seamus," Tressa puts her hand over mine, "All this time, I've been telling you, 'Do life on your own terms.' But that's just junk-rock jargon. It's all talk. There's realpolitik to consider. Know what that means? It means, 'Do what you gotta do to get by.' You gotta compromise, honey. That's what I do. I'm mostly As. That's reality. This, this running off to be that kid on the cover of *Time*, that's not. Or, scratch that: it's *too much* reality. It's more reality than you, my dear, will ever know how to handle. It's slavery."

"Slavery?"

"You'll end up a slave to some pimp and his merry band of pederasts."

"Kirik isn't a slave. He isn't a hooker either. He's an actor."

"Mind telling me the difference?"

"You of all people should know the difference, Tressa. He *was* a hooker, that's true. But now he's an actor. He's not even doing porn. He's getting parts on *Broadway* and they're flying him out to France to do films."

"Stag films."

"I said he's not doing porn! And getting back to what I was saying...if it wasn't for you, I wouldn't even be reading books."

"Yeah, books about smack and sex addicts. So glad I turned you on to that!"

"What? Lawrence, Miller, the Greeks..."

"Hey, I didn't say there was no good shit in the pile, but..." Tressa shakes her head into her hand, "Look, Seamus, I'm not sure those...'role models' are good for you. Maybe for somebody else. Maybe for someone who can handle it. Somebody who takes it with the proverbial grain of salt. Somebody with less to lose."

I pound out my cigarette. "Why are you telling me this?"

"Why am I telling you this?"

"Yeah."

"You got kicked out of school—no, no, *high* school—today. Okay? That's problem number one. And now you're planning to trundle off to the world's roughest city with the lofty goal of working in a *sandwich* shop—a job you couldn't get anyway since you're not sixteen. And you're asking me why I'm telling you this?" Tressa lights up one of my Marlboros now and inhales past her lungs, probably all the way to her pelvis, "Seamus, do you have *any* idea what goes down in New York?"

"Well, I'm about to find out."

"They find kids cut up in dumpsters there every damn day."

"They find kids in dumpsters here every day too. I've managed to avoid it so far."

"Let me rephrase what I just said," she says through gritted teeth. "They find *street* kids in dumpsters there, Seamus. Think, Seamus. Where are you gonna stay? Under the bridge like that actor?"

"No, it's like I've been telling you," I tell her, "that guy Kirik, he went to a place called Oliver's House. They took him in, turned him around. Got him into school."

"So you plan to go to school out there?"

"Fuck no! I'm working in a sandwich shop."

"And then what?"

"Save to go to London when I'm eighteen. Oliver's House gets kids jobs if they don't want to go to school."

"Do you have any idea how expensive New York is?"

"And Oliver's House would give me a free place to crash."

"Do you think you can even get into Oliver's House?"

"Why not? It's not college. It's not like you need a certain GPA. You just gotta be homeless."

"Don't you think they've got a waiting list?"

"Where the fuck are homeless kids gonna wait, Tressa? Do you think they'd turn me away if I showed up begging? I'll go up there, blink some Bambi eyes, tell my sob story, and *voila!*"

"Just like that, huh?"

I sip my cider and smack my lips, "Just like that."

"Well then," she throws her hands in the air and lets them plunk back down on her lap, "There's my answer. You *don't* know shit about the shit that goes down in New York. And here's another news flash: You're not going."

"Oh?"

"No," she says, her crossed leg kicking higher than ever, "You're not going. You're staying with me till we can sort this shit out."

"Whoa-whoa-whoa-wait! I'm staying with you? You and Agatha and Aubrey?"

"And Joshua. Yes."

"Too late. Ruled that one out already."

"Why?"

"Tressa, your folks will cave and turn me right back over to mine."

Tressa looks down at her fingernails, "I can't say that won't happen. But they're also *expert* interventionists. They helped Amnesty International negotiate the release of political prisoners in Mozambique. I'm sure they can open a dialogue between you and your mom and dad."

"You know what happened after my dad busted my lip?" I say. "I told you about it. It was a little over a year ago, a few months before we met."

"Yes," Tressa says, not looking at me. "As I recall, you were up getting a glass of water."

"An iced tea," I say. "It was the middle of the night. I couldn't sleep. My throat was dry as the fuckin' Sahara, so I went to the kitchen to get a glass of iced tea. So I was stirring the mix under the faucet and I heard my dad's footsteps. I didn't turn around. But he put his hand on my shoulder. Not rough. Just normal, like he wanted me to turn around. I thought maybe he needed the faucet. I turned and he sucker punches me right in the fuckin' mouth. Popped me right in the fuckin' mouth.

"Blood gushed down my fuckin' lip. And he just went back to his bedroom, calm as a fuckin' sea breeze, and locked the door. I charged right up and pounded the fuck out of his door. He told my mom not to answer. He ordered her to be quiet. And he stayed quiet too. It was all part of his fuckin' act, see? He was trying to be quiet and calm. That way he could look like the innocent one and I could be the maniac. He was fuckin' l-a-a-pping it up. I pounded and pounded, calling him every motherfuckin' name in the book. I wish I could've broke down the door, but I wasn't strong enough. After a while, I fell to the floor and started crying. When I was all done, I crawled upstairs to my room.

"I went to the police station after school the next day and showed them my mouth. They turned up at our house a couple hours later. Know what he did? He convinced them I had it coming. He said, 'Seamus got up in the middle of the night, looking for a fight. I said, "God Almighty, Seamus, it's 3 a.m. You have school tomorrow. Why aren't you in bed?" and Seamus came at me with the dukes up, saying I couldn't tell him what to do. He took a swing at me so I stood my ground and defended myself.' And the cops came to me and said if all I got was a fat lip, I got off easy. They said they'd put me away if I ever came in lying to them again.

"The next morning, my mom called Dean Russell and had him refer me to a therapist. Not my father to a therapist, mind you. No! Me! Because *I* was fucked up! And she told Russell that, if he sees me with a fat lip, it's because I was going after my dad with a knife. Yeah, she picked up where he left off with his lies. And that's how I met Dr. Strykeroth."

Tressa sighed, "Well, at least something good came out of it. Dr. Strykeroth sounds like a real hunk. And, hey, your dad's insurance is paying for it, so touché to that asshole!"

"After that, my dad tried coming at me one more time, but I beat the living shit out of him. He was going to call the cops, but he would've had to admit to losing a fight. At least kicking his ass kept him from swinging on me again. Now he just calls me puke, punk, and Tinkerbell. That's the level of 'dialogue' at our house, Tressa. And, let me tell you something, the conversation is fucking over."

Tressa pours her tea, looks down and takes a sip. She looks at me after holding the cup in her hands. "Okay," she says, "some things are past repair."

The waiter is setting out dry water glasses next to a pitcher of fresh ice cubes at the counter. Jane's Addiction keeps playing: "Jane says I'm goin' away to Spain/When I get my money saved/Gonna start tomorrow/I'm gonna kick tomorrow/I'm gonna kick tommorrrooow!"

CHESSBOARD TABLE

Winter wind gusts in as I hold the door open. The manager shoots me a dirty look from the counter. I'm going to miss this place.

CHAPTER XXII

Final Session

"So, what do you think Tressa was trying to tell you?" Dr. Strykeroth asks, moving the ashtray closer to me.

I pat the coat pocket where I keep my Marlboros. "No, thanks," I say, "I'm saving them up for out east."

"What did you think Tressa was trying to express to you?"

"She pretty much said I'm crazy. Just like you're saying."

"I'm not saying you're crazy, Seamus. I just don't think you've thought this through."

"Yes, I have. I've told you my whole plan, A to Z, and it's good."

"It's discounting a lot of contingencies."

"A lot of what?"

"Contingencies."

I take out my pen and paper and ask him to spell it for me. "Okay, so, what does it mean when you got a lot of contingencies?"

"A lot of dangers," he says.

I say, "There are dangers everywhere, every day. One time I was standing waiting for the 85A and, right before it came, a fucking crushing gust of wind whipped me right out in front of it. The driver slammed his brakes. Two more feet, I would've been dead. Scared the living fuck out of the driver, the same one who always acts like he wants me dead. But I survived. And that incident changed my whole perspective. Any damn body could cross the street and get hit by a bus, even if they're careful."

Dr. Strykeroth says, "They're a lot less likely to get hit if they're careful."

"I'll be careful. I will. Take my word for it."

"I can't take your word for it, Seamus," Dr. S runs his hand down my leg. "Tressa was right. You have no idea what you'll be running into out there."

"Did my mom call you?"

"Of course she did, Seamus. The school *and* your parents. They're worried sick."

"Do they know I'm here?"

Dr. Strykeroth takes a heaving huff. "No. They don't. I got your message and I lied to them all. So don't go thinking nobody cares about you. I just jeopardized my license covering for you."

"I need some money."

"I thought you got it from Tressa."

"I need more."

"Seamus, you are aware that I'm legally obligated to let your parents and the authorities know if you're planning to run away or hurt yourself in any way?"

"Really?" I say, leaning back. "Dr. Strykeroth, you are aware that I'm legally obligated to let my parents and the authorities know the kind of shit we've been up to in this office?"

Dr. Strykeroth draws back and tries reasoning with me like he's Jimmy Carter or something. "I'm begging you to reconsider your plans, Seamus. It's all fine and good to say, 'Fuck you. I'm going,' *when you're old enough*. But, if you go, I'll be sitting here day after day wondering where you are, how you are, and I'm sure I'll be fielding calls from your mom and dad and the police. I'll have to lie. That'll make me an accessory."

"You won't have to lie, Dr. S. I'll drop my mom a postcard from New York. It'll say, 'I'm fine, I'm on the east coast, don't look for me.' I'll even throw in, 'Dr. S doesn't know where I am either.'"

"But, Seamus, it's more than that." He drops his head almost to his knees, looks back up at me and says, "I'll miss you."

"Oh, Dr. S., I'm sure you'll meet plenty of other suicidal outcasts who smoke and swear a lot."

"Oh, I meet *plenty* of those, but you're different, Seamus."

"I've been hearing that shit my whole life. 'I'm *different*,' whatever the fuck that means. And Tressa's got it in my head that I'm something special too. Well, if I am, now's the time to go out there and prove it."

"Doing what? Busking poems on the street?"

"Maybe. We'll see."

"How far do you think that'll get you, Seamus?"

"We'll see. But I need a little more money first."

"And where do you think you'll get that?"

"How much is our little secret worth to you?"

We walk through the underground shops on North Wacker Drive. He goes to the cash machine, withdraws $300 and slips it into my coat pocket. I tell him, "Thanks. Look, I don't mean to take advantage of you. I just gotta get away. What we had…well, you've helped me a lot."

He looks at me, "Do you want me to recommend you to that Oliver's House?"

"Are you prepared to testify against my parents if the state asks?" He sighs and nods. I say, "Look, don't worry. I'll get in there on my own."

He says, "Well, maybe I can get away and make sure you're set up there. If you can wait a few days."

I shake my head, "And what about your wife and kids?"

"It'll just be a few days," he says. "I'll say it's a business trip. If you can wait a few days."

"I can't. Sorry."

FINAL SESSION

"Well, maybe after you get there," he says, "just to see that you're all settled in and in good shape."

I give him a hug and he hugs me, and I can tell he's looking around, careful to make it all look legal. I wave good-bye as I walk to the L at Washington.

"Where are you going now?" he yells out.

"Home," I yell back, "and remember our deal!"

CHAPTER XXIII
Previews and Coming Aggressions

I know before it even happens that this is a scene I'll never forget. My mind previewed it frame by frame on the 85A back to Ponchitrain Street. All the opening scenes are about to reel before me in 3-D, living Technicolor. I'm opening the door at 6:30 p.m. to find Dad sitting at the head of the kitchen table with a scotch and soda. He twists his wrist up and takes a long, deep look at his watch. Just like that slowly-I-turn-step-by-step-inch-by-inch ham on *The Three Stooges*, Dad turns in his chair and shoots me a look. He's the matador, stroking his lance and peering right between the eyes of a snorting bull who's pawing the dust and turning its horns down at him.

Only I'm no snorting bull. I'm not pawing the dust or turning my horns down. The only reason bulls charge is they think it might be their last shot at living. But I took him once, I can take him again.

Oh, but, fuck! There's something my mental previews never fuckin' showed me. With one long scissor-legged side step, Brody enters the kitchen from the hallway. His eyes are just as predatory as Johnny Rotten's were on that sticker in my locker, but, unlike Johnny, there's no laughter and no smile under his predatory peepers.

Dad has his lance up and ready, and, with Brody behind him, he's got enough brawn to stick it right through me. I start walking to the middle of the room. It's only now I realize I haven't eaten a thing all day, except a hot apple cider and Marlboro smoke, and none of that shit's food. My head's growing dizzy. My heartbeat's doubling, tripling, quadrupling. I puff out my chest and step right toward Dad and Brody, but my steps grow slower. I stumble. I stumble. Before either one can lay a finger on me, I hit the floor with a thud.

I spy a monk. An Asian monk. A Buddhist monk, maybe. He's bald. He's wearing orange robes that fit loosely on his bony frame. He sits on brambles in a forest. He's got his legs folded. He's silent. All he's doing is breathing. The deer and the squirrels and chipmunks come up and nuzzle him. Nothing stirs him. He stays in meditation.

I walk up to the monk. I'm in orange robes too. I do for him what I do for my bedroom poster of Johnny Rotten. I get on my knees and bow. He sits in silence. I sit back on my calves, awaiting his instructions. He says nothing. The forest fades away. So do the animals, so does the monk, and so do I. Everything fades to black. There's nothing. Nothing. And then a single star. The star shines and shines and I hear the monk's voice repeat one word twice, "Unbind. Unbind." That's all he says. That one word, twice. And the star goes out again and everything goes black again. I'm engulfed in blackness again and even my mind fades away now.

My body jerks. I feel a steel claw yanking me up by my scalp. I hear a buzz. A voice: "Errrrugh! All this *shit* he puts in his hair! Here let's run some more water, see if we can get some more of this crap out." I know that voice. It's Brody. I open my eyes and see our yellow bathroom wall tiles. I see the copper floor tiles. I feel my hips being jammed into the sink. Dad's on one side, pressing me facedown into the sink. Brody is shoving my head under the faucet. I twist, I squirm, I jerk. I scream, "Fuuuuucckkkk awwwwffff!" Brody smacks the back of my head, the water makes his whack even louder. He hollers into my eardrum, "Shut up your mouth!" like a mobster from one of his favorite fuckin' *Godfather* movies. He says to Dad, "He's up now. He'll be easier to move, but it'll be harder to keep him down. He's a squirmy worm." Water is washing all over my head. I try to haul off and smack them, but my arms won't budge. I look down to the side and see they've tied my hands behind my back with Mom's bathrobe belt.

Brody starts scrubbing Head & Shoulders into my hair as he holds me under the faucet by the neck. Detergent goop drops into my eyes and I howl, "It's in my fucckkking eyyyyessss."

Dad digs his knee into my back, "Watch your mouth. You're watching your mouth from now, you little punk. I won't have it! And they're not having it either where you're going!"

"Yeah, you little asshole," Brody pipes up, and Dad does not correct his language.

Dad's knee comes out of my back. My forehead is pinned against the bottom of the sink. I scream, "Fuuuccckkk youuuu!" I scream it and scream it as the bathtub water starts sounding behind me. Soon a full pitcher of water comes whooshing down onto my head, and the Head & Shoulders goes whooshing down my scalp and down the drain. Brody keeps washing more and more shampoo out with the faucet water. "That oughta do it," Brody tells Dad.

Dad yanks the robe-belt back; my wrists burn and my shoulder damn near dislocates. I scream and scream. With one hand, Dad throws his arm around my throat. "Shut up," he seethes. I'm gasping for breath. Brody throws a towel over my face. Dad takes his arm out from around my neck and pushes me forward over the sink. Brody claws his fingers into my scalp through the towel as he dries off my hair. He takes the towel off, grabs a handful of my hair and holds me up to the three-panel bathroom mirror. "See!" he says. "See what you get for your bullshit?" I see my hair in the mirror. Huge clumps and patches are missing. My hair is all over the fuckin' sink, toilet, floor, walls, and even the mirror. From the hairline to about the middle of my head, my hair is shaved off in zigzags. A lot of matted hair hangs off the edges.

I scream again and fall over, hoping I can fucking re-faint and revisit my monk. Much as I'd like to faint again and be unconscious for all the shit that's happening, I can't. My adrenaline just goes on roaring as Dad and Brody press my face into the mirror. Dad tightens the robe belt around my wrists. They both arch my body back as Brody lifts my chin with his left palm. The clippers roar in Brody's hand as he shears off the rest of my hair. I want the neighbors to call the cops. I want to scream till the mirrors, windows, and walls break.

But something else comes over me. I start going limp. I drop my head and close my eyes. Half my nerves are relaxing on cue. The rest are roiling with rage. I want Dad and Brody's blood. I want them lying dead as the hair on the floor. But I don't want juvey. Not for them. It's like the monk told me: "Unbind." They got my hands tied behind my back, but there's still time for freedom. And how did the monk do it? He sat still. Yeah, but, shit, he wasn't going through all this shit, he was sitting in a peaceful forest. Well, maybe there were samurais in those hills above him, but they probably backed off, didn't they? His vibe was too powerful. I know. I felt it. I hang my head. I feel like Jesus at his last gasp on the cross, only I'm no saint. Not being a fucking saint's what got me in all this shit in the first place. But I'm not dying as a martyr either, not if I can help it. My blood is going faint but something else is keeping the rest of me awake and alive.

Dad and Brody push me into the kitchen. My hands are still tied. I'm still wearing what I wore to school—the black combats, black pants, and purple flannel. I don't have any hair now, except there's still a lot of fuzz tickling the back of my neck from the buzz cut. It itches like fuckin' hell but I'm not about to ask for a shower. The way the two of them are going at it with me, I'd hate to see what they'd do if I got naked.

The whole time all the shit was going on in the bathroom,

Mom was in the kitchen. She's standing by the lazy Susan now. Right by the table next to her there's a suitcase and Dad's old USMC knapsack. She says nothing but I know they've packed my bags for me. Mom stares at me. I can tell she's feeling sorry for how I lost my hair but proud that I'm paying for the dishonor I've done my mother and father. Still, she cries.

Brody twists the robe-belt on my wrists. "Mom packed up some of your shit," he says, spitting his words into my ear. "You're heading to Wisconsin tomorrow morning. St. John's Military Academy. Better learn to be a man quick, Seamus. They tear sissies like you apart up there."

"Enough, Brody," Mom says, covering her crying eyes.

Hunger washes the blood out of my head as my legs start giving out again.

Dad comes from behind Brody. He stands above me, "So, anything you want to say for yourself?"

I say in a weak voice, "I need something to eat. I haven't eaten all day."

Brody tugs the robe-belt back, "Oh, so now we gotta feed you?"

"You got a lot of questions to answer, punk," Dad growls. "You're not eating a goddamn crumb till you answer them."

"How can I answer if I pass out again?" I say. My legs start crumbling under me. Brody picks me back up and plunges me back on my feet.

Mom says, "I'll get some fruit, make him a fruit salad."

Brody scoffs, "Ah, fruit for the fruit." He yanks out a chair and pushes me into it. I keep looking down. Brody peels a banana and shoves it deep into the back of my mouth, "You gotta eat, huh? Here. Here! Eat this. I know how much you luuuv having things like this in your mouth." I'm choking and gagging.

"Brody, pleeeezze!" Mom begs. Brody pushes the banana

a little deeper against my tonsils before pulling it out. Some of it breaks off in my mouth. I lean forward and cough and spit out banana chunks. I cough for at least a minute as tears I don't want to shed rush down my face. Before I'm done coughing, Mom says, "Brody, please. Untie him. Untie him! Please. Let him use his hands. He needs to eat."

"He's sneaky, Mom," Brody says, giving a push to the back of my head. "He might grab a knife or something."

"Now please, Brody," Mom pleads. "He hasn't eaten all day. He can't even stand up on his own. He's no threat."

Brody whips the banana peel on the table. As he yanks up the robe-belt and starts untying my wrists, he yells at her, "This is no time to be cutting him slack, Mom. You've done way too much of that." He puts his spitting face in mine again, holding up his index finger, "One false move. Just *one* false move!"

Brody puts both my hands flat on the table. "Keep 'em where we can see 'em!" he says. So I keep my palms on the table and look down like a POW who senses it's better to just take the cane than howl in protest. For once, there's only silence as Mom cuts up an apple and peels two tangerines and a banana. Mom puts a fruit salad in front of me and a fork and napkin. I start spearing fruit and gobbling it down. Mom looks closer at my shaved head and catatonic face. She mixes me an iced tea and puts it in front of me. She gets me a Danon blueberry yogurt and a little bowl of Quaker Oats to mix into it. While I pour granola into the blueberry yogurt, Brody walks out of the room with all the knives and scissors in the kitchen. When I'm done, I wipe my mouth one last time and run my hand over my stubbly head. Brody comes back into the room, and I place my palms back down on the table again.

Mom clears away the bowl, the Dannon container, and my half-finished iced tea. Dad takes a seat to my left and Brody to my right. As their faces close in on me, I keep my calm, hoping it'll spill over.

"Now *talk*!" Dad says, "Hey, look up. Look up! Look at me when I'm speaking to you."

I look at him and shrug. "What do you want me to say? That everything at school didn't happen? I don't know what you heard, but I'm sure it's true, so—" I turn my palms toward the ceiling but put them back on the table like a good little POW.

"I was all over town looking for you," Dad growls. "I looked all over 18th Street. All over UIC. Your mother was beside herself. I…I don't even know how to describe how low you've sunk this time, Seamus. Lower than we ever thought you could go and that was already pretty goddamned low."

Once again, I say nothing, I just hang my head. Brody pounds his fist on the table, "He said *look* at him when he's talking to you." I roll my head back up.

"The dean told us you told him you were going to your doctor today," Dad says. "I called your shrink. He said you didn't have an appointment. Is that true?" I look Dad in the eye. I nod. Dad grunts out a chuckle, "There wasn't, huh? Well, who'd you run to then?"

"No one," I say.

"Not even that nigger girl," he says. I just shake my head no. "No contact with her at all?" I shake my head no. "You left your phone book in your drawer, you know." He fishes my little black book out of his pocket and whips it in front of me, "Not many numbers in there besides…what, what's her made-up, negro name? Tressa, is it? Bessa? Odessa? Whatever you call her, we called her parents."

My heart pounds. "And what'd they tell you?"

A smile spreads across his face, "Her folks said you were a nice boy and that they could never imagine you making a scene and breaking out of school like you did. Not a nice boy like you. They also said they were going to call their daughter to see if she'd seen you." Dad pauses and mock-nods in his typical fuckface fashion. "They said they were calling her beeper. Now, what kind of girl carries a beeper, Seamus?"

I don't answer. I just ask, "And what did Tressa tell them?" Even all the new food in my stomach won't keep me from fainting if I find out Tressa came clean.

For what seems like a full minute, Dad lets the suspense build. Then he tells me, "Her parents called me at the office... Tressa claims she hadn't seen or heard from you either." I nod like Tressa has just vindicated me with the gospel truth; inside I couldn't be more relieved that she's still my lying angel. "So where were you?" Dad asks.

I just say, "Walking around."

"For eight hours?" Brody says. I nod. "Where?" Brody asks, looking for lies in the whites of my eyes.

I say, "I walked to State Street and up to Plymouth Court."

"That's funny," Dad counters, "the dean said you ran toward Ashland Avenue."

"I did," I answer, calm as a Valium freak. "I walked around UIC. Then east on Van Buren to State and south to 13th Street. I tooled around Plymouth Court."

"What's around Plymouth Court?" Brody asks, his eyes still searching mine.

"Nothing. So then, I went to Wicker Park. Then I walked into Lincoln Park."

"Through Cabrini Green?" Brody shouts. "Christ, your death wish never quits, does it?"

"Why not," I shrug. "I got nothing to lose." In truth, I'd never fuckin' set foot in Cabrini, not even with the fuckin' National Guard surrounding me.

"That's the one true thing you've said," Dad tells me. "You've got nothing to lose, now that you lost your last shot at

Xavier."

Dad goes on for a long while about how he made a conference call with Dean Russell to a Father Colletti at St. John's Military Academy. Before he entered the seminary, Father Colletti was an army sergeant in the Korea War—and he hasn't lost his commando touch since. Some of his staff will be pulling into our driveway at exactly 0700 hours tomorrow. Looks like they'll take me after all! "I told Father Colletti that whatever he wants to do with you is fine with me," Dad says. "I wash my hands of you. This is what your little rebellion has gotten you, Seamus. You're none of my concern now."

My breath runs a little short ,but I breathe deep from the bottom belly, the way Tressa taught me, the night the skinheads beat me half to death. My body begins to relax, even as it tenses up. "Unbind," I repeat the monk's word, "Unbind." Unfortunately, I repeat the monk's word aloud.

"Excuse me?" Brody says. "What did you just say?"

"Nothing," I say.

Brody kicks his chair over, picks me up by my shirt, and crashes my back against the wall, and, with a shit-eating grin like the puppet in *Magic*, says, "Don't *lie* to me, you little faggot! Tell me what you said."

Even as he pins me up against the wall, I manage to stay limp. My dead weight weighs on his arms. He struggles to keep me suspended above ground. Not struggling causes my neck to fall into the cleft between my open collar button and my second button. My voice crackles as I repeat the word I said at the table, "Unbi-akakakkkk."

"What?" he says, letting me back down on the ground.

I rub my throat as I repeat to him: "Unbind."

"Unbind?" he says, making a face while he gets back up in my face. He pushes me against the wall, "What does 'unbind' mean? Huh? Is that one of your stupid blame-society songs?

You're saying you're 'bound'? " He slaps my face. "Huh? You think you're bound? Think you're one of the oppressed, you whiny little weasel!"

"Well, what do you call all this?" I say. "What do you call what you're doing to me?"

"You built your own dungeon," he says.

"My own dungeon?"

"Yeah, you little shit, you built it with shit grades and a shit attitude. But you say you're 'bound'?"

I stay motionless like the monk. I say, "You're word, not mine."

"No, you little faggot," Brody slaps me hard across the face and pokes his finger hard into my sternum, "your word. Yours. They're probably from one of your moronic Mohawk songs." Mom screams for Brody to stop. Dad tells Mom to shut up, and Brody says to me, "You can't listen to those moron songs in military school, you know, Seamus."

"I didn't tie my own hands behind my back, Brody. I didn't force my own head under the sink. I didn't shave off my own hair while I was passed out. That was all shit you and Dad did to *me*." Brody stops. He says nothing. He pounds his fist into my eye. As I fall over, Mom shouts, "No, Brody, no!" Again, Dad tells her to shut up and stay out of it. He even tells her to leave the room, but she's on the floor crying and Dad's too hooked on what's going on to push her into the dining room. I stand back on my feet, and, even though my own eye is throbbing, I look straight into Brody's eye.

Brody shoves his face in mine, grinding his teeth to yellowing bits. "You're a disgrace, Seamus. A goddamned, limp-wristed disgrace. The first O'Grady *ever* to get kicked out of Xavier. The first faggot O'Grady too." He slaps my head again and starts waving his fingers toward himself, trying to tell me to bring it on so I can give him cause to smack me harder.

Suddenly, I'm thinking, "Fuck the monk." Shit, at this point, even the monk would say fuck the monk. As loud as I fuckin' can, I shout right in Brody's face, "I DIDN'T TIE MYSELF UP, BRODY! You and Dad did. You both looked like you were cumin' all over yourselves the whole time! But get off on it while you still can, asshole. The minute I send the Illinois State Bar snapshots of the shiner you just gave me, they'll rip your law license into fuckin' confetti right before your fuckin' eyes." I can feel the monk tug on me now. He wants me to go back to being limp.

Brody laughs and hacks a glob of spit right on to my nose. As it slides down and drips on to my chin, he laughs some more and says, "You think the state bar's gonna take your word over mine, you little pansy? Well that's the funniest fuckin thing I've heard *all* day." Brody pulls his fist back and I see it coming right back at my face in super slow motion, time enough for me to duck. Above my head, as his fist meets the wall, I hear a crush of knuckles and a snap of bones. "AHHHHHHH-OWWWW!" he howls. Mom and Dad rumble forward. "AHHHHH-OWWWW!" he shrieks and shrieks and shrieks. "AHHHHH-OWWWW!" He holds his dangling arm, screaming and screaming and rubbing it as he steps back and falls backward on to the table, sending the table collapsing and crashing to the floor.

Mom throws her body over Brody's body and the broken table. One minute ago, she was crying for me. Now she looks up and cries, "*This* is the trouble you cause. You reprobate!" She cries over Brody's squirming body like fuckin' Mary Magdalene and Martha shrouding Jesus.

I stand calm with my palms to the ceiling, saying, "All I did was duck."

"Should we call an ambulance?" she cries to my father.

Dad says, "No. I'll take him to the emergency room."

"Go to your room!" Mom thrashes her pointed finger out at me. "Go to your room, *now!*"

PREVIEWS AND COMING AGGRESSIONS

Dad puts his arm around Brody and says to me, "Start writing your apology note to Father Mahoney and the dean. We'll deal with the rest later." I want to say, "A fuckin' apology letter? What am I, fucking six years old?" But I don't. I'm just glad to see Brody squirming. Maybe I can break his other arm too. But I don't have time for that. Besides, I owe him a thank-you. With this new bruise on my face, I'll be in like Flynn at Oliver's House. Brody stands there, doubling over in pain, crying, cursing my name, calling me faggot. Mom takes Brody out to the car. She gives him calming shhhs so Mr. Adamczak and the rest of the neighbors won't hear him carrying on. As Dad grabs his coat and car keys, I walk to the other side of the kitchen and pick up the luggage and knapsack they packed for me. "Where the *hell* do you think you're going?" Dad shouts on his way out the door.

I raise my shoulders and say, "My room. I gotta get my beauty sleep. I got some soldiers coming for my ass tomorrow." I blow a kiss.

"You little shit! Father Colletti's gonna hear about this. Your brother left a meeting with the heads of Merrill Lynch to help us deal with the mess you made!"

"All I did was duck, Dad. All I did was duck."

"You little shit!" Dad says again.

"Dad," I smile, "Brody's making a scene outside. Don't worry. I'll be here when you get back." I take the bags upstairs.

From the upstairs bathroom window, I see Dad starting his Corsica. Mom's in the backseat with Brody. The car pulls out. I walk over to the sink and look in the mirror. I have no fucking hair. Dad hasn't shaved my head since I was ten. It's not a bad look for me. I kind of like it. I see the pink beginnings of a bruise forming under my right eye, though.

I strip out of my clothes, get in the shower and wash off all the shorn hair stuck to my neck, chest, and back. I stay under the soothing warm water for about twenty minutes, crying

203

my eyes out. When I'm done, I step out and look at myself in the full-length mirror. There are many more bruises forming on my shoulders, chest, hips and back. I have rope burns on my wrists too, and there are marks on my neck from when I fell between the buttons of my shirt. But at least neither one of my arms is broken.

CHAPTER XXIV
11:08 pm

The lights go on in my room. Under the muffle of my shag carpet, I hear feet shuffling and the floor creaking. Puddles falls off my legs, but stretches, yawns, and nestles down again, curling one paw under her white-striped, gray breast. I look over to see Mom looking at the suit on my dresser. It's all laid out for the morning. She looks over to me and sees me looking back at her. Her face is a mix of emotions, ones I've never seen her wear all at once.

My alarm clock says it's 11:08 p.m. "I have to be up early," I tell her.

"I know," she says, calmly.

"Can you holler at me about Brody later?" I ask. "I gotta get some sleep if I'm gonna drop and give the sergent twenty when he gets here."

She walks over to my bedside, "I'm not going to yell at you. I just want to apologize."

"Apologize?"

"Yes," she nods, "I called you a reprobate."

"Yes, you did."

She stiffens and breathes, "What your brother did was not right, and I know I've been one to look the other way. I'm admitting that now. And I'm sorry. Oh, Seamus, those bruises!" She comes closer.

"No, Mom, don't," I say. "Don't. Please."

"But...you don't think anything's broken, do you?"

I was doing fine before she said that. Now my face starts throbbing for the first time since I lay down. "No," I say, "and if anything's wrong, I'll take care of it."

"Seamus," she says, "your father's old."

"I know, I know. He's old school, and I know that the nuns used to kick the shit out of him. And I know his folks believed in corporal punishment and keeping him in lockstep."

"No, Seamus," she said, "I didn't say he was 'old school.' I said he's old. He's old. He can only take so much."

I lift myself up on my elbows, "*He* can only take so much? Him? What about me? I'm the one taking the fuckin' heat for Brody."

"Please, Seamus," she says, holding up her palm. "Language!—I'm not expressing myself clearly. Forgive me. I'm a little disconcerted by the events of today. What I mean to say is, your father is old, so please don't make an issue out of tonight."

"What?"

"Please don't try to get him or your brother arrested. I beg of you. Don't try to get the counselors at your new school to take legal action. Just go your way and let them go theirs. You'll be up at St. John's and they won't be bothering you. But I want to spare your father any talk of lawyers and fines and possible sentencing."

"Gee," I say, "not even court-ordered therapy? For him, this time, I mean?"

"He doesn't believe he has a problem," Mom says putting her palm up again. "I know! I know! He has faults, we all do, but there's more to it than that. Now would be a good time to tell you that your father's blood pressure has already reached a critical stage, and the onocologist will be screening for prostate cancer on Thursday."

"Well, Brody's not old," I say. "Here, look at my eye. He's young enough to plant a good right hook."

"Just—please, Seamus. For me."

"No."

"Just," she says, "think it over. We love you, Seamus."

"Bullshit."

"We just don't understand you," she cries.

"Well, like, I don't understand Polish either, right? That doesn't mean I go kick the shit out of the Czernovskis whenever I hear them talking. I don't try bullying them into doing things my way."

"It's not the same thing."

"Yes, it is."

"Seamus, it's just…apples don't understand oranges."

"Then stop thinking you know what's best for me," I say. "If you knew what's best for me, you wouldn't've sent me to Xavier."

She nods and turns her palms up, "Maybe you're right."

"And you wouldn't've kept imposing religion on me."

"That I don't regret," she points at me hard. "You need guidance, young man. And I believe in my heart of hearts that the Church has all the right stuff for saving souls."

"You don't even know what's best for my fuckin' body," I say, pointing to the biggest bruise on my face, right under my eye. "But now you're a fuckin' expert on how to save my fuckin' soul!"

"Language!" she rages. Puddles backs up on the bed.

"And now you're sending me to St. John's so I can get beat up and put down even more."

"I didn't want to!" she cries back. "It was your father's decision. And when you walked out of school today, I'm sorry, but there was little that I could do in your defense. You've been exhibiting extreme behavior, Seamus."

"So have you! You, Dad, and Brody! But somehow you're all exempt."

"I'm not exempt!" she squeals. "I'm apologizing! I'm sorry, Seamus. I'm sorry I let so much happen to you. I've let so much happen that you've been acting out and shattering all of your prospects. And, sweetheart, you're so much smarter and more capable than your record shows."

"So you're sending me to sergeants who'll beat the shit out of me? Is that gonna get me a better record?"

"I'm sorry," she cries some more. "I didn't want it to come to this."

"And where's Dad right now, Mom? Why isn't he up here saying he's sorry?"

She shakes her head sorrowfully, "He doesn't think he has anything to be sorry for."

"Do you agree?"

"It's your father's house, Seamus," she tells me.

"That's not an answer. Did you *tell* him you disagree?"

"Not right away," she shakes her head, looking down. "Brody was under morphine and I waited for Silvia to step out for some fresh air first."

"What did you say?"

"I said that, if someone throws a punch, the other person should duck."

"And what did he say?"

She shrugs, "He said, 'Don't let me hear you talk that way again.'"

"You let that bastard talk like that to you?"

"He's your father, Seamus!" she shakes with venom. "His parents were married one year before his birth. He's completely legitimate and I won't have you insinuating otherwise."

I roll my eyes, "Please, Mom. You know what I mean. Are you going to take that abuse from him?"

"It's not abuse," she proclaims, pointing one resolute finger to the sky like her statue of Archangel Michael.

"You've said that about a lot of things happening under this roof, Mom. Let's not forget, you came in here asking me to help you with yet another cover-up."

She clasps her hands together in prayer, "Just please, Seamus. I beg of you. Don't make an ordeal out of tonight."

"I can't promise I won't."

She runs her hand over my head. She wants to run her fingers through my hair but only finds bristles. "Just go to your new school. Make it through the next couple years. Do well, so you'll have options. Then your life is all yours."

"It's all mine now. But I wouldn't worry. The sergeant guys won't listen to a punk like me even if I do pipe up."

"I'm sorry," she tells me. "I'll miss you." She won't stop trailing her fingers across the top of my head. I stomach letting her do it while she still can. She covers her eyes and starts crying, "I love your brother and I love you, and I just want the two of you to be safe and happy."

Tears flood out of her eyes. I just lie still. Puddles rubs against Mom's arm. Mom laughs and says, "And Puddles wants you to be safe too!"

"You'll take good care of her?"

"I will," she nods. Her eyes and face are puffy with tears now. "I want you to be happy, so I'll make sure she's happy." Mom bends down and kisses my forehead, "And, before Father Colletti's men come tomorrow, I'll pull them aside and tell them to do a mom a favor and not go so hard on her son—"

"Like Dad told them to."

"They'll listen to moms first," she says, kissing my forehead one last time and holding my chin in her hand. "We have that kind of power." She pets Puddles and turns back to me again, "Good night, sweetheart. See you in the morning."

She walks to the other side of the room, turns out the lights, and shuts the door behind her.

CHAPTER XXV

2:35 am

I'm in the backyard. I'm glad I stayed for her to find me in bed. If I'd left earlier, she could've called the cops when there were more of them on duty to stop me. I've got two yards to cross—ours and the Czernovski's. The cold pierces my face and ears and I'm bald! I'll never wear a fuckin' winter cap, though. I look like dog shit in them.

Unlike yesterday morning, though, I made sure to wear longjohns. There's no forgettin' those today. There's no 85A until 5:20 a.m. I'll have to walk the three miles through the Forest Preserve to Jefferson Park. I've done it before. On its own, it's no insurmountable task, but it comes pretty damned close when you got this two-ton USMC sack on your shoulder. I got it packed up with all the shit I need.

The moon is ivory and silver and full of shadows, but, at the same time, it's casting a strong light on the banks of snow covering the yards. Shit, look at me! I'm the worst runaway ever! With no time to lose on my great fuckin' escape, I still stop for poetic contemplations.

My adredaline is surging like whitewater now. The whole trick is to keep going. I hop the fence into the Czernovski's backyard. I hope Grandpa Czernovski doesn't have insomnia. He probably does, though. I can't imagine anyone who did time in a concentration camp sleeps so good, even forty, fifty years later. I hope he's not up, flashing back to the Warsaw roundups while he watches me make off with my haul. I hope to fuck he doesn't whip out a shotgun. There was a time, not too long ago, when I would've hoped he'd gun me down. But now I taste freedom and I'm not letting a concentration-camp crazy ruin my good time.

I hope the crunch-crunch-crunch doesn't stir the other neighbors out of their sleep either. I don't see into any bedrooms from the backyard. People in Jarvis Park keep their living room curtains wide open at night. They think crime can't touch them, not unless it's someone like Andy Payne using their windows for target practice. I myself can't wait to crash in cardboard boxes in all those bad neighborhoods, where people vandalize for better reasons than just that they think you're a faggot. I keep my eyes fixed on the parkway under the streetlight opposite the Czernovski's gangway. It's shining like the Holy Dove, not the Holy Grail. No, that's all the way over in fuckin' London. But once I reach the streetlamp, I'll at least be out of sight of Mom's kitchen.

I'm walking the same route to Jefferson Park as the 85A now. You'd think it could do me a fuckin' favor and just take an early spin down Lehigh for old time's sake. I never thought I'd be doing my last waltz down Lehigh on foot, and I never thought I'd be dancing it so soon. Everything in Jarvis Park stands in full relief, now that I'm not just watching it from a window seat. It all looks so familiar, so familial, all this shit I've tried so hard to put behind me. All thesee dollhouses look so pretty now.

But I like slums. Tressa and de Sade taught me so well. So did you, Johnny. I can't fucking wait to meet you, Johnny boy!

CHAPTER XXVI
Conclusions

It's 6:51. My Amtrak's pulling out right on schedule on Track 9. Right on schedule. This is much more fuckin' efficient than the fuckin' 85A! The wheels are rolling, rolling...and rolling... and—I'm in the clear! In the clear! Thank God Almighty, I am IN THE CLEAR! My USMC sack is stowed away all snug in the compartment above. The train's crowded but, unlike the L, I get a guaranteed seat and no one's come to claim the seat next to me. I can stretch my legs out over Seat B, Row 3, put on my head phones, press play on PiL (*"Don't like the look of this old town/What goes up must come down/Character is lost and found/On an unfamiliar playing ground/Get out of my world!"*), and I don't have to worry about any boring old farts riding with me twenty hours, trying to drag out of me why I'm headed where I'm headed and what's with all the fuckin' bruises on my face.

I'll probably have to turn my face to the window, though, when the ticket taker gets here. I can't make it too obvious I'm trying not to lock eyes with him. Don't wanna make him suspicious. I just gotta hand over my ticket, smile and turn my head lazily to my right while he clips my one-way, puts it under the metal prong, and moves on to the seats behind me. I don't want him looking at my bruises. Then again, when he sees my new 'do, he'll probably think I'm some badass skinhead and run as fast as his little feet can fucking carry him. I should milk that shit for all it's worth in New York while my face is still black and blue.

If I'm as lucky as I have been so far, the ticket taker

CONCLUSIONS

won't be raising any flags on my age. Why should he? I mean, I can probably pass for eighteen, and, anyway, lots of kids travel alone on trains if they're, like, going back to boarding school after winter break or meeting relatives who just became their guardians after their parents got killed in car crashes or some shit like that. The cashier at Union Station never gave me any shit about my age. Never carded me. Never even fuckin' looked at me. I was so fuckin' afraid I'd have to bribe her hundreds more dollars. That would've been a big-ass bite out of my budget, man. But, no, she just yawned, took my money, guzzled a thermos of coffee, and printed out my ticket.

It was about 4:30 when I got to Union Station. All the doors were locked, so I waited out by the loading docks. The bums were sound asleep. Some of them might've been dead. I wanted to get the fuck out of there, but I thought, hey, I'm one of them now. I tried hanging out just for practice for the Lower East Side or wherever else I might wind up in New York, but I didn't have blankets or cardboard houses like the bums got. The Chicago wind kept crashing in as usual and my new bald head and ears were fuckin' burning cold, and I thought, hey, why fuckin' freeze to death when I got cash on me?

I remembered that Billy Goat's is open all night at Jackson and Wells, so I walked over there for an Earl Grey, but they didn't have Earl Grey so I had to settle for an Orange Pekoe. Fuckin' philistines! I thought I might run into a reporter like Royko inside, but I guess not even that crusty old sod is up that early. The Greek guys behind the counter were all howling and carrying on together—so fuckin' early in the morning too!— with all these words and gestures that were all fuckin' Greek to me while I sat there yawning and shivering on the edge of my future, which I'm not shivering about now that I'm on a train that's actually in motion. At about six o'clock, I unrolled my bills to plunk down a dollar for my Orange Pekoe and plain donut and

213

took out a fifty and a ten for a one-way ticket to Manhattan.

But I'm getting way the fuck ahead of myself. Something else happened on the L before Union Station, before we even hit Addison. It was still coal black and starry out, and I started feeling a little wistful for all the neighborhoods I'd be leaving behind on both sides of the Kennedy Expressway. Why I'd miss them, I don't fuckin' know; but, then again, I bet even ex-cons miss their old cells sometimes. Plus cold always makes my ass sleepy, and sleepiness always puts me in sad, sentimental moods. Pulling out of Montrose, I kept slapping myself awake, not wanting to wake up all the way out in fuckin' Forest Park or something and miss my train to New York.

Not even slapping my own face was enough to wake me the fuck up until we hit the next stop, Irving Park, and a guy got on wearing a brown workman's uniform. Lots of other guys from factories were on the L wearing the same kind of shit, but this guy was also wearing a black leather jacket, a black porkpie hat and some kind of black, steel-toed boots. He also had fingerless black gloves on and was warming his fingertips on the piping-hot Styrofoam cup of coffee he came in carrying and blowing on and yawning over, probably one he bought from one of the little Pakistani canteens under the L. I liked the way he carried himself. I liked everything about him, except the factory duds of course. I kept my eye on him. I saw the Murphy's Law logo on the arm of his leather jacket and stood up to look at his face. It was Colby! It was Colby! After all this fuckin' time, I was on the L with fuckin' Colby!

And he didn't have no Blondie or Leopard Print or Sid Vicious/Billy Idol or any other possee with him. I could get him alone. I myself was looking pretty fucking ridiculous with an overstuffed USMC bag at my feet and the musty black ski coat from our attic, 'cuz Dad finally threw out my overcoat while I was passed out. I'm sure I looked even stupider, getting up and lugging everything over to the other side of the car to go sit by him. At least I had my combats on and my hair would be growing back into something that'd look like his in just about two months, tops. At least I could show him that fuckin' much. Colby was right in front of me. It's almost like I conjured him for this one event—this one last shot at us becoming Sid and Johnny or Huck and Jim.

I sat in the two-seater, just perpendicular to his window seat. ('Perpendicular,' see? I did pick up some shit in geometry!) Colby looked at me but just like he'd look at anyone else who was sitting there, staring him up and down. It was pretty fuckin' clear he didn't recognize me. He looked like he wasn't sure whether I wanted to kiss him or kill him. He was still a little red-eyed too and kept blowing on and slipping hot trickles from his steaming coffee cup.

The cuff of his leather jacket slipped down. Just below the hem of his glove, I saw he had a tattoo of a Gorgon. It wasn't there the last time I saw him. I know. I saw both his wrists when I first looked him up, down, and all-around over a year ago.

I knew this was do or die, so I didn't have time to play it cool. "Hey!" I said. He pulled back with a sort of what-the-fuck-you-talkin'-to-me-for face. I decided to play my one and only hand. "Remember me?"

He shook his head and looked out the window, "I'm not that way, okay?"

"No. I…we met before. I had hair back then." I went on and asked if he remembered the night Narc pulled him off the train.

"Oh, yeah!" he said, turning back to look at me. "Yeah. Man, that was a while ago. Were you with us?" His voice was a lot deeper and more gravelly than I remembered it. He talked like a fuckin' Teamster.

"No," I said, "I just saw it happen."

"Oh," he replied. "Yeah, I don't remember much about that night. I think I was trippin'." He drank his coffee and looked back out the window.

"You didn't look like you were trippin'," I said. "You looked sober."

He shrugged and kept his eyes on the cars swooshing by on the Kennedy, "Well, maybe I wasn't tripping. I dunno. It was a long time ago."

I never wanted to think of Colby being on drugs like everyone else. I always thought of him being all creative and straight edge and healthy anarchy. I thought he was *that* kind of god. He wasn't even smoking cigarettes—like I was—the night I met him. "It didn't happen all that long ago," I said, "Maybe a year and a few months ago."

His eyes still on the expressway, he said, "Yeah, well, lots of shit happens in a year."

"Or even a day," I said, "You should see all the shit that's happened to me since just yesterday morning."

He looked down at my bag and said, "Hey, what you doin' out here at…what fuckin' time is it?"

He yawned and checked his watch but I beat him to it and said, "A quarter to four. I have to catch a train at Union Station."

"Whatcha got in the bag?"

"Clothes," I said.

He whispered, "Got drugs in there?"

"No. Just clothes and books."

"Where you goin'?"

"New York."

His eyes woke up, "No fuckin' way!"

"Yeah," I smiled.

"Fuck!" he said, "I'd love to fuckin' head out there some day. Catch some Sonic Youth at CBGB and shit, know what I mean?"

"You can! Train's only sixty bucks. At least, it's sixty one way."

"You're not going round-trip?"

"No," I said, "I'm moving there today."

"Whoa!" he leaned forward. "How old are you?"

"Fifteen," I said.

"You're fifteen and you're moving out there on your own?" I nodded. "Whoa," he said, "you got some big ole balls, boy."

My spirits rose to heaven when he said that. I asked him, "How old are you?"

"Eighteen," he said. So I guess he's not my age after all.

"Well," I told him, "You could move there easy. You're a legal adult."

"Well, maybe I will some day. Who knows?"

"You can come with me right now," I told him.

"Um…thanks," he said. "But…gotta go to work." He took a sip of his cooled-down coffee and looked away when our eyes met.

"Where do you work?" I asked.

"Carnation Sugar. West Side."

"What do you do there?"

He shrugged, "Assembly line. Sucks, but it's easy."

I gave him another once-over and saw a hardcore Prometheus chained to a factory floor, trapped in an ugly-ass uniform. "Then you *gotta* come with me," I said. Not even I could believe how fuckin' bold I was being. I even fuckin' repeated myself, "You gotta come with me!" Who the fuck did I think I was? Jesus with the fishermen? But, fuck, I couldn't help it. How far could Colby go on that West Side sugar assembly line? There's something way bigger out there for him; he just doesn't know it, no one's shown him the travel brochures, the Brecht, the BBC, and I bet he's never even heard of Mozart. I took another look at the Gorgon on his wrist and it started looking a lot more fuckin' desperate than bitchin'. What's he got planned from here on out? Is he just gonna chain himself to an assembly line and make up for the gloom by dropping acid, getting more tattoos, and hitting hardcore shows? How fuckin' dreary can you get!

He turned his face away from the window and looked at me the way I once looked at him, "So, why New York? Why today?"

"I got kicked out of school yesterday," I told him. "I'm sort of running away."

He nodded, "Sorry, man. I got kicked out junior year. I know how it goes."

"I'll be okay," I said. But inside, I was thinking, what'd Colby get kicked out for? Grades? I always pictured him being smart. But there I was, doing the same shit to him that people did to me: thinking smart had fuck all to do with grades and school. So I didn't ask him to go into it. I just asked, "Are you getting a GED?"

"I dunno," he shrugged. "I should."

The L went down the tunnel, heading for Belmont. I didn't know how soon he'd be getting off, so I quit beating around the bush and told him, "I'm moving to London."

"Whoa!" he yelped, "International man of mystery! Thought you were moving to New York?"

"I am. I'll be there till I'm eighteen. Then London."

"Wow," he said. "Well…good luck!"

I asked him, "Did you ever want to move to England?"

"Um," he meditated on the question a second, looking up at the fluorescent ceiling lamps, "I never…thought about it really."

Never thought about it? What the fuck else is there to think about? In the blackness of the tunnel, I asked him, "Are you sure you don't remember me? C'mon, remember? After the Narc dragged you off the L. You came up to me in Medusa's and asked if I saw it all. Remember? And I started talking to you in an English accent."

"Wait, I remember!" he started laughing, even stomped his right foot a couple times, "Yeah, yeah, I remember. You had, like, some Sex Pistols shit going on, right? Yeah, and you were, like, talking all normal and then just like fuckin' whiplash, you're all sounding all Keith Richards and shit. That was fuckin' funny!" He laughed some more. What could I do but laugh along with him?

"It wasn't my shining hour, I admit."

"We still talk about it!" he said, launching into an imitation, "'Yeah, fuckin' cops is fuckin' wankers!' Ha ha ha ha ha!"

"Great!" I said, "like I ain't got enough shit to live down."

"I'm sorry. I'm sorry," he put his palm up, breathing deep to show he was working his ass off not to laugh at me anymore. "Yeah, so what's been goin' on with you, man? What are you, a skin now?"

"No," I said, "Till about ten hours ago, I had the same hair you saw me with before."

"Oh, yeah?" he said. "I thought maybe you went skin. You got a shaved head, black eye, bruises. Figured you must be out fighting with all them. You know Sonny and them?"

I said, "As a matter of fact, I do. They kicked the shit out of me under the Belmont L one night."

"Why?"

"They liked my hat. They wanted it."

"Yeah," Colby said, "they're bad news. Sonny's in jail. He took brass knuckles to a cop's face. He'll be up the river for years."

"Good," I said.

"Did one of his boys do that to your face?"

"No," I said, "my brother did."

"Why?"

"Because I got kicked out of school."

"Oh, man," he said. "I'm sorry. No wonder you gotta get out."

"So, where've you been?" I asked. But trying to not let on I'm a stalker, I cleaned up the question, "I mean, where are you hanging out these days?"

"Not a lot of places," he said. "Can't hang out too much. Got a kid at home."

"Really?"

"Yeah."

"How old?"

"Two."

"Wow!"

"Yep," he said, "I was sixteen. Knocked my girlfriend up. She was living with me at my mom's. Her mom's a fuckin' pothead and her stepdad's a fuckin' lush who tried messin' with her, so she moved in. When you live that close and you're sleeping in the same bed, well, some shit's gonna go down. She kept telling me I didn't need a rubber. She said she was on the pill. She *still* says she was, but one of my boys must've slipped right by her, she says. I dunno. I don't regret it. I mean, the kid's fuckin' unbelievable!"

"What's his name?"

"Joe. After Joe Strummer."

"Nice."

"Yeah, well," he said, "it must be *nice* to get to take off to New York, move all the way to London. I can't. My mom works nights in Franklin Park. She watches Joe during the day while my wife works at Sears and I'm at Carnation."

"Your wife?"

"Yeah. We got married when I turned eighteen, six months ago."

"Oh," I said, looking at a face that once looked so flawless but now looks scared and troubled, "congratulations."

"Thanks, yeah. Well, y'know...Joe's my kid. You gotta

marry the lady if you want rights to the kid after you split. Or else, you just pay child support and never see the kid again."

"You're splitting up?" I asked.

"We can't now," he said. "Neither of us makes enough on our own to give Joe the life he deserves. And it's not like we're always fighting. It's just…we fight a lot. And I see where she's coming from. She's the mom. She comes home all dog-tired from work and then she's gotta shift gears, and being a mom's a much tougher job than working at Sears. But I'm tired too, and I gotta wake up at 3 a.m. to go bust my ass for minimum wage. And my own mom's gettin' tired of us and wants us to move out, but we gotta save up for a deposit on an apartment first. But how do we do that when there's always something new we gotta buy Joe, 'cuz fuck knows we ain't been buying shit for ourselves? So, in answer to your question, no, I ain't been goin' no place for a while now. My advice to you is, don't be a dad till you're ready."

"I never want to be a dad," I said, "ever."

"The kid's unbelievable, don't get me wrong" he said, "but the responsibility…I thought I could hack it, but I didn't know what I'd be up against. So now I'm slinging sugar sacks all day and probably for the rest of my life. My other piece of advice to you would be, stay in school, but it looks like it's a little late for that."

My heart started racing. I said to myself, what the fuck am I doing? I'm a fuckin' dropout now! I'm fuckin' homeless. Right before my fuckin' eyes, my teen-idol Zeus just became a plebe Prometheus! Worse, he's Ed Norton! Give him ten or fifteen years, he might end up growing a gut and becoming Ralph Kramden! I thought, shit, maybe I should turn back now, but I kept my seat as the L crept out of the West Town tunnel. Colby's head hung down. I wanted to say something to make him feel better. I couldn't think of anything except the stupid shit I blurted out next: "Well, you still dress cool, Colby."

He chuckled a little and said, "Yeah, when all else fails."

Then he looked up, "Wait, how'd you know my name?"

I had to think fast. "Um, didn't you just say it?"

"I don't think I did," he said. "Wait, did I? Man, I prob'ly did. How else would you know it? See? I'm so tired busting my ass all day, I don't even know half the shit I'm sayin' anymore. Take it from me: wear a rubber every time and get your ass back in school."

I looked out over West Town. All the severe, cagey fire escapes and the graffiti glowing in the dark and the Mexican dads, about to wake up from an hour's sleep between whatever under-the-table jobs they could get to feed the too-many mouths at their tables, and there were the random apartments that were lit up even at this ungodly hour, probably with all sorts of Cassandras and Oresteses in them, calling it a night after whatever kind of after-hours, head-trip soirees they must've all been throwing.

Colby took out his wallet and showed me a picture of his son Joe. What can I say, he was a cutie like all babies. He looked like he had Colby's eyes. I said, "He's a great little guy!" and Colby said thanks. He showed me a picture of his wife. It was Blondie. Fuckin' Blondie is his wife now. She's still got her curls but they got all mussed up into "mom" hair, and what the fuck's she doing working at Sears? What a fuckin' nosedive! Still, I said, "She's pretty," and Colby said thanks.

We made it to Damen. I stood up to take one last look down at North Avenue and a little speck of a building a couple blocks away called Café de Sade. I sat down and smiled sadly. I said to Colby, "Ever hang out around here? I mean, whenever you *do* get to hang out?"

"No way," he said. "Here? Why? I'm no Mexican."

I turned my head away a little, my hands folded, my sad smile still on, my eyes grazing the floor. The train descended into the downtown tunnel. Colby got up and put his hand on my shoulder, looking at me just the way he did in Medusa's hallway. "Take care of

CONCLUSIONS

yourself," he said, "in New York…and London, right?"

"I guess I can't talk you into coming," I said. He smiled, took another swig out of his Styrofoam cup and shook his head no. Of course the answer was gonna be no. He's a dad, he's got Joe. But I can still dream, can't I?

The L pulled up to Division and Ashland. Colby adjusted his black porkpie hat and waved good-bye as he stepped off the train, clad in leather and a shit-brown uniform that looked more and more like an orange prison jumpsuit with each step he took toward the stairs. I waved back. I think Colby was glad he ran into me. Not that he remembered who I was right away. It's just: he looked at my bruises, figured I understood problems, and knew he could unload.

If only I knew Colby before Blondie got her hooks in him, he'd be in a lot less trouble. Shit, he couldn't get me pregnant! I could've told him my Plans. If he'd known me, he never would've known life at the sugar factory. I would've made damn fuckin' sure of that. Maybe he'd be sitting next to me right now on the Amtrak, waving good-bye to the South Loop and the Chicago skyline, the one he sees every morning on his way to the sugar factory, the one I saw every morning on my way to Xavier.

Colby's eighteen. If I'd known him before Blondie, maybe he'd be in London by now, feathering a nest for me to land in in three years. It's a little after seven o'clock. The sun is rising in the east. Soon I will be too. After all, I got the luck o' the Irish! I get bounced out of bad scenes so I can get bounced into better ones, I guess. Colby must not be Irish. Whatever he is, it doesn't look like the poor guy will ever get to England.

THE END

ABOUT THE AUTHOR

Kyle Thomas Smith is a writer in Brooklyn, New York.
Visit him at www.StreetLegalPlay.com and www.85Anovel.com.